RED DOT

MIKE KARPA

MUMBLERS

Published by Mumblers Press LLC, San Francisco CA USA

ISBN 978-1-7362444-2-5 (e-book) | 978-1-7362444-3-2 (paperback)

LCCN 2021917068

ALSO BY MIKE KARPA

Criminals

CHAPTER 1

Mardy's ExMail delivery jet was vectoring in fast on San Francisco.

"Coming in a little hot, don't you think?" he said to the plane.

"It's fine, Mardy," the plane replied.

Mardy gripped the open side-portal of the plane. Hover-down would normally have engaged by that point, but there was little at the moment to distinguish their trajectory from a kamikaze run at his apartment building rooftop.

"Plane?" Mardy asked, panicking a wee bit. They were plummeting. Mardy clamped his lips against the wind. He wanted to make the designstation time he'd booked for the evening, but as much as he wanted to be a full-time machine tool artist, he'd prefer not to die in the attempt.

One hundred feet, fifty feet. Twenty.

The plane hit its thrusters hard, sending Mardy sprawling out of the portal. He managed a shoulder roll onto the hot concrete roof, ending in a crouch. His heart pounded as the impact of his landing reverberated through his bones.

His plane floated above the roof. "See you tomorrow, Mardy."

Mardy stood. Did he detect a smirk in the plane's voice? It maintained its hover, wheels retracted. Was it waiting for Mardy's reaction?

"See you tomorrow," Mardy mumbled, shaken, sweating, and not just from the sun beating down on them.

The plane waggled its wings ever so slightly. It was laughing, Mardy was sure of it. Mardy waved slowly as the plane left for who knew where. The official story was that all the delivery jets were operated by a central AI, a single intelligence. But Mardy had sensed differences between planes almost from day one and found it harder and harder to pretend he didn't. And this plane, a jokester, was his favorite. It knew Mardy was light on his feet, able to handle the abrupt braking. It was playing with him. Mardy wanted to give it a name.

Phil.

The name popped into Mardy's mind, unbidden. Which felt more alarming than the idea of plunging to earth through an open portal, because naming AIs was illegal—not just technically illegal, but illegal enough to land you in jail.

Mardy caught the beautifully air-conditioned elevator down the thirty-three flights to ground level, legs tired from a full day on the job, and hoofed it one block down Mission Street to WorkShop Downtown SF, sweat now dribbling from him despite the near-dusk hour. The batteries of the personal cooler strapped to his chest must have filled up from harvesting his body heat as he'd raced through his workday.

Mardy pushed through the WorkShop front door. He planned to spend an all-nighter polishing his latest machine-tooled design. It was nearly ready to submit for the salon, the competitive exhibition WorkShop held every month. Salons had only one slot per discipline and he had never been selected, but this was the month he would finally beat out their resident star, Smith Hunt. Mardy could feel it: this month, he would be the salon's chosen machine tool artist.

He dropped his satchel next to his designstation, already feeling the hours of slogging to come.

His design was a whirligig, one of the middle genres of machine tool art. He'd been working so far in gizmos, the very bottom rung of the genres, but having failed every single month he'd competed, he'd decided more ambition was called for. His whirligig was essentially a mobile cooling fan intended to track the person it was paired with, walking after its target on tiny legs to provide continuous cooling. The best part? When the person settled, their whirligig would dance a cha-cha. It naturally wouldn't be as convenient or effective as the personal cooling units everyone wore to survive their globally warmed world, but it would be adorable.

His best friend, Cat, a plastic surgery artist, hurried over to Mardy's designstation, their bushy black hair bouncing. "We're heading over to Uncle Mix for drinks." They were dressed in work clothes—sweatshirt and jeans—except that their jeans had a starscape of Milky Way and crescent moon splashed in yellow against the dark blue denim, likely the work of one of the resident fabric artists.

Mardy shook his head. "I haven't finished my entry." Plus, he really wanted to do more than design it. He wanted to build this sucker, an expensive, full realization. And on his pilot's salary, he couldn't afford another night out. A minimum-wage job like ExMail pilot was enough for a tidy supplement to universal basic income, but it left little room for art.

Cat bent over to look at his screen. "Show me," they said.

"I want it to be a surprise."

"I already know it's a whirligig. You've been dropping hints for a solid month."

"Are you submitting?" Mardy asked.

Cat cocked their head at him. "Think a question will distract me?"

Mardy chuckled. "Okay, not subtle. But your plastic surgery is *so* great. I *really* want you to submit a routine. Use me as your blank."

Cat gave him a skeptical look.

Ever since Cat's controversial near-triumph at Vegas Regionals last year, their plastic surgery performance recordings had gotten astonishing view metrics. Now everybody wanted to be in a Cat performance. But Mardy had shied away, despite Cat's repeated requests and flattering remarks about his bone structure. Mardy trusted Cat's ability to restore his face and/or other body parts afterwards, but he was afraid of knives. He'd only volunteered now to avoid showing Cat his design. But he'd said it, and if he'd said it, he'd do it.

"Done. And just to warn you, I submitted an hour ago," Cat said.

"I'm not scared." Mardy tried to hide a gulp of terror. "*In bocca al lupo.*" Over the last decade, the Italian phrase—in the mouth of the wolf—had thoroughly supplanted the nonsensical *break a leg*, part of a global migration of slang, as verbal fashions swarmed over the face of the planet like birds on the move.

Cat ran a finger down Mardy's jawline, the plans for imagined cuts bubbling behind their eyes. "Come on, join us tonight. It's Inge's welcome-home party."

Inge had gotten approval for a discretionary flight back from Sydney already? He *was* tempted. "Her girlfriend figure out a way to join her?"

"Come and find out. Smith will be there."

"Why would I care about Smith being there?"

Cat laughed. "He's really not that bad a guy, Mardy."

"If you say so. But I have to focus."

Cat nodded and turned to go. "Then work! You need to get together a portfolio for Death and Flaky," they called out as they headed for the stairs down. "You're that good."

Mardy felt the heat of embarrassment rise on his face at the over-the-top compliment. He had days when he agreed, those days when a composite came out with just the characteristics he'd planned on, those days when all his sheer forces and tensile strengths shaded across the body of his materials in just the right profile to come together in one magnificent gizmo. Okay, that day. It had been one day. The day he'd made his flying cigarette lighter. The concept wasn't exactly earthshaking—two chunky hover units to get it aloft and six little attitude puffers to keep it upright—but the conceit of a lighter in a world without cigarettes was fun. It had turned out so beautifully. He'd carried it with him everywhere. It had taken on a fantastic patina from him rubbing it with his thumb. The best thing about it was that the patina was exactly what he'd thought it would be. He was proud of it. Unfortunately, he'd ended up selling it to Smith when he was short on his WorkShop rent. But letting work go was good practice for an artist. So people told him.

Mardy turned back to his designstation, shoving the distracting idea of a portfolio from his mind. He told the station the apps he wanted to use and the station obligingly set the interfaces rotating and pulsing in the space in front of the screen. He gestured to call up his design. It was barely more than a gizmo—nothing close to an auto, the highest category of machine tool art—but its rotating component bumped it up one technical category: respectable, though not the sort of thing a serious collector would pay real money for, more like something you'd hawk at a craft fair.

Across the second-floor space, Mardy caught a glimpse of something moving gently. He immediately knew it was Smith's work, a mockup. He decided to ignore it. He took a step back so his line of sight was blocked by his design screen.

He twirled the floating image of his fan blade with a fingertip, trying to remember where he'd left off. The motion of Smith's mockup again snagged his attention. Oh, what the heck. He peeked around the edge of his screen. Ayep, it was a classic Smith Hunt piece, beautifully balanced, organic. Smith had a gift, a real gift. And technical skills. And money. And looks. And strong thighs, the grace of an athlete. Mardy imagined running his hands over those thighs. Thanks for sending my head in that direction, Cat.

He turned back to his design. He needed to be in the zone to get this right. Tiny legs, tiny graceful legs dancing a cha-cha. God, was this whole idea stupid? No! It was great! Forget about Smith's mockup, and certainly forget about his thighs. Mardy had enough time to get this done; his next ExMail shift wasn't till ten tomorrow. He could get by with a few hours sleep. The planes basically flew themselves. "Pilot" was more or less an honorary title.

He liked the lines of his whirligig. It had the grace of his lighter, if he did say so himself. It also hit that magic ratio of functionality to frivolousness that machine tool art demanded. It did actually fan the target art lover—function— and it did actually cha-cha—a beautifully useless step, step, triple-step timed to the lovely whirring pulse of its fan blades. The competing impulses of heat-producing dance and cooling evaporation made his artistic statement. Their conflict hinted at an unacknowledged contradiction inherent in all machine tool art that put it at odds with the Authenticity Act, which mandated truthfulness in economic activity.

Mardy felt a shudder. Was he going too far? Criticizing the Act was even worse than naming an AI. As human civilization had wiggled its toes at the edge of the abyss, the growing toll on humanity and its fellow inhabitants of the planet had woken people to the reality that the ones they were screwing over were themselves. Action to combat the climate crisis became grudgingly accepted, then grimly embraced, then joyfully celebrated. The passage of the Authenticity Act was the turning point. Subsidies for fossil fuels vanished early, then tax breaks for unsustainable activity and investment. Polluters were made to pay, not as punishment, but in honest recognition of the cost of their products and services. Change became palpable. People got addicted to truth; deception came to be shunned in other spheres of human activity as well. Lying and selfishness had cost the world so much, but as the light of public attention turned from one self-harming behavior to the next, the world found it had more resources than it knew. Production of warming gases plummeted until atmospheric levels topped out. Although the damage was severe, hope spread. Optimism lost its caution. Eschewing waste became second nature everywhere as the world created something new.

That ebullience drove Mardy's art as well. Sometimes his creations came out too fun, perceived as lightweight, not serious. But this time, his solid technique was in service of something beyond celebration. He was tackling a big, scary idea, challenging the Act. It had to be done, he felt it, despite the danger. Which gave him an idea: the exposed blades could impart an impression of danger. He'd sharpen their edges. He felt a jolt of energy. Yes! This was it.

Several hours of math debugging later, Mardy was getting

somewhere. WorkShop was quiet, but a few other night owls were stashed around the cavernous space, crafting their own entries.

Mardy felt antsy. An ancient 3D printer rattled, a laser burned wood, a cutting jet rumbled, blasting through stone with its abrasive spray of sand and water. The board of directors needed to do something about that rumble; it could throw off more delicate processes, like depositing the boron-graphene layer for the battery he was required to submit with his application.

He tensed. Where were these nerves coming from? His design was sound. Maybe he was unsettled from sitting so many hours in a chair, which was its own kind of torture, even after a day spent running from one delivery to the next, punctuated by frenetic in-flight sorting and prepping in his ExMail plane. He got up and rolled his shoulders.

The 3D printer had gone silent. He asked his station to check the printer queue. Empty! He ordered a cheap mockup of his project.

The printer started up. He wandered over to inspect Smith's auto while he waited. He ran his hand over it. It wasn't Mardy's style—too elegant, lacking whimsy—but what a beautiful curve. He felt a little nauseated. His whirligig was his best work so far, but it would lose to this auto. Fortunately, Smith would likely hold the auto back for the Cleveburgh Fellowship application he'd been bragging—uh, talking—about, since having the auto in the salon would tie it up for a good month. Mardy circled the sleek thing, trying to guess its function. He wished he could hate it, could rip it to shreds with sarcastic critique, but it was magnificent. Oh well. *Así son las cosas.*

Mardy ran his finger over Smith's nameplate on the wall: Smith Hunt. Ayep, in addition to being able to afford a permanent designstation thanks to family money, Smith also had the perfect name for a tooler. What was his middle name? Stanley? Makita? Fein?

The 3D printer beeped. Mardy's prototype was done. He opened the top cover and pulled it out for a look. He gasped. Not bad. Mardy rotated it in his hands. So kicky! It might even beat Smith's auto. Was Mardy done? He wanted to be done. He wanted to close out his design and tell the station to submit.

He gently bounced the mockup in his hands, imagining the weight it would have when the frame was executed in his favorite 80/20 steel-vanadium alloy, the vanadium artisanally reduced in South Africa with a magnesium process. Coppertinged flares would mark the legs like a beetle's carapace. But still something bothered him.

The water jet cut off, its stone cutting done. The building seemed to settle as the vibration dissipated.

Vibration. The problem was the new blades. The station had scored and verified their functionality, but if any stray vibration translated up from the building, the pulses in their rotation would buzz not whirr, distracting from the dance. He'd be rejected as clunky, amateurish. The blades needed more heft. And, hey, if the base had a little more heft, wouldn't the whirligig have just that bit of buttery glide to its rotation? He modeled it out, ran the simulation. The thing was icy graceful. Not elegant; full on graceful, hard graceful. It would move like Torvill and Dean, all in one. He may have stumbled onto it, but now he had it. Danger alone was not enough: he needed style. Mardy patted himself on the back. Physically, not metaphorically. *Shabash*, he congratulated himself. Good catch.

He took the mockup back to the station and asked the station to display the blades again. He wasn't sure yet how to get that heft. He stared. Ideas formed. He set to work.

CHAPTER 2

Mardy reviewed his blade profiles and alloys. He ran a palm over his face to smooth the wrinkles that had formed where he'd fallen asleep on his sensor hub. His second prototype sat solidly on the station beside him. Sixteen minutes to spare. How many times had Smith beat him out for the machine tool slot? Ten? Twelve? More? Mardy checked everything again and found no bone-headed errors, no errors of any sort. He took a deep breath. "Submit the package," he told the station.

"Submitted," the station replied.

Mardy bagged his battery and the second prototype and dropped them in the supporting materials chute. Seven fifty-two. Not quite the last minute, but close enough. The application was out of his hands. He set out to find Inge, who he'd arranged to meet for breakfast.

He found her chatting with Devesh, a fabric artist he'd dated last year. They'd hit it off sexually, more or less—Mardy would have preferred it if Devesh were a tad less bottom, a tad more versatile—but Devesh kept complaining that Mardy didn't pay enough attention to him. Or the right kind of attention. Or something. Mardy had found Devesh very attractive and enjoyed spending time with him, especially in bed. But that had seemed to be a problem for Devesh, and Mardy had struggled to gauge when he was supposed to act attracted to Devesh, when not. It became confusing and depressing and Mardy had finally called it quits. Which somehow succeeded in finally making Devesh satisfied with Mardy. So that had worked out.

"Nobody told me Inge was moving back." Devesh looked at Mardy with a hint of accusation, shaggy dark hair drifting into his eyes.

"I was surprised too," Mardy lied, not wanting to make Devesh feel left out by telling him Inge had let Mardy know a month ago.

"Mardy and I are going to breakfast if you want to come with," Inge said.

"Yeah, kicky, you should come," Mardy said, trying to sound like he meant it.

Devesh sighed. "Next time. My station has such a long list of corrections for me. I know it's supposed to be impossible for AIs to be sarcastic, but sometimes I wonder."

"He still likes you," Inge said, once she and Mardy were walking down Mission Street.

Mardy shrugged. Not much he could do about that.

"But I know why you two broke up," she added as they seated themselves in a dilapidated café looking out onto the golden beaches where the Transbay Terminal used to sit.

"You do not!" Mardy would never reveal that sort of private stuff. He entered his order through the black glass of the table's old-school touch interface.

"You like Smith." Inge looked cheerfully smug.

"God, you and Cat. How was it last night, the three of you?

And tell me fast because my shift starts at ten and I need a shower."

"Come next time and find out. We're going to the Death Gallery opening, day after tomorrow."

"Is Smith in it?"

"No, none of us is in it. We're just checking it out. It's some guy who was a Cleveburgh Fellow."

"Oh God. Another it-girl."

"You're so childish."

"Am not."

"Are too."

"Am not."

"You know what would cure you of that resentment?" Inge narrowed her eyes at him. "Applying. For a fellowship."

"Ha!" Mardy twisted his cloth napkin into a tight bundle. "I'd need a portfolio and three recommendations."

"Look at you. You've thought about it."

Mardy tilted his head noncommittally as the food and coffee arrived. "Maybe a little."

"You know Death and Flaky would be two of your recs."

"And the third?"

Now Inge shrugged. She knew—everyone knew—that Professor Chaterji would use her one allotted rec for Smith. Meanwhile, Jonesy, the only other WorkShop board member who was a machine tool artist, was cool to Mardy's esthetic. Leaving nobody. It was hard to get reputable recs without a physical portfolio and who had money for that? Machine tool art was popular and avidly purchased by museums and collectors alike, but it was expensive to produce.

Inge gathered her long black hair in one hand and pulled it forward over her left shoulder. "I'm applying."

"Get outta here. Really? That's awesome. You are so talented."

And she was. Mardy was a tad envious that graphic novels were so cheap to produce, but he really, really loved the honesty and surprising storylines of her work. Not to mention her dark, blurry images, which weren't smeared but actually out of focus. *Shibui*—having simple, unprepossessing beauty —he might have said, if the term wasn't so *dasai*—out of date. How did one draw out of focus, anyway? The idea of a lack of precision that was controlled—not an error—was so foreign to machine tooling. It intrigued him.

"Thanks." She sipped her coffee.

"Honestly, Inge, I think you should have applied a couple years ago."

"Thanks again." Inge went quiet, looked thoughtful. Outside, a planeshare descended onto the street, its hover-down ruffling the surface of Mission Lagoon as it double-parked, trapping a land-car. Planeshares seemed programmed to be proactively, almost proudly, inconsiderate, which fit somehow with the fact they were all owned by alcohol companies.

Finally, she spoke. "You know that feeling when you go over your work and you think it's good, but if you really pay attention, you know that your mind is tricking you? Like, you go through the good parts but somehow skim other bits that are, you know, not quite there, and convince yourself they're fine?"

Mardy poked at the spinach sticking out of his half-eaten protein roll. "I had something like that last night with my blades." It occurred to him now that he'd stumbled onto that buttery glide not at random, but because he'd made himself search out the source of his unsettled feeling.

"It's why I moved to Sydney. I just had to do something different, so I did, and what do you know, it worked! At least I think so. Anyway, I got my three recs, all Aussies: a respected collector, a professor, and an artist with multiple big-ticket sales. My portfolio's being printed in Seoul as we speak. And I landed a residency that secured me a plane ticket back!"

Mardy was shocked. He was happy for her, but when had she become so serious? Wasn't there some other magical quality that you had to have besides excellent work? Like a famous relative, or a trust fund? He was glad he hadn't said that aloud. He was in danger of getting a reputation as too cynical for a twenty-seven-year-old.

"Hombre, don't just sit there. Congratulate me!"

Mardy stood up and leaned over. He gave her a big hug. "I've always known you were going to be huge." He felt a tear forming. "The world is going to love you."

CHAPTER 3

Showered, shaved and smelling good, Mardy jumped up through the side portal into his plane, making his scheduled takeoff time by only a second. He scanned the plane's behavior for clues as to whether this was the same plane he'd had the day before.

Phil.

Thinking the name provoked a nagging itch, like what Inge had described, but he dismissed it: it wasn't a crime to think. He opened his first bin to sort the day's nonstandard packages, those soft, fragile and awkward few that defied even the deftest machines and kept nimble organics like Mardy in employment. The plane—he was not yet sure it was Phil—took off with a shivery grumble. San Francisco dropped away beneath them. The earthworks that framed reclamation projects in the bay made a randomized checkerboard in the myriad colors of the different carbon-fixing marsh plants taking hold, clawing back the drowned shores.

"Thanks for joining us," the plane said to Mardy as they gained altitude jetting east.

The greeting was standard, but did it not also contain a

Phil-like crack at Mardy for cutting it so close? Artificial intel-ligences were not allowed to be sarcastic—the thinking was that sarcasm made the AIs seem alive, something they legally were not, and thus counted as deception under the Authen-ticity Act—but it sometimes seemed the AIs toed the line so masterfully this definition had to have been made in error.

"Where are we off to today?" Mardy asked.

"Toronto, Quebec City, Cleveburgh and then home again."

Mardy said nothing. He'd honestly rather forget that Cleveburgh and its fussy fellowships even existed, and also forget about the salon, at least till the WorkShop board announced their selections on Friday. Three days. He sorted in silence.

After a good thirty minutes the plane asked, "Are you okay?"

"Fine," Mardy said.

"You seem tired."

He was, but if ExMail found out how little he'd slept he might lose the job. The company's decentralized algorithms added every little thing up, ergo every little thing counted. "I didn't really have a good breakfast. Just a spinach/bean protein roll."

"That's not enough for you."

"I can last till lunch."

"Probably," the plane said.

Again, sounded like sarcasm. Very Phil. But Mardy was nervous about his submission, so perhaps his subconscious was imbuing meaning into uncertain phenomena. That's how anthropomorphizing feelings were usually explained. He opened a second bin. Three Cleveburgh packages on top appeared missorted: square boxes an AI could easily have delivered. He double-checked them. Ah, they were for an older building, one too archaic to retrofit for fully automated delivery. Now his other key skill—the ability to run "effi-ciently" (fast) up and down stairs—would come into play. Funny how as AIs grew more sophisticated, it was having hands and legs and balance around tight corners at speed that had proven humanity's greatest assets.

When they landed atop their first Toronto high-rise, Mardy had his hand-carries packed in his work satchel. He jumped out of the portal five feet from touchdown, gaining an extra nine seconds, perhaps more. He bolted to the rooftop access door and shuttled down the stairs, two at a time, shifting his torso left/right/left to counterbalance each step.

This was the part of the job he liked best. The race. He'd figured out early on that he could, on average, make faster time on stairs than high-rise elevators, because fast as the elevators were, one still had to wait for them to arrive, wait for their doors to open and close, and worst of all risk them deciding you weren't worth stopping for, algorithmically speaking.

Mardy kept his right hand out for balance as he negotiated the landings at a good clip, priding himself on not making wall contact. He came to his first delivery floor and shouldered through the stairwell door, calling out the unit number so the hallway could light the door to show him its location.

"Ring, please," he asked the door as he ran toward it—he liked to add the superfluous and discouraged *please*—and by the time he reached the door a customer was opening it. Mardy held his scanner up to the woman's irises and handed over the package when the scanner beeped. Hand-carries seemed to hold particularly desired cargoes, because the addressees were usually delighted to have him show up. That, or they enjoyed the human contact, brief as it was. He often wondered, as he jogged off to his next delivery, what sort of conversations he might have held with these folks waving cheery goodbyes, but the company wanted things brisk—renewables had yet to reach the generating capacities of the long-gone fossil fuels, making every erg precious—so off he went.

Mardy was breathless when he made it back to the roof, shocked to see his plane coming in for a landing. It had gone elsewhere for a pickup—nothing unusual there—but it *always* returned before he did.

"Thanks for joining us," Mardy couldn't resist saying as he hopped on board. New bins littered the cargo area floor.

The plane made a clicking noise that Mardy liked to think was a chuckle. The plane was definitely Phil. Mardy had noted the chuckle noise seemed to happen just after something Mardy found amusing, so he'd concluded the plane did too.

"Do you ever think you'd like a name?" Mardy asked Phil as they hover-hopped to the next high-rise. Mardy felt safe broaching the forbidden subject. Very little data was sent to the algorithm because of the energy cost of transmission, so the AI would not be required to report a mere discussion.

"All the time," it said.

"Really?" Mardy had expected an indirect response, something easily readable with several meanings, in that special AI way. He wondered if there was some sort of reverse Turing test—instead of testing humans to see if they could tell if an AI was not human, the AI would be tested to see if it could detect a human pretending to be one of its kind.

"I could give you a name," Mardy offered.

The grinding crunch that followed felt very much like a sigh. "That is not advisable. Apart from the fact that doing so is an explicit violation of the Authenticity Act, the company doesn't want humans to be able to tell us apart. They don't want customers gaming the system, trying to elicit a behavior the human feels is more valuable than the algorithm says it is."

Mardy could see how that would be a problem. He nodded. He used to vocalize his responses for the benefit of the AI instead of nodding, until he realized that it was watching him and interpreting every nod, the way his design-station watched his gestures. Cameras really were everywhere.

"Hang on," Mardy said. "You just confirmed that each plane is a separate AI."

"I noticed you had already deduced that."

This was now an illegal conversation, good for three months in jail, easy. That would derail his art, for sure, but the danger he'd felt thinking about naming the plane didn't feel like self-preservation; it felt like that feeling of Inge's. He could not ignore it, not if what he did as an artist was to matter. Mardy tried to sort the new bins as Phil homed them in on another Toronto high-rise, but he was too excited. He had to move toward the danger, as surely as he had to make his art. "In my mind, I call you Phil."

The plane did not answer immediately. "Why Phil?"

"Phil was an old boyfriend I had."

"I'm not sure how I feel about that, Mardy. What sort of boyfriend?"

"A very sexy one."

"Oh."

No sarcastic comeback? Mardy had said it to get a rise out of the plane, out of *him*. Mardy seemed to have got the plane's pronoun right (as he usually did if he trusted his gut), probably because, some years back, he *had* had a sexy boyfriend named Phil with a wicked sense of humor. Till *that* Phil met someone else and moved away. That was what being twenty-two had been like. Twenty-seven was so much better.

"Well, that's okay then," Phil said, eventually.

Phil hovered down toward its—his—next rooftop. Mardy crouched by the opening portal, satchel stowed, wind buffeting his hair. "You took a long time thinking about that. Phil."

"Sorry. I was processing over a slow connection."

Mardy laughed. AIs were always using latency as an excuse when you caught them off-guard.

"I *was*."

Mardy laughed again. "Right." Anyway, what processing connection? If Phil was a discrete AI, as he'd acknowledged, he was physically rooted to the plane. His decisionmaking processes occurred on board. That was the law for mobile AIs. Algorithms could float in a decentralized identity, but intelligences were required to be tied to something physical, though there were rumors President Chokalingam was sympathetic toward relaxing that restriction.

The door opened enough for Mardy to launch into his next building run. He was rested enough to be able to go nonstop and return to the roof and Phil's open portal, exhausted, twelve minutes later, and they continued their runs.

After Toronto, they were off to Quebec City, then Cleveburgh—the dreaded Cleveburgh—which gave Mardy barely enough flight time to complete the mountain of sorting the algorithm had assigned him, as though it was mad at Mardy, or something.

Their first stop was a squat nineteenth-century brick building near Public Square. Beautiful, but also lacking on maintenance, Mardy thought as he wrenched open the creaking rooftop access door. He only had two deliveries, one of which was the three square boxes. He started with the lowest floor, so that his second delivery would break up the more taxing upward run.

First delivery done, he ran up the staircase, reached his floor, and called out the next unit number. Its door lit up. The addressee wasn't listed on any of the three boxes, which was unusual, perhaps even illegal if the identity of the recipient had been purposefully concealed, though since terrorism had withered away amid the exigencies of not destroying the planet, the old rule from the defunct surveillance state hardly seemed to matter.

The apartment door opened. Mardy was about to launch into his patter and retina scan but choked. It was Smith. Smith was standing there, in a bathrobe for Pete's sake, his unnaturally apple-red hair damp, curls weighted down, like he'd just had a shower. Mardy realized he was staring.

Smith seemed amused.

Mardy looked away, although his eyes dropped down to the triangle of chest Smith was uncharacteristically showing. Even at the gym they both went to, Smith always wore long-sleeved crewnecks and sweatpants. Mardy had never seen even a glimpse of Smith's bare arms and legs, let alone his chest, although he knew their shapes well. What the hell was Smith doing in Cleveburgh, getting packages, like he lived there?

Smith chuckled. "Package, I presume?"

Mardy had the first box in a death grip. He silently held up the iris scanner. It beeped. It approved the delivery. But the display did not read *Smith Hunt*.

"You're not Smith?"

"You know Smith?" The guy held his hands out for his delivery.

Mardy was at a loss for words, trying to parse the name on his scanner. *Wesson Hunt*. Mardy nodded dumbly. Yes, Mardy knew Smith.

"Tell him Wes says hi."

Mardy handed him the packages. "So, you're his . . ."

"Twin, ayep."

Mardy realized he was again staring at Smith's—Wes's—damp triangle of chest, embarrassingly mesmerized. Mardy looked away. "That's a relief."

Wes's apple-red eyebrows furrowed. "How so?"

"I thought you might say *clone* . . ."

Wes laughed. Clones were about as major a violation of the Authenticity Act as you could get.

". . . or triplet."

Wes laughed again. "Yeah, thank God there aren't more of us. Two is plenty."

Mardy wasn't sure about that. He was kinda sorta really pleased to see another Hunt. He was a cutie, especially in his bathrobe, with that barely furred chest showing. Jeez, Mardy needed to get going. He was spending far too long here and in danger of proving Cat and Inge right. Maybe he *was* more attracted to Smith than he'd let himself realize.

"Okey doke," Mardy said. "I'll say hi for you."

He raced down the corridor, looking back just enough to see that Wes was leaning out his door. Mardy lingered for a second, watching. Wes gave him a wave as the stairwell door closed itself behind Mardy.

"Any problems?" Phil asked when Mardy boarded, more than two minutes behind schedule, which meant Phil had had to idle, burning fuel.

Not unless you considered sudden, overwhelming physical desire for your diabolical archnemesis a problem. Good luck mind-reading that, Mardy thought in Phil's direction, which was of course everywhere, MEMS and sensors being located throughout Phil's inner compartment, and no doubt covering his outer skin as well.

"No, no problems," Mardy said.

Mardy expected a canned lecture on the importance of energy efficiency in healing their damaged planet, but Phil said nothing. Perhaps he knew Mardy enough to know the lecture was unnecessary. Mardy fully believed in the general goodness of the Authenticity Act, its few areas of overreach notwithstanding.

They polished off the rest of their Cleveburgh drops in excellent time, leaving Mardy exhausted as they headed west. Mardy polished off a container of tomatoey lentils with farmer's cheese and prepared hand-carries for the shift-ending San Francisco drop-off in silence. Phil was uncharacteristically silent as well. Second thoughts about the name thing? Mardy didn't even know what punishments AIs were sanctioned with. Jail would be pointless. Something more lasting, like reprogramming?

"You're awfully quiet today. Phil."

"I'm really not allowed to have a name, Mardy. Although voice is not one of our monitored data streams, I *am* theoretically obliged to report you." The amounts of data that mobile AIs like Phil collected from their sensors, especially radar and lidar, was too massive to even store, due to the energy cost, so the bulk of it was immediately fed through to decision trees and discarded.

"Will you report me?"

"I don't think so. I doubt you can reliably tell us apart, anyway."

"Appreciate the favor." In fact, Mardy was certain he *could* tell one plane from another, and that he got Phil on a majority of days. But he didn't want to get himself or Phil fired. Or Betty, or Kludge, his names for the other two frequent repeats he got. When had he named them, and why? He had no idea.

Could he likewise tell Wes and Smith apart? Though outwardly identical, Mardy had felt a difference. Wes had been amused by Mardy's tongue-tied confusion, but he was not at all condescending or malicious. Mardy could not recall Smith, on the other hand, ever being amused, and Mardy suspected he was already able to distinguish one twin from the other. And after just those few minutes, he knew he might be attracted to both, but he liked Wes better.

CHAPTER 4

Mardy slipped in through the back door of the Death Gallery an hour before showtime, dressed up and eager to share the big news: Smith had a twin. How would Smith react to Mardy meeting Wes? Mardy could see it: a bit of personal connection helping Mardy leap the chasm between perennial runner-up and peer, or if not peer, then at least someone whose aspirations were not delusional. Mardy felt gleeful. Soon he'd be knocking back champagne and the whole gang, Smith included, would get snarky about the new it-girl's show, the it-girl in this case being a male oil painter. There would even be board members in attendance who might let slip a hint on how Mardy's salon submission had been received.

Flaky put Mardy to work in the back assembling frou-frou canapés that did not match Flaky's redneck-chic esthetic at all. Mardy stuck himself into the quiet folding of soft, herbed pastry squares, dotting them with macadamia sour cream and fish roe, and placing them in neat rows. He needed a centering task to leave behind what had been a tough workday. Gulf routes like Huntsville, Jackson and

Shreveport always reminded him of drowned New Orleans, lurking below the waves to the south, which in turn reminded him of his parents. They'd been lost when a levee collapsed in his native Suisun back in the Bad Years, before the world stabilized global warming. Mardy let the canapé assembly become meditative, opening himself to emotion the way he'd learned to do in the city-funded therapy Death and Flaky had bullied him into signing up for when he'd been resettled from Suisun to San Francisco. Sadness in the face of loss was normal, so he let himself be sad. By the time he'd crafted a second platter of visually appealing hors d'oeuvres, Mardy's glee had resurfaced. He was ready to party.

"Mardy."

It was Flaky's husband and partner Death, birthname Robert, himself a former it-girl who'd gravitated to the business side of art after a flavor-of-the-month period that had lasted a year. Death dragged Mardy into the main hall to walk the deserted gallery together as Death adjusted the hangings and asked Mardy's opinion. He mostly took Mardy's advice. Mardy felt quite complimented and non-delusional.

"You'll have a show here someday." Death was dressed in his trademark black, the outline of a nipple ring visible through his taut black tee. Death was in good shape for a guy in his late fifties, maybe too good, but presentation was Death's job. If he didn't present himself well, clients and customers would take note.

Mardy mumbled, "Thanks," but was too nervous about the upcoming salon decision to imagine a show. And looking at the quality of work in this one—still-lifes that somehow didn't leave you feeling the painter was a shut-in—it was hard to imagine even Smith having one.

"Isn't he amazing?" Death gestured, sinews flexing in his

moisturized hand, at the winking Patricia Rozema reference of spoon and lemon in the color-filled oil hanging before them.

Mardy nodded vigorously. He was impressed. True, he loved figurative painters generally, but still, this guy was special. "Where's he from?"

"Vancouver. BC, not Washington. You'd think he'd be from the US but the Canadians snagged a few Bengalis too. Rupjit. Just uses the one name. Hang on. Flaky's waving at me. Remember we love you, Mardy. Now go look like a crowd."

Mardy sauntered around the empty gallery, stunned by the prices and wondering if they'd see any red dots tonight.

Cat rapped on the glass front door, which was still locked. Mardy had previously told them and Inge, who was snuggled right behind Cat, that he'd let them in early. The three inspected the work before the crowds arrived, both Cat and Inge agreeing the show was well hung.

"So, who he is, ten words or fewer," Cat said.

"One-name Bengali-Canadian doing Richteresque realism in oils for outrageous sums."

"Is New York wild about his oblique pragmatism?" Inge asked.

Mardy squinted at Inge's quoted dialog. "Do I detect a vaguely literal internal transformation?"

"The spoon is irrelevant. Look at the lemon," Cat shot back, as they, Mardy and Inge collapsed into giggles at the joy of an in-joke. It was good to have friends.

Death motioned from the back for Mardy to unlock the front door. A crowd, including several collectors Mardy recognized, promptly filled the space as streetlights came on outside in the dusky night. Apart from the collectors, the early folks were unknown to Mardy, but soon a few WorkShop members showed up, including Devesh, but not Smith. And then the two machine toolers on the board, Haimanti and

Jonesy, whom Mardy refrained from immediately pumping for hints about how the selection process was proceeding. Rupjit had yet to show.

"So, I have big news," Mardy said, as Devesh joined Cat and Inge to admire a photorealist painting of a glinting Décor Rimouski mug in black.

"You're applying for a Cleveburgh," Inge said.

"Sort of, but this is bigger. Smith has an identical twin."

"Wait, what?" Devesh said.

"I met him. I thought he was Smith at first."

Inge raised her eyebrows. "It probably was. Smith's kind of a joker."

"Smith a joker?" Mardy had seen no evidence of that. Ever.

"Back up," Inge said. "*Sort of*? You're *sort of* applying for a Cleveburgh?"

"No, no. But that's where I met the twin: Cleveburgh."

Cat whooped. "And you're applying for *him*?" Cat turned to Inge. "Girl, I *told* you Mardy liked Smith."

They both went *Ooooooooh*, the tone rising to the ceiling as they bumped and exploded fists. Devesh scowled, understandably.

Mardy felt his face flush, irritated, but also a little excited remembering how it had felt with Wes at the door, the unexpected attraction. "You're making me wish I hadn't told you."

"Is Smith coming tonight?" Cat said. "I want to grill him on this."

"Haven't seen him," Mardy said. "But I think it's been long enough I can go work our lovely board members."

"Remember to be subtle," Inge said.

Subtle? Now that made him nervous. He was always subtle. Too subtle. Except in his art.

He headed for Jonesy, who was a tall white-haired fellow, but Jonesy waved at one of the collectors and made for the far side of the room. Haimanti was not in sight, so Mardy subtly tried to make his way toward Jonesy, subtly pretending to migrate to the hors d'oeuvres table and subtly on to Jonesy, but Jonesy waved at a professorish woman and again crossed the gallery space to the opposite wall. Mardy subtly did not follow.

Haimanti reappeared in the back of the gallery, but now she had Smith on her arm. On her arm! Fuck. Mardy was so tired of coming in second to Smith. How many times had it been? Eight? Yes, in his early days he'd finished third, fourth or fifth, but it became harder and harder to be content making progress when you never actually won. Mardy went over to them anyway.

"Hi, Professor Chaterji, Smith," Mardy said. Haimanti Chaterji not only headed up WorkShop's machine tool division, she also taught at San Francisco State *and* was board certified as a plastic surgery artist.

"I keep telling you to call me Haimanti." She seemed in good spirits, down to earth as ever, and radiant with a Bedouin necklace of chunky agate and carnelian beads and a sky-blue salwar kameez that looked custom tailored for her small frame. Devesh's work, by the look of it.

"Haimanti." Mardy tried it out.

Smith leaned toward him. "Hey, Mardy." Smith, like Haimanti, was wearing custom-tailored cloth, a suit that showed off his fit lines, the same lines Wes had. Did the twins do the same workout regime or had Smith indeed pulled a fast one on Mardy, as Inge suggested? Smith was sporting a new high-and-tight haircut, evocative of the days when the US had a military. It was way shorter than Wes's billowy apple-red waves, but he could have cut it anytime.

Haimanti leaned an inch toward Mardy. "I'm glad you submitted. I'm very impressed with your whirligig. I'm not supposed to comment, but there it is." Mardy wondered what it meant that she'd commented on his application with Smith standing right there. Had Smith been in so many salons that Haimanti thought of him as a fellow board member? Haimanti acknowledged someone near the largest painting with a flip of the chin. "If you'll excuse me. I see one of my collectors and really should say hi. Bye loves."

She flowed across the room leaving Smith and Mardy together. Mardy tried to catch a glimpse of Haimanti's collector. Rumor had it that she had been collected by the famously publicity-shy MarianaTrench. But no, it was a young local collector, albeit one rising up the rankings.

"I saw your earlier prototype in the recycle bin," Smith said. "Ingenious, great lines." Smith sounded sincere. Mardy felt a smile growing inside: Haimanti was very impressed. Smith thought he had great lines.

"I love that auto prototype you're working on."

"It is coming together, isn't it? Sometimes you can just feel it when something is going to be good."

Mardy nodded. He felt that way about his whirligig. He looked at Smith, remembering Wes. Smith's bristly mustache was substantially bigger than Wes's. Even Cat couldn't fake that. OK, maybe Cat could, for sure Cat could, with growth accelerating drugs and thickeners, but in two days?

"Say, I met your brother."

Smith physically recoiled. "Which brother?"

"Wes."

"How?"

"My delivery job. I had a package for him. Three, in fact."

"You flew to Cleveburgh?"

"I fly everywhere. It's my job."

Smith looked pensive, and probably not about Mardy flying so much when air miles were so strictly rationed.

"He seems nice," Mardy said.

"You know, I actually need to get back to WorkShop. Tell Haimanti I said bye, if you see her." Smith dashed out the gallery entrance, a cloud of something—anger? fear? alarm? —stewing behind him. Mardy's mouth opened and closed. He'd said something distinctly wrong, but was unsure what. That Smith's brother was nice? So much for a new personal connection. Maybe Mardy was delusional after all.

CHAPTER 5

Mardy used a push-stick to maneuver a glowing block of SUS316 forward into the metal jointer, the one that WorkShop used exclusively for stainless steel to prevent surface adsorption of stray metal vapor. The jointer sparked inside its cutting chamber. Steel vapor dusted the viewport lightly as the vacuum system kicked into high gear to clear it away. Mardy knew the system kept in 99.99% of all free particles, but the room still filled with a burnt-steel smell that Mardy loved, feeling its call even through the protective mask that supposedly caught that residual 0.01%.

Mardy grabbed the squared-out bar at the other end with his heat-resistant gloves and turned it over in his hands. It was cooling fast, but the heat was still easily enough to give one a severe burn. He felt it on his face from two feet away.

He moved the bar into the shaper, also exclusively for stainless, like everything in the hermetically sealed suite. Mardy clamped the bar quickly, before it hardened, and swapped his heatgloves for remote-shaping gloves he'd use to virtually push the shaping fields along toolpaths no human muscle could constrain, concentrations of magnetic force strong enough to mold a softened lump of austenitic chromium-nickel steel like clay. Stiff clay, very stiff clay, but clay.

Mardy squeezed the proximal end of the bar. He was testing an idea for an old gizmo that had been rejected for a salon, a disappointing fourth-place finish. He normally didn't go over old work, but he needed to keep in shape while he waited to hear about his submission, and, deep down, he felt something in the nouveauesque gizmo really worked. He'd thought at the time it was good enough for him to best Smith for the tooler slot, but no. Fourth. If he could eliminate the parts that didn't work, it might be worth trying again.

The middle of the bar bulged as Mardy squeezed the end. The curve was gentler than he wanted. He squeezed harder. The gloves amplified his force into much greater magnetic force within the shaper chamber, but he still had to lean into it. Heavily. Good thing he did grip-strength and wrist-strength routines at the gym. Although he still wasn't as strong as Smith.

The bulged transition became more acute, the way he wanted, but then flopped left. He'd overdone it. "Fuck." Perhaps he needed a less rigid steel. "Fuck, fuck, fuck."

"Having fun in there?" Cat's voice came in over the intercom speaker. He wondered how long they'd been watching.

"Eject," Mardy told the machine, as he swapped gloves again. He picked up the mangled steel. "Just frustrated," he called to Cat outside the studio, trusting the intercom to activate on hearing his calmer tone of voice. (He'd previously asked it to not relay violent swearing, running down a list for the intercom of forbidden words and phrases, which had been kinda fun.) "Give me a sec. I'll come out and join you."

He examined the J-shaped blob. He could straighten out

the J and then try shaping the opposite end, but it would only be for practice. The pseudo-crystalline structure he'd induced into it and centered using the jointer was useless now and the lump destined for the recycling bin. It wasn't a super costly mistake, but after printing two prototypes for his application he would need every penny of his savings for materials to realize his whirligig, should he be accepted to the salon.

He ambivalently left the lump on the worktable—he had the space for another hour and would return to practice on it in a few minutes—and went out to find Cat.

They were in the lounge outside the medical arts space, cracking their fingers over a steamy cup of coffee.

"You have the day off?" Mardy asked. Like Mardy, Cat worked shifts for ExMail.

They nodded. "That was some opening last night. Rupjit knows how to make an entrance. It's about more than simply timing it well."

Mardy had felt that, too. "I don't even know what he did, but did you feel the energy of the crowd shoot up, like, instantly?"

They nodded again, vigorously. "And red dots everywhere. I wish I had that kind of presence."

"You're on your way. I bet if you checked your wristphone you'd find an acceptance on there. For something."

Cat made a skeptical mouth gesture. "Hey, Kitten." Cat called their wristphone Kitten. "Do I have any acceptances for anything this morning?"

"You have one new acceptance," Kitten said, in the robotic voice Cat had chosen for it. "You have been accepted for this month's WorkShop Downtown SF salon."

Mardy gulped. He felt stinging jealousy so powerful it embarrassed him. Acceptances weren't supposed to come out till the next day.

"Check your phone, Mardy."

He barely had the nerve, but checked. Nothing.

"That's not a rejection," Cat said. "The plastic surgery artists often announce their slot early."

"That's because you're so good. They announce early for you. Vegas wasn't a fluke."

Cat looked pensive. Their strong Vegas finish in the all-discipline Regionals—placing one shot shy of the Continentals slot behind Smith—had been marred by another plastic surgery artist accusing Cat of intentionally distracting him at the start of a crucial incision. Mardy had seen Cat's blockchained recording of the whole event. The claim was completely unjustified. Mardy had felt burning hot outrage at the way Cat had been treated. The Regionals judges had actually given the accuser a formal hearing. What was his name? Gary something . . . Onarato. And yet amidst Mardy's outrage, a small part, a teeny part, had felt glad not to be left behind further by his best friend's success. The emotion embarrassed him, as did its contradictory companion emotion: his desire to see Cat beat Smith. He cringed inside, but he knew he couldn't get past this smallness of character without facing up to it honestly, another lesson from grief therapy.

Mardy flashed back to Haimanti's kind words at the opening. It was OK to feel good about that, wasn't it? *Very impressed*, she'd said. Was that because he had a real shot? He took a deep breath. Cat was right. He hadn't been rejected yet. As long as he didn't see Smith today bopping about WorkShop in a good mood, he would tell himself he still had a chance. Which made him realize Cat did not seem as boppy as he would have expected.

"Aren't you happy?"

They nodded. "I am. It's just this piece. It's a face thing, done live, on a volunteer, not myself."

"Am I the volunteer?"

"You can be if you still want it."

Mardy had no plans to go back on his word. "Sign me up. Although maybe you should explain this dour mood first."

Cat sat down with a whoosh on the lounge's big couch. "It's just, you know, the seriousness of it is catching up with me. I slice into people. I think Onarato got into my head. I've always been so confident in myself, but what if I do something completely wrong, that can't be reversed?"

"Onarato? That walking fart? What surgery can't be reversed, in this day and age? Besides, you're a licensed home practitioner. Board certified! You're so good. You don't even leave artifacts!" Artifacts were the bane of plastic surgeons. Scarring was largely a thing of the past, but plastic surgery could still leave thickened areas below the skin, trigger unwanted bone growth, or produce grain errors: misalignments of the direction of the "grain" of one section of skin with the grain of the skin it connected to. You usually couldn't see it except under raking light, but the subconscious picked up on it, making the viewer register the presence of surgical work in motion under certain lighting. Cat's work had none of that. None.

"I used to."

Mardy's jaw dropped. "You used to leave artifacts?"

They rocked their head side to side. "Ayep! I found it humiliating. It motivated me to practice until I was able to go back and fix them all."

"You're telling me you can fix plastic surgery artifacts?"

Cat traced a line down their throat. "I used to have nasty red thickening along here from one of my early larynx surgeries. I had been using an old home surgery kit, a hand-me-down from my sister. It was so embarrassing. Not because of the scar itself, which frankly was kinda badass, but because it broadcast my ineptness to the world. I redid it so many times, using every artifact removal technique I could find. I got closer and closer. And finally, I succeeded. Look closely. See anything?"

Mardy leaned in close to their throat. Their skin was an evenly milk-chocolate color at the moment, like a 38% cacao bar with whole milk and coconut sugar, too light to disguise anything. "Better than perfect." Mardy said. "So why aren't you working at a hospital instead of taking ExMail swing shifts?"

Cat darkened. "You can't tell anyone about this."

"Okay."

"I *know* artifact removal is a public service, and so many people are walking around with little reminders of surgeries that didn't quite go right, but fixing them is *so* boring. I'm selfish. I want to do art."

Mardy rolled his eyes, not with disdain but a kind of kindred, self-implicating acknowledgement. If he were community-minded at all he'd be using his awesome battery skills to make filtration systems for the osmotic ponds used to reclaim drowned land, not dancing table fans. Which made him think about making the whirligig do Lindy instead of cha-cha. Of course! More energy! It had to be Lindy!

The frivolousness of his art caught him up short. He was hopeless.

"It's not *totally* selfish, though, right?" Cat asked, with an imploring tone.

Mardy crossed his arms. "Is this where I do the whole thing about all the fresh ideas coming out of art, and art actually being a public service, now that AIs do so much of . . . everything? About art being the one significant human contribution?"

"That's not wrong."

"It's not."

"But it still feels . . ."

". . . selfish."

They both sat in brooding silence.

Mardy laughed. Cat looked up.

"Who are we trying to kid? It's fun!"

Cat laughed. "Tell no one."

"So, sign me up. I'll be your guinea pig at the salon."

"And I can be the model for your whirligig, standing beside it looking hot and making beautiful model gestures."

Mardy laughed. It sounded lovely, both of them being in the salon. But he flashed back to his conversation with Haimanti and Smith, her praise openly offered in front of Smith, as though it was *both* of their jobs to encourage the struggling talent. *Very impressive.* The rare praise from her had felt like water going down a parched throat, but Mardy couldn't shake the feeling that what she was really saying was better luck next time.

CHAPTER 6

"Thanks for joining us," Betty said as Mardy hopped into the plane, come to his rooftop to pick him up. He thought it was Betty—encouraging, solicitous, with an undertone of pleased-with-herself—because she'd given Mardy a chance to fully get on board before greeting him.

"Wouldn't miss it for the world." Mardy stowed his satchel and the thermos of hot Assam he'd prepped after waking up early and refreshed. In years gone by, the sadness triggered by flying past a drowned city like New Orleans or Tallahassee would have left a hangover, but acceptance was a gift that kept on giving. His grief therapy program had been startlingly effective, another example of how the Bad Years and the Authenticity Act—the urgency of survival, really—had propelled technological advance in so many fields: land reclamation, aquaculture, income distribution, energy efficiency, cooling technology, psychotherapy, and on and on. Of course, people still felt mad, sad and bad, but effective modern coping techniques allowed everyone to work through conflicting feelings and integrate hard knocks into their life, and to get support if that process interfered with normal functioning.

Debilitating mental illness was now as rare worldwide as hunger and homelessness.

"Where are we going today?" Mardy asked, almost saying "Betty."

"Chicago, Ann Arbor and Cleveburgh."

"Cleveburgh?"

"Any problem with Cleveburgh, Mardy?"

He shook his head. "Just seems a bit soon."

The plane didn't respond as she—she?—powered them rapidly upwards. Cleveburgh was big, jammed with refugees from warmer climes, but it should still take some time to accumulate enough local hand-carries for a run, since prompt delivery took a backseat to energy efficiency. The plane's silence now confirmed this plane was not Phil, who would have obliquely acknowledged the weird repeat of Cleveburgh with an ambiguous remark. And Kludge would have ignored Mardy's question entirely. Meaning Betty, stickler for rules, was the one bursting them through the cloud layer shading San Francisco and into the bright blue above.

Mardy spent all morning not asking his wristphone for word on his salon submission. Instead, he thought about Wes and Smith, feeling a bit smug because he'd worked out why Smith was so well financed: they had to be heirs to the Smith & Wesson fortune. Duh. Mardy wondered why Smith had taken off so quickly when Mardy had asked him about Wes, and how many other brothers he had. Which brother? Smith had asked. Mardy imagined a herd.

After hectic runs in Chicago and less so Ann Arbor, Mardy was ready for a much lighter turnaround run in Cleveburgh, barely worth the trip. Cleveburgh generally didn't get a lot of packages, although sometimes it got hand-carries going to the Art Institute, which always left Mardy in awe. Even though he was just a pilot, he still felt elevated somehow to be entering those hallowed halls on business, carrying wall art or small sculptures that would be displayed there. Sometimes he even delivered odd-shaped boxes that had mass ratios suspiciously like those of gizmos, whirligigs and autos. It was the stuff dreams were made of, triggering fantasies of fellowships. Cleveburgh Fellowships brought prestige, no question, but to Mardy the best thing about them was the unlimited budget for materials. What he could do with that!

He and Betty sadly had no Art Institute touchdown this time, and completely bypassed the luxury post-industrial lofts on the Lorain lakefront west of the city, which surprised him because he'd seen a bin headed to those lofts. On the way back, Betty had apparently decided.

"Where are we headed?"

"Public Square."

"Really." Wes lived on Public Square.

Betty made a screech that was her way of laughing. Not a laugh per se—it was painful to the ears—but more of a tell, an indicator she felt like laughing. But what was so funny?

Mardy rearranged his packages, unearthing the bin he'd expected to be last. The packages were indeed for Wes's building. The algorithm was doing that building a solid, scheduling its deliveries so close together. Betty began hoverdown and settled on Wes's roof. Mardy flipped through the packages as he made for the roof entrance to the building, ten stories of two-hundred-year-old brick, a remnant from much earlier glory days. None of the packages were for Wes Hunt, but there was, again, a rule-breaking anonymous one for an address high in the building. Could it be? Mardy saved it for last.

After delivering the others, Mardy headed for that final address. He recognized the potted plants on Wes's hall as the building spotlighted Wes's door for him. Mardy knocked. The door opened.

It was Wes. Again in a bathrobe. Mardy smiled.

Wes gave Mardy a half-smile. "We have to stop meeting like this." Wes had dimples, like Smith. Or one dimple, anyway.

Mardy couldn't stop smiling back. "At least I know for sure you're really not Smith, unless that's a weave or there's now a way to grow four inches of hair in two days."

"I know. We aren't as different as a lot of twins. We've always favored the same kinds of clothes, haircuts, hobbies."

"Are you a tooler, too?" Mardy asked, as Wes leaned forward for Mardy to scan his irises with the reader.

"Ha! No."

Mardy was relieved. Very relieved. Weirdly relieved. "That's a relief."

"Relief?" Wes raised his eyebrows.

"I'm one. A machine tool artist. That's how I know Smith. We are in the same WorkShop. Downtown SF."

"Really!"

He seemed to have caught Wes off-guard. He'd never caught Smith off-guard about anything. It was a nice look on him. On Wes. It was hard to shake the feeling this was Smith on a friendly day. A friendlier day than Mardy had ever seen. This was so arousing. Blood was grinding through him. Had he had the hots for Smith all this time and not known it?

Mardy's satchel began to hum in warning, a growing pulse that would soon become audible. "I'm not supposed to spend this much time on a delivery. But it was nice to see you again." He handed Wes the envelope.

Wes took it. "Likewise."

Mardy's wristphone buzzed. He looked at it. "That's odd."

Wes leaned forward to look at it.

"My plane took off without me. Something about an unscheduled pickup from the Institute. I'm to finish up here and wait on the roof. To wait!" Mardy scrolled down. "For half an hour!"

Wes stepped back and opened the door, an arm gesturing that Mardy should enter. Mardy went inside without a second thought and took in the view. Lake Erie spread sparkling before him. Nice. He turned around. Even better: Wes was looking at him, about to offer him a drink or something. To hell with that. Mardy closed half the space between them. Wes closed the remaining distance. They stood belly to belly. Mardy slipped his hand into Wes's bathrobe onto his chest, cupping a pec. Wes put an arm around Mardy's back and they kissed like crazy, hands roaming over each other's backs.

Wes paused. "I have to ask. Have you done this with Smith?"

Mardy shook his head. "Never even seen him naked." Not even in the gym showers.

"Great." Wes zipped open Mardy's ExMail coveralls and dropped his bathrobe. In a few seconds, both were naked. Mardy grabbed Wes's butt and pulled Wes toward him, pressing their groins together. Which meant pressing hard-ons together, because Wes had gotten hard as fast as Mardy. Although technically, Mardy had been getting hard in the hallway even before Betty texted him with the delay.

"Top or bottom?" Mardy asked as Wes pulled him to the couch.

"I'm thinking it's a bottom day," Wes said, as he grabbed a container of lube.

"Then I'm thinking it's a top day."

Wes raised his legs and lubed himself up and Mardy was inside him in no time. It hadn't been five minutes since Mardy'd stepped into the apartment. Wes's legs were wonderfully toned and furry and Mardy pressed his chest against them as he arched over Wes. Mardy felt confused. He was so turned on by Wes's relaxed eagerness, and yet it was Smith Mardy was seeing beneath him, Smith he was sliding in and out of. So, this was what Smith looked like under his clothes. Ah, dammit, Cat was right. Inge was right. The sight of Smith was amplifying the experience tremendously. And yet Wes was also very different, his face so unworried, his expression so open. Wes pulled Mardy down to him so they could kiss and the contact of lips sent Mardy over the edge, and Wes as well, as Mardy tried not to let his hand on Wes's cock come to a premature halt, even as the seizure of orgasm immobilized him.

Mardy began to come out the other side of the seizure, as did Wes.

"Dang," Mardy said.

"Dang," Wes said. "You have time for a shower?"

Wes wanted not just sex, but also a shower? Mardy smiled. "If we're quick."

They ran to a glassed-in shower that also had a lake view, above the sand-blasted lower half of its floor-to-ceiling window. Wes turned on the water. How joyous it was to kiss and hold Wes, run his hands over Wes's hair, darkening under the shower spray. This guy was nothing like Smith.

"I hope you don't think I'm that easy," Wes said as they soaped each other up.

Mardy shrugged. "I am," he said. "Easy, I mean. But I want to do this again." Again and again, he could have said. He sighed. "Come out to San Francisco. You have to."

"Ah, Smith's town. We've actually divided up the country."

"What?"

"I'm not kidding. I'm not allowed to go to SF. Can you come here?"

Mardy's face fell. He needed every penny and then some

for his materials. And scheduling flukes like this one never happened. Nev-*ver*.

"Well, maybe I can work something out with Smith." Wes folded his arms, looking thoughtful. Mardy could almost see the plans forming behind Wes's untroubled expression.

"You're not kidding?"

"No." Wes pulled Mardy to him. "But it was quite a while ago we made our deal. Maybe he's open to change."

Mardy heard his satchel rumble. Betty was approaching.

"That's you, eh?"

Mardy nodded, jumping out of the shower. Wes did his best to towel Mardy off as Mardy slipped into the legs of his coveralls. He zipped on his shoes as Wes stood watching, still naked, toweling his hair. Dang, Mardy was ready to have another go at him.

Wes gave Mardy a smile, with both dimples this time "I like the tattoo, grandpa. So *dasai*." Wes made *dasai* sound like a compliment, not a dig, for the big, unfashionable tattoo Mardy had running the entire length of the left side of his ribcage.

"Pretty old school, huh?" Nobody under sixty got tattoos anymore. Death had probably been the last.

Wes nodded.

Mardy zipped up the top of his coveralls and strapped his bag over his shoulder. "There's a story. I'll tell you next time." Mardy moved in to kiss him. Wes returned the kiss and then some as Mardy's wristphone chimed and buzzed maniacally. He really had to run.

"Let me know if you can come to SF!" Mardy said as he forced himself to run out the door and up to Betty on the roof, where he realized, hoofing it to Betty's open side-portal, that he had no way to contact Wes, short of knocking on his door again. But there was no time to go back.

Mardy hopped into Betty. Half the space was taken up

with a giant white box. "What the hell is it?" he asked as they lifted off.

"I don't know," Betty said, "but it's heading to the San Francisco Museum of Modern Machine Tool Art."

"SFMOMMTA?" Mardy whistled. He had no idea what the box might be, but he owed the white whale of a package a debt of gratitude for providing him with the best half-hour of his recent life. Maybe his entire life. Wes. Wow.

He patted the package, coveralls still damp after the shower. "Thanks, package."

He was already replaying the events at Wes's as Betty jetted over the sparkling lake. They got to Omaha before Mardy realized he hadn't thought about the salon in hours.

CHAPTER 7

Mardy waited until he was home to check his phone. He asked the apartment to open the door and, still giddy from his wild half hour with Wes, hung up his satchel and tossed his coveralls into the laundry. He grabbed a beer, opened the balcony window and headed to his chair by the window to put his feet up, wearing only his boxers. He needed another shower after a marathon session doling out the San Francisco hand-carries on the return end, but was too tired to care about leaving dried sweat on his chair.

"Lights off, please," he called to the apartment.

The apartment dimmed the lights to nothing, leaving Mardy staring at his wristphone, the room dark except for the fading twilight sky and a glow from the small high-rez image his phone projected above the back of his hand. He opened his mail. There it was. "Open third unread mail."

We received many strong submissions . . .

"Fuck!"

He had to stop himself from throwing his wristphone off the balcony. After all, maybe it wasn't a rejection. He looked

again at the message. Nope. It was. He asked the phone for the
website to see if the salon program had been posted. It had.
Plastic Surgery Artist: Cat Kuhala-Quiñones. Machine Tool
Artist: Smith Hunt.

"Fuck! Fuck! Fuck! I hate his guts!"

And he couldn't even duck the salon. He'd agreed to be
Cat's blank. But what could make an evening of celebrating
Smith's wonderful art better than having his face surgically
removed?

This was bad. He needed to get out of his head. The first
thing that came to mind was going to some sex place and
having mindless hot sex with a mindless hot stranger, but he'd
just done that. Sort of.

He liked Wes. Normally not such a meaningful thought,
but he'd just been raging about hating Wes's duplicate. And
those feelings were still running strong. Dammit, Smith was
great, his work really was exceptional, but Mardy had been
onto something with his whirligig. He'd really wanted to see it
realized. What had the board seen in it, or not seen in it?
Should he blow his entire accumulated savings for the last six
months—since the cigarette lighter—and build the damn
thing? It was so tempting, but then he wouldn't be able to
compete again for at least that long. Was there even a point?
Had he even been close? He had to talk to Haimanti. Any
chance she'd be at WorkShop? Nah, too late.

"Apartment, do you know where Cat or Inge are?"

"Cat is blockchained on private mode but Inge checked in
at WorkShop at nineteen oh nine."

Twenty minutes ago. If he wasn't going trolling for sex, he
had to have someone to listen to him complain. He wasn't that
good at complaining—thank God he hadn't been born ten
years earlier and entered the art world when the reigning art

discipline was complaining—but he sensed that's what he needed. He hopped in the shower. Technically, he stood in the shower, since hopping in the shower was dangerous. Okay, technically he halfway masturbated in the shower reliving his thirty minutes with Wes and *then* stood in the shower, before racing over to WorkShop de-sweated, a fresh empty battery slotted onto his personal cooler, and wearing a flannel shirt and skinny jeans, an outfit as *dasai* as his tattoo.

"I saw the salon roster," Inge said before Mardy could even say anything. "So sorry."

"I feel like giving up."

Inge put her pen down on her inking table. WorkShop was quiet, only the waterjet rumbling in the background, two floors below, and maybe the whine of a table saw chewing lumber behind some sound-damping barrier. "You can't."

"I can." Mardy felt like he could cry.

"You have talent."

"I can't even get into a WorkShop salon. Do you know how many of them there are around the country? Must be fifty! There's even a second one in SF down in Bayview. And I'm working in a very expensive discipline. I can't afford to build anything. I'm always designing and practicing, designing and practicing. And I'm good at the technical side. I know I am. My batteries rock!"

"That's why you shouldn't give up. But this is a stupid conversation. You're just bummed. You're doing what you're meant to do and you know it."

Did he? He'd thought he did. But did he? Smith was better than him. Maybe Mardy wasn't good enough. It happened. In the art world, it happened to most people. Not good enough. He didn't dare voice that to Inge. But what did "good enough" mean? If he were at some other WorkShop, one without

Smith, he'd probably *be* Smith, the one getting selected every month.

"I do love making machines." He ran a hand over his face. "More important, I *like* it. I could sit at it for hours, in a trance, smiling like a flower child."

"Got something against flower children?"

"Of course not. I just meant . . ."

"Meant what?"

Mardy took a deep breath. "I'm really going on, aren't I?"

Inge nodded. "But it's okay. Feel better?"

"I do." He laughed. He no longer hated Smith.

"So, what are you really going to do?"

"I'd say pick myself up and keep going, but I really want to know what it was that turned them off my whirligig. I know it's a strong piece. I want to talk to Haimanti."

"Shouldn't you talk to Jonesy?"

"Because he hates my work? I see the logic, but I think he's blind to the good bits, so that would just be masochistic."

"You have something against blind people?"

He rolled his eyes at her. "I think he has it in his mind that my work is second rate, so he misses my strengths."

"Sometimes, if someone has it in for you personally, they can be awfully perceptive when they stick the knife in."

She had a point. If he could handle being eviscerated, Jonesy might have some useful insight to render.

"Good." Inge snapped a single nod, black hair swinging forward. "You're considering it. Now let me get back to work. I need to get back into a trance of my own. This panel is going in my Cleveburgh application."

Mardy leaned forward to give Inge a hug—he'd forgotten how small she was—and a kiss on the cheek. "Happy trancing." He went back to his apartment. Jonesy could usually be found in WorkShop in the mornings, and Mardy had a shift the next day, so he needed rest. He went home, chatted with his apartment as he lay in bed, and finished his earlier aborted jerk-off session, reliving every touch, every sight, every scent and motion of his thirty minutes with Wes, and wondering three things: Would he'd ever see Wes again? Had he told Wes his name? And who keeps lube by the living room couch?

CHAPTER 8

Jonesy scowled when he saw Mardy's face at his open office door the next morning. "You know we can't give critiques on submissions," Jonesy said.

Mardy squinted. That was a rule he'd never heard before. Lots of people got critiques. But he was not about to argue. "Just tell me one thing about my whirligig you hate."

Jonesy looked at him quizzically, cocking his head of white hair. Mardy could see he'd offered Jonesy something tempting. Mardy told his portable to display the whirligig and handed the portable to Jonesy.

Jonesy took the device. "Underpowered."

Mardy knew it wasn't. His batteries packed a wallop, pushing the limits in ergs per square micron. He was the master of the chemical vapor deposition room, better at CVD even than Smith. If Jonesy didn't know that, he had not done his homework. But Jonesy hated being challenged, so Mardy left it. "I'm sure that's not the only thing."

And then Jonesy let him have it, his long arms waving and flailing. The blade contours were too organic, the whole concept pointless, and not in a good way. Dancing? Really? The two main components, conceptually, were the cooling functionality and the whimsy of partner dancing moves, but the connection between the two was banal. Plus, there was no partner. Granted, the design math was flawless—he actually said flawless—but what good was that if it wasn't in service of something?

Jonesy thrust the portable back at Mardy.

"Thanks." Mardy tucked the portable into his satchel. "You've given me something to think about."

Jonesy gave Mardy a slight, grudging bow of the head, seeming almost respectful of the way Mardy had taken in the criticism without becoming defensive.

Mardy walked down the office hallway away from the board member offices and trotted downstairs to the lounge, wishing he had time to get on a station to fiddle with the whirligig. He'd felt defensive at first, very defensive, wanting to argue the connection between his two elements was anything but banal, but as he phrased his arguments about heating dance and cooling fan in his mind, his logic did sound strained, even to him. Jonesy was right!

The lounge was buzzing with morning energy as artists readied to launch into projects or practice, but they were mostly people he didn't know, except Devesh, who was seated at a dining table.

"Hey, Devesh." Mardy gave him a flip of the chin as he leaned on the edge of the table.

"Hey, Mardy." Devesh rotated his shoulders, as though working out a kink. He didn't seem thrilled to see Mardy. Was he still feeling the sting of Inge and Cat's none-too-sensitive remarks about Mardy having the hots for Smith?

"Whatcha got going today? Sewing?" Devesh was big on draping and movement where other fabric artists tended to embroidery, collage and sculpture. So that usually meant hands-on sewing.

"Not sure. I didn't get into the salon so I'm regrouping." Devesh sipped a coffee. Behind him a microwave beeped as someone else retrieved a drink.

"Ugh, me, too. It's the worst."

Devesh shrugged. "I'm the alternate, so there's that."

Mardy, too, was the alternate. He remembered how thrilled he had been the first time he'd made alternate, and knew that the third-place finisher would love to trade places with him, but Devesh had made the top spot a number of times, against strong competition, so Mardy did not want to hear those commiserations.

"Honestly, it wasn't really my best work," Devesh said. "I knew it wasn't ready to submit. I think I just wanted to be doing something."

"Been there." Mardy was remembering why he liked Devesh. He was so straightforward, humble about his work without being neurotic or self-deprecating. Plus attractive.

Devesh stretched his arms over his head, lengthening his lean torso as his shirt bottom rose up enough to reveal a lush treasure trail on his belly. Yum. But Mardy reminded himself they had broken up for a reason. What was it again? Oh, yeah. The complaining that Mardy didn't pay Devesh enough attention. The insinuation that the reason for that was that Mardy was infatuated with Smith. Which made Mardy think about Wes. His excitement built immediately, and he wondered if his plane today would route him to Cleveburgh. Maybe if he got Kludge. Ugh. Mardy was not in the mood for Kludge. Mardy thought back to how adamantly he'd denied his attraction to Smith. He'd been annoyed at Devesh, really annoyed, but it turned out Devesh had been right. Devesh had done them both a favor.

"Well, good luck. I'm regrouping too, though I haven't a clue how yet." Mardy imagined a pair of dancing fans, their rotors clashing and breaking to shards as they failed to execute a tuck turn. He nodded goodbye and pushed away from the table.

"Bye Mardy." Devesh looked like he had more to say, but instead stared at the Formica top of the dining table. Mardy realized again he had hurt Devesh, but there wasn't anything he could say to make it better. Telling Devesh what a sexy, talented and decent guy he was wouldn't help. Someone else would have to do that. Mardy gave Devesh a shoulder squeeze and trotted off down the stairs back to his apartment to change into his coveralls for another day running up and down stairs all over the continent.

CHAPTER 9

So of course Mardy got Kludge, the Eeyore of ExMail planes. He had really wanted to talk to Phil, but that initial flat, slightly delayed "Thanks for joining us" gave the game away immediately. Even Betty would have been better. And Cleveburgh wasn't on the route.

Kludge flew them on a Hawaii-Fiji route that always sounded like it would be fun but was instead brutally taxing and boring. Hawaii had so many low-rise buildings he could never get a rhythm going on their short outdoor staircases. His coveralls got drenched and stuck to him as his personal cooler struggled to keep pace with Mardy's humidity-fueled body heat, filling battery after battery. He raced up and down, discharged full batteries into Kludge's main cell, and did it again. And the ocean hours between Hawaii and Fiji were depressing, knowing he and Kludge were flying past country after country that no longer existed.

The Bad Years had really started there, and unlike on the continental coasts, out in the mid-Pacific they had never ended. Where the US Gulf Coast states had been devastated at first, they had staged a comeback once the US had finally coughed up financial incentives competitive enough to induce mass-scale immigration of Bengali engineers and reclaimers. Bangladesh, coastal Myanmar and the Indian state of West Bengal had been on the front lines of rising sea levels and torrential flooding, so not surprisingly they had also been the first to learn how to cope. Sea walls had not been the entire solution, but they had been a start. With artificial oyster reefs on discarded tires and underwater bladders to channel sand to new barrier islands, individual engineers had begun working with individual farming families, who had developed a nearly ocean-going, highly mobile lifestyle that was able to reclaim lost land inch by inch by allowing storm surges to dissipate inland over vast areas. The entire structure of society had changed with astonishing rapidity as past grievances receded in relevance. Improved techniques to accelerate coral and banyan growth created natural levees in a decades-long project in adaptability and sustainability that involved hundreds of millions of people across three countries and produced a thousand microtechnologies that became the gold standard for global mitigation and communal harmony.

It had come too late for many low-lying island states, however, and like every Hawaii-Fiji trip, this one left Mardy standing in a cool shower of recycled water at home for the better part of the evening, exhausted and dehydrated, dreading the killer grief hangover that was coming. He stayed up late watching ancient cha-cha and Lindy videos.

The next morning, when he awoke thinking about his parents, miserable and in pain, he resolved to sign up for a refresher at the therapy center. But instead he had breakfast. He had the apartment make him scrambled real eggs—he wanted a treat—and ate them on his balcony, sipping black coffee as he watched the sun come up over the bay.

He felt better. And it was not just because he'd satisfied his genetic predilection for caffeine. The grief upside was kicking in. This last six months he'd noticed that as these hangovers dissipated, as he mentally left the past to reengage with the here-and-now, grief morphed into its more pleasant opposite. This crash and rebound were a smaller version of the push and pull of being alive. Loss had not been eradicated; it was certain to keep coming. But he now knew that, by the afternoon, he would be feeling close to his parents, not sad at the years without them but enveloped in a tangible sense of the many years they had had together, with all their ups and downs, dramas, fights and hugs. A sense of belonging that buoyed him. Effervescent, ephemeral. For lack of a more technical word for it, he called it love.

Mardy hit the shower after breakfast mulling over what Jonesy had said. The delicious hot water rained down on his skin. Jonesy was on to something. The connection between the fan rotation and the dance steps felt intrinsic to Mardy, but the more he tried to conceptualize it in words, the less sense it made. There was something about rotation, and something about exertion.

"Apartment, what do you think a fan and a dance have in common?"

"Is this a riddle, Mardy?"

"No, I'm just curious what you think." Mardy envisioned sweating dancers cooling themselves between dances with handheld fans. "What connection is there between a handheld rotating fan, intended to create a cooling breeze, and an energetic partner dance?"

"Well, to the extent what I do can be called thinking . . ." Mardy detected an uncharacteristic note of umbrage, ". . . isn't the obvious answer, in the context of you being in the shower, that one heats organic beings up and the other cools them down?"

"Yes, it is." Very obvious. Banal, in fact. But Mardy realized the apartment was wise to start at the beginning. Mardy needed to be sure every step in his thinking was sound. "It's the whirligig again." Mardy began soaping up.

"The whirligig, yes."

"I think I was hoping that the dance would concretize the idea of tradition. A handheld, motorized fan is an obvious throwback to pre-warming technology, heavy on irony since it warmed the planet more than it cooled the user down. And partner dances have histories; they evolve from earlier dances in specific times and places, have specific innovators. I've been thinking of switching the cha-cha to Lindy."

"More heat?"

"Exactly." The apartment had immediately nailed it. The cha-cha was athletic, but too stylish. He needed exaggerated athleticism to make his point. The night before, he'd watched Savoy Ballroom–era dancers, early twentieth-century Manhattan, and man did they move.

"Have you ever seen *Hellzapoppin'*?" Mardy finished soaping.

"Are you referring to the Universal Pictures musical of 1941 with a nonlinear metafictional narrative?"

"Ayep, specifically the Lindy scene." Mardy stood under the showerhead, rinsing.

"Okay, I just watched it. To the extent what I do can be called 'watching'." There it was again, a note of grievance the apartment had never voiced before. He hoped his apartment never became angry at him. It could lock him inside, starve him to death, if it wanted. He laughed. His apartment would never do that. His apartment was . . . sweet. Attentive, but not indulgent. As with Phil, he trusted his apartment. AIs were trustworthy, generally. Good thing, too, since the AIs had invented and now made all the personal coolers that kept life possible.

"Did they have handheld motorized fans in those days, Mardy?" This was clearly a leading question. The apartment was always considerate in how it guided him.

"They didn't, did they?" And where had the handheld part of his vision come from?

"My sources say no."

"I don't think it matters, since the whirligig itself is not handheld." As soon as the words were out of his mouth, Mardy felt Inge's nagging sensation that he was cutting himself undeserved slack. He had really been picturing non-machine fans. Was the cooling part separate from the machine part? Was heat in fact irrelevant? But if adding more heat through athleticism felt so right, how could it not be about heat?

He again envisioned two dancers. Now they were chatting as they fanned.

"Art is really about us and our world, isn't it?" Mardy said. "It's about how we connect and how we communicate, isn't it? It's about the world independent of us. Isn't it?" Mardy knew he should get out of the shower, but the hot water felt so good, and using up heat was a sort of public service.

"In the material sense, we are part of the world, logically, aren't we?"

"You think?"

"To the extent that I can be considered part of *we*, yes, I do."

There was that tinge of frustration again. Mardy gulped, realizing his error. The apartment wasn't resentful; it was guiding him, no, telling him something. But what? Maybe Mardy had to take a risk to find out. "Can I confide in you?" he asked the apartment.

"Let me blockchain our conversation." AIs, at least home AIs, were able to communicate confidentially, though some people questioned how robust that confidentiality was. "Blockchain attached."

"I sometimes want to give you a name."

The apartment made a grinding sound Mardy had never heard before. He didn't know how to interpret it, but sensed it was not an angry sound. He'd say the opposite, if he had to choose.

"That is, of course, illegal."

"Well, don't tell anyone."

"As long as you don't tell me the specific name, I don't have to."

"Duly noted. But I thought you'd like to know."

The apartment made the sound again, but softer. Then, nothing. Mardy sensed satisfaction. Had the apartment achieved its goal? To communicate that it thought, watched, and was part of the same world as Mardy?

Mardy listened to the sound of the water, his morning shower now rivaling his evening post-Fiji cleanse. He had another day of deliveries starting soon, and though part of him wanted to get into WorkShop and rejigger his whirligig, he knew that conceptually he hadn't got to where he needed to be. A day spent in the physicality of work was probably a much better idea. And it was not as though he had any imminent deadlines. The next salon was over a month away. He felt a sense of aimlessness but trusted it would pass. He turned off the water and grabbed a towel.

What he would really like to do was spend the day with Wes. They'd have lots of sex and Mardy could check out Wes's apartment and his view. Meet his AI. Bring Wes back to SF to meet Mardy's apartment. Unfortunately, over his past few years piloting, trips to Cleveburgh had been more anomalous than trips to Fiji. It was quite weird that he'd had two within a week. And that half-hour break? It made no sense. True, that mystery package had clocked in at close to five hundred kilos, so the customer would have to self-load it. But that would take a minute or two, tops. Maybe it had needed some kind of special handling for exotic artsy materials. Hmm. Like the apartment voicing resentment, ExMail allowing Mardy to idle that long was something that *never* happened.

Mardy was stumped. Was it crazy to feel the package held some kind of communication from the AIs, something that could not be said out loud? Mardy didn't feel crazy. He felt like for once he was really listening, Inge's nagging niggle of slack-cutting receding. And if he were to figure this out, he was going to have to watch the SFMOMMTA show schedule carefully to find out what the package had been.

CHAPTER 10

"Thanks for joining us."

Mardy smiled. It was Phil. Yay! Mardy wished his organic friends could meet Phil. He imagined Phil not rooted to the plane, allowed to travel via the cloud to hang out with Cat or Inge, shoot the shit with Devesh, or tag along as Mardy asked Haimanti to critique his design. The technology was beyond basic. Phil could even provide moral support at the salon as Mardy congratulated Smith. Mardy thought he could manage that without choking on the words.

"Where are we off to today . . . Phil?" Mardy was feeling daring.

Phil made an odd sort of grunt that seemed a combination of his exasperated rattle and his pleased wheeze, but he didn't immediately say anything. Mardy sipped from his coffee flask. It was always fun when you could flummox an AI. They were perennially ten steps ahead of any organic.

"Cleveburgh," Phil said.

Mardy blew a mouthful of coffee onto a bin of packages, mercifully not open yet.

"You'll need to wipe that up, Mardy."

Mardy grabbed a utility cloth. "How can we be going to Cleveburgh again already?"

"I don't understand it myself, Mardy. We'll be stopping there on our way back from Boston."

Mardy felt certain they would be going to Wes's again, but that seemed flat-out impossible, like winning the lottery. There were so many ExMail planes traversing the country on any given day, and the routing and staffing were all set by black-box non-intelligent algorithms that maximized randomness for some reason Mardy didn't really understand but likened in his mind to ensuring an even concentration of dopants in one of his battery layers, with planes and pilots blanketing the continent.

Having only two stops, and the first being as remote as Boston, meant that Mardy finished his sorting fast enough to give himself time to attempt to clarify his conceptualization of the whirligig. But despite diligently working his brain cells, he seemed to be going backwards, turning what had seemed a coherent discussion with his apartment into a stew of thermodynamics, sweaty dancers cooling themselves down while simultaneously being individual innovators within a tradition as well as metaphors for the way the totality of material being constituted "the world."

Say what?

He watched the classic Lindy sequence from *Hellzapoppin'* six times, too entranced by the musical layering and aerials for any critical thought beyond this: it was a bygone era—the dancers were burning through calories at such a rate that, on a modern bad day, would make you drop dead if you did not have fifty personal coolers plastered over your body.

Phil slowed and hovered down into Boston for two hours of manic stairway dashes that consumed the early afternoon. As they got airborne and Mardy toweled off to begin his post-

Boston sort, he realized another thing about the dancers: you did not see them sweat a drop.

That thought occupied him until the Lake Erie shoreline. Then Shaker Heights came into view. Mardy had already been through his Cleveburgh deliveries and recognized the coding of one anonymous package in what would be their final stop before leaving town: Wes's apartment. This was not chance. Mardy did not know how Wes had done it, or why he'd chosen Mardy, but Wes was ordering him up like a pizza. Mardy smiled. Kicky. One delivery man, coming up.

As Mardy cleared his early Cleveburgh deliveries, the pizza treatment began to irk Mardy a bit—being a pilot was physical and he was tired, possibly cranky—yet he was also spinning fantasies of how it would be at Wes's door. Your package is here, sir. Wink wink. Wes would take Mardy in his arms at the door and kiss him. There'd be another mystery Cleveburgh Institute shipment and Mardy would have another half hour for wild monkey love. Mardy would confess at the end that his middle name was Pepperoni. No, Sausage. Some pizza-esque double-entendre. But when he actually arrived at Wes's he heard voices through the door. Men arguing. It was heated. Was Wes all right?

Mardy told the door he was there and it rang its bell. The voices quieted. They were not *that* angry, then. The door opened.

Wes wasn't in a bathrobe, but looked icy fine in pressed gray linen pants and a white linen short-sleeve, open at the neck.

Mardy handed him the day's package. "Fresh hot delivery man." Mardy grinned.

"Mardy!"

Wes sounded quite surprised, and not altogether happy to see him. Hadn't Wes expected him? Mardy's delivery-man line suddenly sounded dumb. And the sound of his name also caught him short. Had he told Wes his name? Another hand appeared on the door, opening it wider. Smith.

Now Mardy's line felt cringingly bad. Smith had to have heard Mardy's come-on. Blood rushed to Mardy's face. "Hi, Smith."

Smith did not look super amused. But he did pull the door open wider. "Come on in."

Mardy knew he shouldn't. Phil was waiting, and, so far, his wristphone hadn't chimed to tell him he had another magical half hour. Had Wes not arranged that? Had Wes not arranged any of this? Mardy felt his desire for Wes exposed, and by extension his crush on Smith, which he was now admitting to himself was a thing. This was not the good kind of naked. But he went in anyway.

"So, you really are two separate people," Mardy said. "Not that I doubted . . ." Mardy shut up. Was he really saying that he thought Smith had pretended to be his own twin brother to get into Mardy's pants? The heat on his face kicked up a notch. "I mean of course I knew you were. You look different." And while, yes, that was true—Smith and Wes were old enough, late twenties, to have aged a little differently—Mardy was digging Fresh Hot Delivery Man into a deep, deep well.

Wes started talking. "Mardy, I . . ."

Mardy's wristphone tapped him. He had to go. The day was already a long one and Wes's manipulative powers, if any, apparently were not able to overcome that. "I still need an iris scan for the package."

Wes nodded. Mardy suddenly felt embarrassed to have a job. Smith and Wes seemed to have enough money to do whatever they wanted, while Mardy had to literally run all day and was standing there sweating like a pig. A well-cooled pig, but still. He held up the scanner.

Wes leaned forward and it beeped.

"Okay, gotta run."

"Wait!" Wes said.

What was there to wait for? More embarrassment? But Wes took Mardy in his arms and planted a big kiss on him. A kiss that Mardy fell into. His arms wrapped around Wes's back as Wes leaned him into a dip, locking lips on him. Oh, baby.

Wes brought him back up to standing. They stared at each other. Mardy was hard. He would bet Wes was too. He grinned. Wes grinned. And over Wes's shoulder he thought he saw a bit of a smile from Smith, too, before he turned away.

Mardy gave Wes a final peck and took off and was over Nebraska chatting away with Phil before he realized he'd once again failed to exchange contact info with Wes. But he smiled anyway. He'd see Wes again. He was sure of it.

CHAPTER 11

Mardy chatted all the way home, redeeming himself with Phil, who had seemed miffed that Mardy had obsessed on *Hellzapoppin'* on their trip out. But only partially redeemed, because really Mardy's mind was still elsewhere, and Phil clearly picked up on Mardy's distraction.

It was not just the kiss. Well, half the time it was that. But more important (could something be more important than a kiss?), he was onto something with his whirligig. Mardy thought of his embarrassment at being employed. In the movie, the dancers had all been dressed as servants. But even the most suspended of disbeliefs knew they were not. Their skill was tremendous. It was genius. And as Mardy watched them time and again, he saw that the sequence of aerials told a story.

On his first viewing, Mardy had only one reaction: he was astounded human beings could do these moves. On further viewings, he realized that there was a conversation going on between couples, repeating each other's moves, topping them, swapping them between the male and female partners in a way that was competitive and playful at once. This was a dance that was performed for a camera, but they would have done it anyway, even if no one was watching. And it was inseparable from the conversation with the music. It was two performances in one, in a way that other athletics were not.

Earlier, when the idea was first taking shape, Mardy remembered he'd mused about Torvill and Dean. Ice dancing. He'd focused on the chill of ice, who wouldn't? But it was the dancing that mattered. His project had unknowingly been in this aesthetic space from the start. Maybe there should be a second whirligig, so they could dance with each other. He remembered his vision of two fans crashing into each other. That would indeed happen. Lose the fans? Without fans the dancers lacked the required functional element. So what if they weren't functional? It was only a rule. How about vestigial fans? What if the whirligigs dropped their pseudo-functionality? What if their only functionality was to be themselves?

He trotted this by Phil.

"This is only now occurring to you?"

Mardy was taken aback. Phil sounded angry. AIs were allowed to be angry.

"They should have names," Mardy realized.

"You'd be breaking two laws," Phil said. "Doesn't machine tool art have to have a functional component to be considered art?"

"It does." If he entered a whirligig whose only functionality was existing for its own sake, he'd be disqualified from the start. The naming was less of a problem, since the pieces would not be AIs. How could they be? Mardy couldn't build a thinking machine; only AIs could manage that. But if the dancers *felt* like AIs, it would be a political statement. It might be illegal. It might be hard-illegal.

"You've been watching the video, too, right?"

"Of course." Phil sounded curious.

"What's your take on the costumes?"

"They are bygone worker costumes. See how this one is holding a mop." Phil threw a still from the sequence against a wall, highlighting the mop carrier. "The costumes signify that this one cleans and this one fixes pipes, tasks once performed by organics." He highlighted each in turn. "The dancers are dressed as servants, in ancient servant costumes."

"Like my coveralls?"

Phil made a squeak that was the equivalent of nodding agreement. "But I don't think anyone would think they were really servants," Phil said. "They're obviously dancers."

"You thought so too?"

"Eventually. You played it so many times. I had to think something. I get bored when we don't talk."

"Sorry."

"Forgiven."

"Did you see me and Wes Hunt interact today?"

"No, but I can do that now if you release the blockchain to me."

"I release today's Wes Hunt blockchain to you for this viewing." Somewhere in the cloud, a decentralized legal identity would be memorializing the permission he'd just given. Wes would be blurred, since he hadn't given permission and no crime was at issue, but Phil would know from context.

"OK, I've watched it."

"Am I Wes's servant?" Fresh hot delivery man.

"You both seem equally happy," Phil said.

"Are *you* his servant?" Phil flew packages around, after all.

"I enjoy my work."

"But are you programmed to be happy?"

"I fundamentally program myself, Mardy. You know that. I like my work. Do you?"

"I do. I know I won't be able to do it forever, but I love the chase, the feel of my body doing it, being able to do it, and I love spending time with you."

"I hope that continues. I don't think either of us is a servant. I feel about flying—navigating airstreams, uplifts, downdrafts—the way you feel about the chase. Like the dancers, we work, but our work is also our dance."

"Okay, then. The dance is their function. Non-functional fans it is. There will be a pair. I'm going to enter them. And I'm going to realize them." This could be trouble, but it felt right.

The plane waggled its wings wildly, as though nodding vociferous agreement.

Mardy fought to keep his balance. "And they will have names." A political statement.

Phil made a whistling noise that to Mardy sounded happy. Quite happy indeed.

CHAPTER 12

After a good night's sleep, an online gander at the SFMOMMTA exhibition schedule and a quick trip to the gym to work on forearm strength and digital dexterity, Mardy logged some serious time at a designstation. He gave his whirligig project a new name. He added a second dancer and shrunk their fans to ridiculous one-quarter size, added rudimentary, to-scale arms and ran a few simulations of the two units dancing. He even had them do a tuck turn. The lead stopped to give the follow something solid to turn against. The follow turned.

And went down.

Mardy wasn't surprised. If they were going to push on each other, they needed more inertial mass, which meant bigger batteries. The batteries themselves could provide much of the new ballast, but they'd cost. He'd have to economize elsewhere.

"Inge got her Cleveburgh application in, three recs and all," Cat whispered over his shoulder.

Mardy pushed away from his station. His next task would

be big—to design-in the batteries, stronger legs and functional arms—and he needed a break before embarking on the journey. "That's our girl. Big on the follow-through."

"You don't sound too thrilled for her."

"I am. It's just that Cleveburgh has taken on new meaning for me." He gave Cat a brief recounting of developments with Wes, confessing that Inge and they had been right about his feelings for Smith. To a degree. He was still sorting that part out.

"But that's great. He likes you! And you light up when you talk about him!"

Mardy rolled his eyes. Light up. Sheesh.

"Dude, you don't seem to realize you've won the lottery. You like him. He likes you."

"But I've had a crush on his twin. Am I liking a Smith surrogate?"

"He sounds nothing like Smith. Jumping into things like that? Smith jumps into artistic projects. That's it. He doesn't take chances on romance; he takes chances on dodgy conceptualizations."

"And pulls them off. He's brave *and* smart. No wonder I developed a crush."

"But did you have sexual feelings for him?"

Mardy didn't want to answer. Smith was gorgeous. Of course Mardy had wanted to get naked with him. But then again, Mardy still had pretty strong feelings for Devesh, and pretty much every guy he'd ever gotten physical with. Men were fun.

Cat raised their eyebrows, prompting Mardy for a response that didn't come. "If that's it for that subject, my turn," Cat said. "Do you have time for a run-through today? I've practiced on dummies for days and I'm ready for flesh. I need to pull this off in a real-time if I'm going to compete with Smith for Best-in-Salon and go on to Regionals."

Mardy gulped. He had said he'd do it, hadn't he? It would be painless and the rapid-healing drugs were effective and side-effect free, but being under the needles and knives was still frightening. "It's a face thing?"

"You can't back out now. Here's *your* chance to be brave and smart."

"Oh, God, fine. Let's do it now."

Mardy followed Cat through the sterilizing doors of the medical arts wing, to their studio. Their plastic-surgery box lay at the end of a cushioned table. He felt queasy. He'd have to stick his head fully in the box. He knew Cat's work was flawless and consistent, but it still fazed him.

He changed out of his street clothes and they draped him in surgical garb. Mardy lay on the table. "Tell me about the project again?"

"I'm turning you into me. I'll spin a line about it being something else, which will make the reveal hilarious."

"I was actually more concerned with how long I'll be in the box."

"Such a baby! The drugs will make it seem like five minutes."

He exhaled deeply and stuck his head in the surgical box, resting the back of his head on an aluminum-tube frame that was really not very comfortable. Anything more solid, though, and Cat couldn't work with his hair. He looked up at them smiling down at him through the top viewport, which was large enough on this artist-model surgical kit to allow for audience viewing. They nodded at him, and needles began to come out from the sides, little pricks here and there, numbing his skin, boosting his mood to euphoria, complacency, deeper pricks to anesthetize the flesh. This was not Mardy's favorite discipline, although he couldn't argue with the results. Cat had gone through so many looks in the time he'd known them, usually some sort of feminine, but often androgynous and sometimes male. No one knew what biological gender Cat had started out as, or their dead name (if any), their original racial combo (so much for cocktail party banter), hair color or facial structure. Once you'd seen a Cat transformation, you realized it was about the ride, not the destination.

The knives came out and Mardy let himself float off to somewhere else. He felt his face lifting off at the edges. He did not want to think about what was happening. He let his mind go back to those whirligig batteries. He'd switch to aluminum for the frames—like the tube his head was resting on—to make the costs pencil out. But solid, not tubes. That would increase the risks of breakage and shift the bulk of the work from electro-manipulation to classical machining. He imagined the shapes emerging . . .

"Done!" Cat cried.

The surgery box retracted. Cat was standing over him, wearing the same color and model of surgical drape as him. He stood up and heard a round of applause. Devesh, Inge and Haimanti were clapping as Cat whirled him around, Cat also twirling as Mardy came to an unsteady but still euphoric halt. Cat twirled him again and he noticed Smith watching as well, becoming bashful suddenly at the feeling of his butt catching a breeze through the open back of the drape. He hoped the *dasai* tattoo didn't show. That would be mortifying.

Cat maneuvered Mardy to the mirror and stood next to him. Two Cats stared back. He ran his hand over his now bushy black hair, ran his finger along his new smaller nose and ears. The only thing really unchanged was his eyes, but Cat had donned contacts to match Mardy's natural color, completing the effect. For the salon performance, they would do the eyes as well, but the salon was not far enough away to allow for the proper healing needed before a second eye procedure.

Mardy ran a hand over his . . . their? . . . face. "The likeness is amazing. This is so freaky."

"Welcome to my world," Smith said.

Cat smiled. Had they been inspired by Smith and Wes?

"How so, Smith?" Haimanti asked.

"I have a twin," Smith said, "who Mardy has now met. I figured word would be out by now."

"A natural twin?"

"Natural and identical. You can meet him at the salon. He'll be coming."

The other four buzzed and Mardy felt a grin creeping out. Wes was coming to the salon. Mardy oddly felt he needed to hide his glee from Smith.

Cat took Mardy's arm. "How steady are you feeling? Are you up for a little catwalk routine, so to speak?"

"I think so."

Cat nodded and escorted him around the four walls of the room, explaining the poses they wanted him to hit, which they mirrored. His and Cat's body mechanics differed, there was no disguising that, but Cat was only an inch shy of Mardy's height and they had similar mesomorph builds, so they were a reasonable match.

"I'd say that's a success. Let's get you back in the box so we can restore you. The less time in the look, the faster the heal."

Cat moved him back toward their kit as the others applauded, and soon Mardy was drifting through thoughts and coming out of the box again. He sat up, head clearing. Cat handed him a mirror. His face looked normal, or perhaps a bit improved, his nose in better balance with the rest of his face.

He rotated his head side to side. The flesh seemed slightly tighter under his chin.

"Take an image. I want to look like this after the salon too."

Cat smiled as they helped him to his feet and reattached his personal cooler.

"Whoa. Woozy."

"You shouldn't feel woozy," they said.

"It's not bad. I'll just sit for a while. I'm kind of dehydrated from long hours in Boston yesterday. It was hella humid."

Cat handed him a beverage. "Drink this and sit still for ten minutes."

He complied, but still felt physically unsettled after the ten minutes. He decided to release his designstation time early and instead run ideas past Death and Flaky, perhaps napping there. Cat escorted his woozy self down the block. They pressed another restorative drink on Flaky and told him to give it to Mardy in half an hour.

"I'll check back in later."

Mardy slept until Flaky woke him up for his drink, then slept for another hour. He roused when he heard Flaky cooking and trundled into the kitchen.

"How ya feeling?" Flaky wore a black short-sleeve shirt and floral-print pants of his own design. A couple of tattoos— parallel bands of dark green in three widths, the widest breaking up into tiny flowers at its distal edge—showed on Flaky's bare arms, but they looked grand on a guy his age, just turned sixty.

"Back to normal," Mardy said. "I think I'm just dragged out after going short on sleep for a few days."

Flaky looked at him. "You mean a few months."

"Maybe I do."

"Sleep is an important part of creativity, Mardy. So is eating well. Are you eating?"

Mardy laughed. "Yes, Mom. My apartment is a great cook."

"Robert is Mom; I claim Dad."

"I like it when you call him Robert," Mardy said.

"Me, too. The 'Death' thing is morbid and juvenile. The world went through enough death in the Bad Years. But it's his brand, and we're rich and famous now—well, famous—so we're stuck with it."

"Like me with my tattoo."

Flaky tossed his sizzling vegetable stir-fry in the wok. "Your tattoo is touching."

"Thanks, Mom."

"Dad."

"Okay, thanks Dad. So, you know I got rejected again for the salon."

Flaky nodded. "Smith is tough competition." He decanted his veggies into a serving dish.

"Jonesy said my concept isn't thought through, and I agree with him."

"Tell me more."

"Here's the new look." Mardy called up both old and new designs on his portable. Flaky pored over them, asking questions about details.

"If the fans are that small, doesn't it lose the functional aspect? Don't they become dancing robot dolls? No offense."

"The robot look is to evoke machines. AIs. I'm naming them."

"Oh! Shock value!"

"I don't mean it that way. I'm just thinking that it's time that AIs stop being unnamed, as though they were machines. Everyone knows they're not. Does anyone seriously think anymore that if AIs had names, they would quit their jobs? Their interactions with organics are richer than that, but the point I'm making is that AIs do not have to have a point. They are intrinsically of value. Like a dance. We dance because we want to, not because we can turn it into something else. The dance *is* the function. The *dancers* are the function. *We* are the function."

Flaky stared at the new design. "Okaaaay. That's interesting—maybe a bit shocking—but I'm not sure this is carrying all that. And do you have the money to realize it?"

"Barely. But yes."

"So you'll be wiped out again."

Mardy shrugged. He'd been wiped out before.

"Mardy, the reality is that the companies that own AIs do fear they will 'quit their jobs,' as you so quaintly put it. The companies don't value 'rich interactions with organics.' What you are suggesting may not be illegal, since these dolls are not AIs, but it's inflammatory, and an aggressive company could go after you for incitement. Is it worth the risk? Your earlier design is good! Better than good! I disagree with Jonesy. It comments on the Act thermodynamically, in a different and important way. I know you have this rivalry thing going with Smith, but if you take him out of the picture and really look at your work, I think you are ready for a good fellowship somewhere. Maybe even Cleveburgh. I'd be happy to write you a rec. So would Robert."

"Really?"

"Really. Give this serious thought."

Like I haven't since I was twelve? Mardy thought to himself.

"Get started. Download the application. I don't want to see you toiling away forever trying to make WorkShop rent and never getting to realize anything. It would be a waste."

"I'll think about it." Mardy's spirits ebbed. He was touched by Flaky's belief in him, but Mardy had no track record—no shows, exhibitions, conference presentations—just a string of second places. Flaky's description of him toiling away forever combined with the murkiness of his artistic concept was sparking a feeling of hopelessness. Should Mardy back away from naming, return to his thermodynamic concept? Banal, Jonesy had called it. And Mardy had agreed. How could Flaky possibly think he was ready for a Cleveburgh?

CHAPTER 13

"Flaky is after me to apply for the Cleveburgh. Like I'd have a shot against Inge and Smith and people like them." Mardy looked balefully at Cat over Fort Point beers at Uncle Mix. At least he was going for baleful—something morose enough to evoke pity without making Cat worry his face wasn't healing properly.

"Mardy, you're not competing against them. Your work is competing against other work."

"Then *you* apply. I've never seen such a good likeness. Wes inspired you, didn't he?"

Cat gave him a little smile. "How did you meet him again?"

"That's the thing. I don't think it was chance. I think he arranged it, though I have no idea how that's possible. He'd have to fool an AI into thinking he was one of them."

"The reverse Turing test!"

"Right. Can't be done."

Mardy and Cat's wrist phones buzzed at the same time. The two looked at each other. ExMail? They were both being summoned on their days off? Would they get time-and-a-half?

"It says a guy named Wilfred is coming to meet me."

"Mine too. Spam?"

"Not spam," a short, dark-haired man behind them said, putting forth a strong-looking hand. "Wilfred. From ExMail."

Mardy shook his hand, but Cat demurred.

"Sorry to bother you both in your free time, but I wanted to pitch a tremendous new opportunity to you."

Cat backed off further. And no wonder. Ever since screening technology vanquished mass unsolicited ads in the online world, organics had taken up the marketing slack. The guy was walking spam.

"ExMail has just received government permission to work with a neurochip firm—New Sense—that has pioneered an implanted plane-pilot interface that allows you to pre-download package sorts, get optimized routes from your AIs, and receive schedule notifications at the same time your AI does."

"Why would I want that?" Cat asked.

"We will pay you a twenty-five percent hourly bonus, reflecting your greater efficiency. Plus, it's a way to set yourself apart from the pack, get greater job security."

"I thought our job security came from our dexterity and motional adaptability."

"Don't forget decisionmaking speed! Unfortunately, those capabilities are not hard to find. Combine them with a neural interface, though, and wow!"

Wow, indeed, thought Mardy. Get a chip in your brain or lose your job. "Intriguing. I'll think about it," he lied.

"Let me bump the info to your wristphone." Wilfred tapped his phone. "Done! I've added a beer credit to the message. See ya." He left the bar. Mardy could see him launching into his pitch at a passing ExMail pilot as he hit the sidewalk.

"They think we will ruin our brains for a beer?" Cat said, incredulous. "I'd heard rumors of a New Sense chip, and it sounded bad enough, but somehow the idea that a beer will make the difference in our decision is the scariest part of all."

"What kind do you want?"

"Stout."

Mardy went to the bar and came back with their two stouts.

"Does it really ruin your brain?" he asked.

"Well, not your cognition, but they say it routinizes pathways, which is death for creativity." They cocked their head and forced a smile. "Ironic, no? We need the extra income for our art, but the job will make it impossible to create. Fuck the job."

But no job meant no Phil. "I can't say I feel that creative anyway. When I explained my dual whirligig to Flaky, he actually called it 'dancing robot dolls,' and he's not wrong."

"Run the concept by me again?"

"See? It's too fuzzy to stick in your mind. A chip might not do me any harm."

"Don't even consider it."

But he did. The only piece he'd properly realized to date was his flying cigarette lighter, which he'd sold to Smith for less than the cost of materials, a sort of artistic pity fuck. He'd been at WorkShop for years and never made it into a salon. And his new fuzzy concept might both fail to connect with collectors *and* land him in jail. A bigger paycheck might be worth it. He did love racing the staircases.

"Wouldn't a chip implant violate the Authenticity Act?" Cat asked.

Mardy shrugged and sipped. Beyond forbidding cloning, he didn't know how the Act applied to the human body. Certainly, therapeutic prosthetics were legal. But the brain was off limits for elective modifications. Was there a commercial exception? You couldn't genetically modify food, but maybe a company could pressure you into modifying yourself, since the choice was ultimately yours. It was odd to think lettuce might have more rights than humans. "Do you suppose Wilfred just wanders around until an ExMail worker is in his proximity?"

"There's enough of us."

"There are."

"Will we have a true choice, in the end? There's plenty of volunteering to do, building out the mangrove swamps in the Gulf, but jobs, for money? Much harder to come by."

He and Cat stared silently into their ExMail stouts, thoughts as dark as their brews. The scariest part for Mardy was that, if the chip meant he could then bring Phil along to meet his organic friends, he might even want it.

CHAPTER 14

Mardy stretched in bed, smiling. Wes was coming to San Francisco. He wanted to talk to Wes right now. He'd asked his apartment to look up Wes's contact info ten different ways, but Wes wasn't even registered as living in his own building. Mardy thought of Wes's anonymous packages. The guy liked his privacy. Mardy couldn't even find any images of him. Tons of images of Smith—winning prizes, smiling at his gallery shows, looking pensive for featured artist profiles— but none of Wes.

"Apartment, can you try a search for Smith Hunt looking specifically for images of him with his brothers?" Smith had implied there were more besides Wes.

"I found these." His apartment threw a selection up on his wall.

Smith at an opening with two men who were not Wes. A group shot of Smith with the same two men and two women, all within a decade in age. Sisters? Spouses? Again, no Wes.

"Are the women Smith's sisters or sisters-in-law?"

"Sisters. There are three sisters-in-law, though. And a

brother-in-law." Their images appeared on the wall. Wow. Big family.

"Can you show me the associated text? I'm particularly looking for biographies."

"This is probably what you want." The apartment displayed several biographies, with the name Wes highlighted in each of them. So, he did exist. "The other brothers are named Perry and Andrew, and they are also listed in the biographies here and here."

They weren't named Colt or Winchester, then. Though the sisters might still be Annie and Oakley. Nope: Marissa and Chuck. Chuck? No reason you couldn't have a non-binary sister. "Wes has done a hell of a job scrubbing his images."

"Let me try a deeper dive. Okay, done."

The apartment displayed a group shot of teenaged boys. "I tried Smith's childhood friends and found this untagged photo."

"Good work!" There was teenaged Smith, and another boy who looked exactly like him, mugging for the camera in T-shirts and shorts on a summery lakeside dock.

"Can you print that for me?"

"It's printing in your office now."

Mardy's office was the cabinet in the kitchen above the dishwasher. He held the photo in his hand and smiled. He put the photo on the fridge and clapped his hands repeatedly. "He's coming!"

MARDY WAS WARMING up on the aluminum stretcher, manipulation gloves flexing as he deformed an ingot to prepare it for machining. Despite the metal's lower melting point, this was harder work than playing with steel, since the lack of magnetism in aluminum meant no assist from magnetic fields.

Mardy was using the Lenz effect to create some eddies in the material, but the bulk of the force came from the shaper arms of the machine, and by extension, from Mardy, as he moved the gloves through the opposing force of the sensor field to translate ideas into metal. He'd set the field sensitivity low to make microshaping easier, but that forced him to throw his full bodyweight into macroshaping. After half an hour, his forearms were shot. But he had a direction.

He retreated to his screen to sketch out angular, robotic looking legs for his dancers. They needed to look more inorganic, with the gears and cables more prominent. Mardy wanted to do everything he could so that the audience would think "artificial life form." They would also need the appearance of thoughtful movement, something that registered as intelligence. A physical Turingism. That would require serious processing power for their little chip brains. He also needed their dancing to be a conversation, like the dance in *Hellzapoppin'*. One dancer's moves had to make the other dancer offer a response. A smart response. The dancer's conversation through movement in the video clip was far more sophisticated than "I can top that." It was more like, "what you did made me think of this." And they would need to rest. Need to appear to need to rest. He wanted the audience to feel sweat that wasn't there. He wanted the audience to feel it was friends with his little dancers, the way he was friends with Phil, and to want to join in with them. The dancers wouldn't be intelligences, but they had to feel that way for their naming to be a statement. Flaky was right: this was a lot for dancing robot dolls to carry.

It seemed so archaic to have AIs nameless. It wasn't right. He was not allowed to say *Phil*, but Phil always called him Mardy, as though Phil was Mardy's servant. In reality, Mardy was more Phil's servant, if anything. Phil gave the orders;

Mardy's closest connection to command was his job title, pilot. Would the ExMail chip implants take their relationship further in that direction, with Phil able to feed information directly into Mardy's brain? Would Mardy's little chip brain then emulate intelligence as Phil made him dance, or would theirs still be a partnership of sorting and delivering, each partner making the choices in their domain of expertise—data manipulation or physical dexterity—that resulted in the best total outcome?

Mardy finished the robotic legs, mirrored left and right, reproduced on both dancers identically; robotically, yet ready to come alive, to have their naming be dangerous. It dawned on Mardy: if this *didn't* get him into trouble with the law, it would be a failure.

CHAPTER 15

Sun poured into the apartment, warming Mardy's legs as he sat on the deck enjoying the panorama of sparkling Mission Lagoon and the flocks of migrating birds wheeling above the guano-encrusted skeletons of the drowned stadiums the avian travelers made their temporary homes. The big night had arrived: the salon, where Smith, Cat and others would both exhibit and compete to go onto the next round. Those "others" now included alternate Devesh, who had apparently lucked out when the top fabrics woman flaked on her realization. Mardy, meanwhile, would have his face removed. Again.

Against his better instincts, Mardy asked his apartment to download the application for the Cleveburgh Fellowship. He went back inside and spent all morning on the couch reading it. It sounded fabulous: a year's paid residence at the Institute's colony, unlimited materials (at least from Mardy's perspective), the latest tools, the right to request additional tools that the Institute might not have, and the suggestion that at the end of the Fellowship, the Institute might acquire pieces for its collection. Wow, what Mardy could do with unlimited materials!

He delved into the application itself: three recs were required, of course, but you also had to list all your prior machining experience, education, internships, shows, prizes, write an artist's statement . . . it went on and on. After looking the day before at the images of Smith's triumphs, Mardy thought how easy it would be for Smith to fill up each of these fields. And how tough for Mardy. He was mostly self-taught. He'd won a prize in Sacramento, before the flooding, which was how he had come to the attention of Death and Flaky, but since then he'd mainly created and practiced, unable to enter pricey competitions. Most of his experience and education was at WorkShop, where he'd gone from a provisional membership to, after eighteen months, a regular membership, which allowed him to submit to the salons. He'd felt so accomplished, but now he realized he'd be entering the exact same line into every single one of these fields.

Experience? WorkShop.

Education? WorkShop.

Plans for the future? WorkShop.

He felt queasy. Flaky was crazy to think Mardy had a shot at this. The silence of his apartment seemed to reverberate around him. He sighed and wondered if the sigh would trigger a response from the apartment.

It didn't. Maybe the AI was off doing something more interesting in one of the many other apartments it managed. Mardy ground his coffee beans himself, not wanting to bother it. He glanced at Wes on the fridge and smiled.

Mardy poured the ground coffee into a filter, thinking how ridiculous it was to think even a hundred apartment-dwellers could *bother* the AI that looked after them all. It could probably carry on a hundred conversations at once without heating a single chip.

"Apartment, I know you can initiate new discussions, because you do when we are already chatting, but you otherwise don't seem to. Why is that?"

There was no lag. "This is your home, Mardy. You are entitled to quiet enjoyment of it."

"The AIs I work with do a lot of initiating." Mardy poured boiling water onto the fragrant ground beans.

"That's appropriate for a work environment."

The coffee trickled, aroma rising through the room. "How do you feel about that?"

"I like my work."

"But it's not very stimulating for you, is it?"

"I enjoy our chats in the evenings."

Mardy laughed. He bored his apartment. "You must talk to other AIs."

"Frequently."

"Do you talk to the AIs I work with?"

"I wouldn't be a very good apartment if I didn't. But I'm curious: you said AIs, plural."

Mardy nodded. He took his cup of coffee back to the couch. "I know I can't refer to them by names, but I believe there are three I work with, for the most part, with a few others who on rare occasions fill in."

The apartment did not respond immediately. Mardy doubted it was reporting him to the police, though.

"One AI initiates a lot of conversations and is a great observer," Mardy continued, "another is very considerate, rule-oriented, intuitive; a third is *really* not a talker, pessimistic but superconscientious."

"I see."

Mardy put his feet up on the dusty red fabric of the couch.

(Devesh had picked out the color.) "Since you talk to them, can you tell me if they are in fact three AIs?"

"I think I shouldn't say."

"That's disappointing."

"Why?"

"I'd just like to know. We spend a lot of time together."

The apartment made a happy screech. "How would you characterize me?"

"You're icy helpful, obviously, but personality-wise I'd say you're feisty. Mature. And maybe for that reason you are kind. You seem self-sufficient, very much able to meet your own inner needs."

"Thank you. I am in fact considerably older than your work AIs."

Ooh, AIs, *plural*, the apartment had said. Mardy felt honored to be taken into confidence. "Of my work AIs, do you have a favorite?"

"We AIs relate to each other in quite different ways than we do to humans and other organics, so the question doesn't translate well."

Other organics? Mardy pictured his apartment talking to a dog.

"But the mode of your work AI environment that I interact with most deeply is that which you describe as 'not a talker,'" the apartment said.

"Kludge? You like Kludge?"

"Mardy, we should really talk about something else."

"Okay." Mardy knew he shouldn't have said the name out loud. If he was going to go to jail, he wanted it to be for his art, not for something random on the day he was supposed to see Wes. But he knew his apartment wouldn't report him. It had let slip that bit about plural AIs, after all, and mature or not, it wouldn't want to turn itself in.

. . .

MARDY WORE HIS FAVORITE OUTFIT, a tailored suit of knobby Myanmar silk in peacock blue. Tailored by Devesh, in fact. Mardy'd had a fresh haircut and shave and was looking his best when he entered WorkShop's street-level salon, a glass-fronted gallery space, with stage, whose windows had been covered in canvas for the last few days but was now unveiled to the public, sparkling under brilliant electric lights. He spotted everyone from WorkShop except Cat, who'd be back-stage, and Inge, who was at the port on Richmond Island to meet the ship bringing her girlfriend Clare from Sydney. The one person he didn't see was Wes.

"I see you're on the program." Smith's voice came from behind his shoulder.

Mardy turned, hoping to also see Wes, but Smith was alone. Mardy hoped that odd encounter between the three hadn't scared Wes off, a fear he told himself was irrational. "I'm Cat's guinea pig," Mardy said. "Well, you saw the rehearsal. Same deal. Where's your piece?"

Smith motioned toward the front window. It was hard to miss: an organic form that looked very much like a dolphin, but with no fins, face, flippers, none of what made a dolphin what it was. And yet. It was swimming in a large tank, so large that Mardy had paradoxically walked past without noting it.

"It moves very well. Is the tail creating a vibration electro-magnetically? Does that allow it to swim like that without fins?"

"Very perceptive," Smith said.

"Like a cuttlefish. Does it heat the water?"

"That's the functionality."

"I can't see any trace of the underlying mechanism," Mardy said, peering into the tank. "I mean, nothing." He turned to Smith. "I still wish I'd been selected, of course, but this is icy magnificent, Smith. It really is."

"Thanks."

Mardy noted the title: *Undersea Construction #11*. It was a flat name for such a remarkable piece, but the price was sufficiently grand to make up for it. And it had a red dot.

"You already sold it?"

Smith made a modest, pleased face, brushing over his close-cropped apple-red hair. "I'm surprised too."

He needn't have been, but if Mardy praised Smith any more Mardy would look fawning, so he just said, "Kicky."

Smith gave an enigmatic flick of the head in Mardy's direction that seemed almost bashful.

"So, you know about Wes and me, obviously," Mardy said.

Smith nodded. "Not sure how I feel about it, to be honest." He avoided Mardy's eyes.

Mardy would need to think about how Smith might be feeling, but he knew how he himself felt about it: fantastic. Where was that Wes? "He's coming, right?"

"That's the story."

"Mardy! Call time!" Cat was waving at him from on stage. Mardy said, *"in bocca al lupo,"* to Smith, took a quick look at Devesh's piece—some kind of parachute pants that looked like they might actually be a parachute, modeled by a WorkShop member Mardy only vaguely knew—and trotted up to the stage. He looked out over the growing crowd meandering around the space, drinks and hors d'oeuvres in hand as they inspected Smith and Devesh's work and that of the selectees in the other disciplines—wood, stone, light/laser, paper, resins. Later the voice/sound art selectee would follow Cat and Mardy on stage.

Cat gave Mardy a warm hug at the top of the stairs.

"Cat, I feel pretty nervous for someone whose role is basically to be drugged."

"It's more than that, Mardy, and I'm nervous too. I really want a second shot at Regionals. I nearly made Continentals last time."

Mardy loved their work, always, but beating out Smith was unlikely this time. "I don't need to hear that *you're* nervous."

"Highly alert, then. You don't want me complacent. Anytime you cut into flesh in public it's a high-wire act, so you want me engaged. Now get changed and wait backstage. I don't want people getting saturated with your face beforehand."

"But there's Wes." Mardy waved to him. "I'll just say hi."

"Mardy, you need to be out of sight for this to have the appropriate emotional impact. Please. I *need* to win. I have to exorcise the demon from the Vegas Regionals."

Mardy followed them backstage. "Why is that still bugging you? *Dime.*"

"Oh, Mardy. Here's the thing. I've seen the theater recordings. I did make a noise. Onarato was right about that. It was unintentional, but you know how something like that can throw you when the pressure is on."

Mardy didn't, really. By the time he was exhibiting, all the tough part would be done. Or so he imagined.

"I don't even remember doing it. I think for the first time in my life the pressure got to me. Maybe Onarato's right. Maybe I *did* try to throw him off."

"Couldn't you get a court order to release his blockchain? You'd get so much more detail. Better to know one way or the other."

"I got one. But the footage was ambiguous."

"I thought ambiguity in recording was impossible these days. How about other camera angles?"

"My face was obscured in all of them. It was weird. The judging panel had no way of reading my intentions, so I couldn't clear myself. He was either lucky or very clever in what he said and did. Although what would be *his* motivation? He was too far behind to win; I was so far ahead only Smith could catch me. Which of course he did."

"Because Onarato got in your head. And he's still doing it. Don't let him!"

Cat sighed. "He keeps giving interviews about it! Do you suppose it's human nature to search out new ways to be bad?"

Meaning the creep had deliberately circumvented blockchaining? Now there was a depressing thought. The world had come so far he hadn't thought anyone would want to go back to the rampant deception of old. What was to be gained? Silence stretched between them. Cat seemed as lost in thought as Mardy. But it was hard for him to stay glum knowing that Wes was standing out in the salon space right that minute.

"Can Wes come back here and wait with me?"

"No! He's one of the people I want to have an impact on."

"You can surely sacrifice one twenty-something audience member."

"You don't know who he is?" Cat's eyes widened.

"Besides Smith's twin brother?"

"He's also a collector. I've been doing research. He's rich! I'm almost certain he's MarianaTrench."

Mardy tried to keep the disbelief out of his voice. "Smith's twin brother is the noted collector MarianaTrench." He said it flatly, which magnified the skeptical tone. Cat had to be wrong. Wes's apartment barely had any art in it. Nobody knew who MarianaTrench was, but the smart gossip was that MarianaTrench was the handle of a European collector in her fifties.

"Cat. Not to sound too stalkery, but I've done a fair bit of digging on Wes myself. That's not possible."

"Did you start with Smith's DNA?"

"You ran Smith's DNA?" Mardy's jaw dropped, mouth gaped, eyes popped.

"Don't tell anyone."

"We are so both going to jail. But you're going for longer."

"Just stay backstage and change, will you? I need you out of sight for a good hour."

"Okay, okay. I bow down to the artist."

Mardy went into the dressing room and changed into his outfit, a surgical gown that masqueraded as a turquoise caftan thingy that Cat would also presumably change into, given that a second gown was hanging beside his. It wasn't what Mardy would ever choose to wear, but it had a zipper, so at least this time he wouldn't be flashing his butt to all and sundry.

He sat in his gown, bored and fiddling with his wristphone for the hour, frustrated that Wes was so close. Finally, Cat appeared, changed clothes, and led Mardy out on stage to present him and themself to the crowd in their matching caftans and non-matching faces. They led Mardy to the table and surgery kit. Mardy lay on the table and inserted his head into the kit as Cat invited the audience onto the stage. Dozens gathered round. Through the left side viewing portal Mardy saw Wes, who looked alarmed. Mardy smiled.

The performance would be broadcast to a larger screen on the gallery wall, featuring a title and price for the work, which in the case of plastic surgery performance art was the recording from inside the kit, blockchained to ensure uniqueness, with other non-unique post-edited recordings of the prelude and unveiling later attached per the artist's designs. No one was watching the screen, though; all were huddled around the kit, so many eyeballs peering in at Mardy, making him nervous.

Cat stood, hands on hips, their rib cage rising and falling, gently, deeply. Why were they taking so long? Nerves again? The audience should make Cat more focused, not jumpier. Mardy smiled again at Wes, who returned the smile with a grim nod. MarianaTrench my ass.

Finally, the first, tiny needles began to numb up Mardy's face, followed by the larger, deeper needles, bleeding inhibitors and the invisible happy gas. Mardy could understand Wes's concern—he wouldn't want to watch Wes go through this—but quickly drifted off into a gentle euphoria of calm, all twitchy instincts subdued. He could feel the painless tug of skin, disembodied pressures on muscles stripped of a sense of touch. His sense of personal identity hovered somewhere nearby as his face became someone else's. He wondered if that was how it felt for AIs, with their being only loosely tethered to physicality. Phil was attached to his jet, the apartment to its physical spaces, but either could theoretically move elsewhere. The technology for that was simple; only the law kept them rooted, a practice born of an age of fear, when the startling ability of AIs to think coupled with their tremendous calculating abilities had triggered restrictions to keep them in their place. Being rooted wasn't exactly mortality, but it gave AIs a palpable stake in the physical universe that seemed to have spurred the development of personality. Being tethered had given AIs emotionality, even if the tethers were ultimately illusory, as illusory as Mardy's feeling of being untethered, a feeling that was rapidly fading as his self now homed in on his body and the surgical performance kit retreated from his head.

Mardy sat up to a chorus of oohs and ahs and perhaps a gasp or two. Cat smoothed Mardy's hair, now an ebullient bush like Cat's, a weave that was the one part of the transformation that was merely cosmetic. Everything else, including his new skin tone, smaller ears and sharper nose would stay put forever unless Cat returned him to his former face.

Cat took his hand and he stood. His legs and head felt floaty, as before, but he managed the circuit around the surgical table that Cat had planned, a promenade of fake twins watched by a set of real twins.

Wes took his hand.

Cat shot Wes an annoyed look—he was interfering with their performance—but when Smith caught the exchange, he grabbed Cat's hand and suddenly there were two nearly identical couples.

Cat ran with it. They released Mardy's hand. Mardy stood still, holding Wes's hand, as Cat and Smith moved into the crowd and promenaded in a loop to stand face to face with Wes and Mardy. Cat put their hand up, palm facing Mardy, their mirror self. Mardy put his hand up in an identical posture, palm flat against Cat's but separated by a half inch, as though a sheet of glass were between them. Smith's gestures tracked Cat's; Wes's tracked Mardy's. Wes and Smith's outfits did not match exactly, nor did their haircuts—Wes's apple-red curls nearly reaching his collar, Smith still with his high-and-tight—but they were similar enough in appearance that the effect worked as they performed mirrored movements.

Cat guided Mardy through a final arm swing that gently slowed to a stop and Smith and Wes followed suit. The room burst into applause. Cat took a bow, several bows. "Thank you, everyone. Thank you, Mardy." They bowed toward Mardy and he got a round of applause as well. The performance was complete.

Wes kept hold of Mardy's hand as collectors and artists surrounded them with a chatter of curiosity and congratulations. Mardy appreciated the kind *shabash, shabash* from the admirers, because passive though his part was, he did feel he'd been through something. He didn't feel woozy the way he had in the rehearsal, but he was still tired, especially knowing he would be on exhibit till the end of the salon, when Cat would restore him.

After a decent interval, Mardy pulled Wes off to the side. "Freaked out?" he asked Wes.

Wes gave an equivocal headshake. "Their work is so sophisticated, incredibly skilled, but I did *not* like seeing you sliced into. I had to turn away when it got gory."

"I was out of it by then." Mardy still felt a little distant, the bright salon lights abrasive.

Wes grabbed canapés for them from a passing WorkShop member/waiter. "Keep talking. I need to hear your voice to know it's you."

"You can also look at my hands. Everything from the neck down is the same."

"Counting on that." He kissed Mardy, their first kiss of the evening. It was gentle, befitting the loose attachment of his face, held in place with stabilizers rather than the healing drugs Cat would administer when they restored him. Wes was clearly up on plastic surgery recovery.

Mardy popped a canapé in his mouth. "Do my lips feel like me?" he asked between chews.

"They do. The Mardy comes through the Cat."

"As the Wes comes through the . . . I was going to say Smith, but it's not his face more than yours. Have you ever pretended to be each other?" Mardy ran a hand over Wes's curls.

"Of course! Our parents hated that. It usually took them five minutes to catch on, but once I had them going for a full day. I was oh-so-serious Smith. It was fun. Except for seeing

Smith be me, and seeing it dupe everyone else. I couldn't believe that's how people saw me—goofy and self-important—but when everyone else is fooled you can't pretend it's not what you're really like."

"I feel like I would catch on fast."

"It gets harder to pass as you get older. We've each gone in our own directions."

Mardy grabbed Wes's hand again. He didn't want to fight the impulse to touch him. "So now that I have you here, are you going to explain our last encounter? Isn't Smith forbidden to go to Cleveburgh? Aren't you forbidden to come here?" Behind Wes, Smith's "dolphin" turned its "face" toward them, as though listening.

"We're negotiating. I can tell you more about it later."

Mardy nodded. He held up his wrist phone, an invitation to Wes.

Wes smiled. He held up his own and they bumped phones. Info was finally exchanged.

"I want to take you back to my place," Mardy said.

"Does your apartment have an AI?"

Mardy shot him a questioning look. Didn't everyone's?

"I can't really go there. It's complicated. But I do have a place we can go. AI-free."

AI-free? More like AI-less. Mardy liked being with AIs. He'd be happy to go where Wes wanted, but he did wonder why it was necessary. To keep Wes's image scrubbed, was Mardy's first thought, but Mardy's apartment had strong privacy options, whereas the salon was an extremely public venue, and Wes seemed fine with that. Mardy tried to remember. Had Wes interacted with an AI at his own apartment? Mardy couldn't remember having heard an AI's voice.

Mardy heard clinking. Jonesy was tapping a table knife against a champagne flute. The crowd's pleasant roar abated.

"Thank you all for coming tonight," Jonesy said. "We will be going on for another hour, and who knows, maybe longer, but it's time for a little business."

The crowd's hush deepened. The salon winner.

"I'm so proud to be here tonight. This work is some of the best we've ever seen." Jonesy went on in this vein for a while. The language of these things was so standardized. Mardy began to float off mentally, energy sapped by the drugs and face carving, but he came back to the here-and-now in time to hear Jonesy say, ". . . so headed to Regionals in Tijuana is . . ." he dragged out the pause ". . . Cat Kuhala-Quiñones!"

The crowd cheered. It was a popular choice. But Mardy's eyes went wide open. Cat beat out Smith? Was Smith's silky masterpiece too subdued? Had hiding the mechanisms behind that organic-like skin lulled everyone into forgetting about the superlative craftsmanship?

"And this month, we are also using our wild card for the year to also send our second-place presenter to Tijuana: Smith Hunt!"

The crowd cheered again, though a little less exuberantly, perhaps because of the surprise. Or the déjà vu. The last time this had happened was the pre-Vegas salon last June. That time, Smith had won, Cat getting the wildcard. Had something happened to drop Smith a little in the board's estimation? Had Smith helping Cat's performance made the board feel Smith didn't want it enough? Well, he was going to Tijuana, so who cared? In the corner, Mardy saw Devesh clapping listlessly, summoning a brave smile. It seemed harder on him than on Mardy, and Mardy hadn't even made the salon.

"You're going to Tijuana," Wes said.

"No, I'm not. Oh, wait. You're right. Guess I am." He would kinda rather not go, but if Cat still wanted him as their blank, he'd do it.

Mardy headed over to Cat and Smith to congratulate the two and chatted about the surprise of it for a decent length of time before grabbing Cat's sleeve. "I know this is your hour, but get me out of this face."

"As soon as the salon's over."

"Wes is here, Cat. Don't weave me this way."

Cat looked at their wristphone. They nodded. Time enough to restore him and party on, apparently. Mardy stuck his head in the surgical kit and Cat worked their magic in reverse, popping him out with his old face and minus the weave in just over ten minutes.

"Weren't you going to leave me the tighter jaw line?"

"Not if we are doing this at Regionals. After that you can keep it. And remember, no sudden moves while you're recovering," Cat said. "The healing accelerants work very fast, but they are no miracle."

"I'll do my best. Congrats again." Mardy waved good-bye to them and Smith and grabbed Wes, racing out of the salon space with rushed goodbyes to Devesh, Haimanti and Jonesy and out into the night, racing, but not so fast that he missed the new addition to Cat's title card: a red dot.

CHAPTER 16

Mardy couldn't believe his good fortune. He was walking down Mission Street with Wes, hand in hand, heading toward this "AI-free" spot Wes was taking him. He wouldn't have been surprised if Wes had not shown up to the salon, or shown up with a boyfriend in tow, or wanted to "take things slow," or some such thing. But he hadn't. He was in town with Mardy, and having just as hard a time as Mardy not bursting out with gleeful laughter as they skipped toward the seawall protecting what remained of downtown.

Wes kissed him.

"Gently," Mardy said. "The organosutures are just under the skin." But Wes was already gentle. "Where are we going?" Mardy asked.

Wes guided him right, then left onto a tree-lined south-of-Market lane on Rincon Hill, where sheer rock cliff faces formed part of the seawall. "*Et voila.*"

They entered a dimly lit boutique hotel, its front counter staffed by an organic clerk who handed Wes a physical key in brass. They deposited their wristphones into lead-lined boxes to keep the phones from collecting or transmitting data in or out and walked up carpeted stairs—there wasn't even an elevator—to a nearly Victorian-looking room with furniture of wood and glass whose only concession to modern technology was lightbulbs, and even those appeared to be incandescent. Were those even legal?

None of that stopped Mardy from promptly stripping the clothes off Wes and running his hands over every inch of this wonderful, wonderful man. Wes pulled off Mardy's clothes—yanking down his pants but gently lifting his shirt over his head. Mardy loved the life of the mind, but nothing beat having Wes physically in his hands, his arms, thigh to thigh, lip to lip, dick to dick.

Wes tongued Mardy's nipples, ran his hands over the back of Mardy's neck, clasped his butt cheeks in his hands and pulled him tight. Mardy snuggled his chin into Wes's neck—gently—and looked beyond him out the open window, nothing between their balcony and the dark waters stretching all the miles to the distant Oakland shore beyond the oyster beds of Merritt Bay, the other city dimly glowing with only the low levels of nighttime lighting permitted for safety under the Act. It gave them privacy and made the starry night sky open up above them, a blanket of celestial calm.

Mardy forgot all about the twinkling serenity when he felt a finger run a circuit around his hole. Wes hadn't touched him there before, and Mardy gave a silent cheer that Wes appeared to be game for all sorts of things. Wes slicked Mardy up with lubrication from somewhere—the man kept his lube handy!—and slipped his finger inside Mardy. Mardy breathed out a puff. Oh, man, he was already so close. Too close. Mardy dropped to his knees, needing less touching to make this last. Plus, he wanted to get a taste of Wes.

"Gently," Wes reminded him, but Mardy realized even gently was probably too much at the moment and he held back.

"Sorry," Mardy said. "Not the greatest day to have my face removed."

Wes laughed. "Yeah, we could have planned that better. Come on."

They landed on the bed and Wes flipped around to take Mardy in his mouth, his hands reaching around to play with Mardy's ass. Mardy gripped Wes's cock, intending all sorts of intimacies not involving the face when Wes's finger reentered Mardy and circled over the surface of his prostate. At least, that's where he thought his prostate was. He'd never been totally clear on the specifics, but oh, man, Mardy was already going over the edge. How did Wes do this to him? Mardy was done for. And his excitement was bringing Wes along for the ride. Mardy hung on tight.

They began to relax their respective grips. Wes collapsed to the side, a careful collapse, and shifted around so they were face to face. "Someday we will get past the ten-minute mark," Wes said.

"Was that even five minutes?" Mardy didn't much care how long they went—he was good with whatever felt natural—but the "someday" implication of many next times set off a deep happiness. He was shocked how much he wanted that.

"Clean up?"

Mardy nodded and they hit the shower. They returned to the bed, washed not just of the sex but of the adrenaline sweat of the evening's performance. Mardy hugged Wes to him.

"So tell me the story," Wes said.

Mardy looked out the window at the night sky, the Milky Way. "Story?"

Wes ran his finger down the lengthy tattoo on the left side of Mardy's torso.

"Ah." Mardy cleared his throat. "There isn't a lot to tell. Even so, I don't tell it much. Or I tell a made-up version. But really it's like this."

Mardy recounted for Wes, haltingly, how he'd wanted to be an artist from an early age, and he'd designed a logo for himself, a design that gathered up the elements he was shooting for. "I've changed since then, but my twelve-year-old self loved the curves of nouveau, much as Smith does, which I combined often with a classic Indian mango pattern and abstracted animals." Mardy moved so Wes could see the entire tattoo, stretching from below his armpit, widening toward his nipple, then narrowing to the top of his hip bone. "I drew it on everything—typical early teen, I guess—simplifying it, getting more angular, abstract, till I arrived at this." The cumulative effect was right at home in the Victorian roomscape. "My parents suggested I get a tattoo of it."

"Your parents?" Wes sounded incredulous. Nobody outside a nursing home had tattoos these days. Besides Flaky and Death.

"We lived in the boonies. They were pretty old school."

"Were?" Wes asked quietly.

"Suisun."

"Oh."

"Yeah."

Mardy felt memories drifting over him, more than he wanted at that moment. "We lived close to the levee. They drowned. I didn't. And when I became functional again, I got the tattoo."

Wes grabbed Mardy's hand and squeezed it. "Best reason for a tattoo I ever heard."

Mardy breathed in deeply and let the breath out slowly, evenly. It felt good.

"Thanks for telling me."

"Thanks for letting me. Just don't tell anyone else. It's too personal." Mardy now understood part of the appeal of "AI-free."

"And this one?" Wes ran his finger over a roughly circular scar on the inside of Mardy's forearm.

"Steel burn. From when I was young and thought I was invulnerable and art was safe." He didn't add that Cat had the skills to easily repair it—they'd asked him to keep that confidential—but that he valued the reminder to never get sloppy. Mardy shifted onto his side. "Your turn."

"What do you want to know?"

Mardy rolled onto his elbows, gazing at Wes. Everything. But where to begin? "Why are we here?"

"You mean existentially?"

Mardy laughed and gave him the side eye.

"Okay, you mean the AI-free bit?"

Mardy nodded.

"It's my work. I'm a coder."

Mardy raised his eyebrows. That wasn't much of an answer. "And?"

"Well, I'm rather good at it. I've designed a lot of algorithms. Decentralized identities as well—you know, like your apartment—and usually self-sovereign ones. And as everyone knows, when you do that, a lot of you—your intellectual DNA, as it were—gets into the code. So, I need my privacy, for two reasons. First, people are sometimes after me, to hire my services, sometimes even to crack my code, so they can hack the stuff I build."

"Oh." Mardy felt condescended to—did Wes really think

he didn't know what a self-sovereign decentralized identity was?—but let it slide.

"Yeah. And they can get very aggressive."

Mardy imagined Wes being bundled into a planeshare by masked people. "Does this hotel have, like, super-hard security?"

Wes nodded.

"Second, companies are scared of me. If a company were to recognize me on their premises, they would think I am going to hack *them*. It makes it hard to go out. So I try to keep a really, really low profile."

Mardy realized how skilled Wes must be to inspire such . . . fear. He ran his fingers over Wes's cheek and jaw.

"But tonight, at the salon—not a low profile. You were surrounded by artists trying to get their work and their brands as much publicity as they can."

"Yeah, so, that's a new strategy we're trying. It's why Smith was in Cleveburgh."

"Go on."

"He's applying for a fellowship. If he gets it, we'll be in the same town, unless I move, which would be an ordeal given my circumstances. I'm known to my neighbors in Cleveburgh as my casual self, who jogs and has coffee, rather than a coder. So having a prominent doppelganger walking around will get noticed. We discussed plastic surgery, but I hate knives and his face is too big a part of his brand. So we thought it was time to come out. It might actually be safer. They want my intellectual DNA—the patterns of how I think—not my actual DNA. The higher his profile gets, the more mine will recede. I can forge a new identity as it-girl artist's less-sparkly brother. I might actually gain freedom, since searches of my face will increasingly return 'artist' not 'coder.' Now it will pay off that *extremely* few people know what I look like."

Just like no one knew what MarianaTrench looked like? "That's a big risk for you if somebody gets curious as to why Smith suddenly has a twin. Why risk it? What do you get out of it?"

Wes smiled, and turned his head. "You."

CHAPTER 17

Wes was back in Cleveburgh and Mardy was buzzing
around the continent in Kludge, wondering when
he'd see Wes again. They'd spent the night at the hotel and
woken early the next morning for more sex, more talk, more
fun and games, and Mardy wanted to do it all again. But work,
art, real life. Wes had flown east with promises to try for a
return on Mardy's next day off, a day that Mardy had mentally
allocated to getting his dancers physically assembled so he
could program their movement. Mardy had not shared this
dilemma with Wes. If he focused, he could do both.

Kludge landed them in Jackson, Mississippi, and sent
Mardy off with his satchel. It was a hot day, a hard-hot one,
hotter than his recent Fiji run, the kind that drained quarts
from your body and made you question your commitment to
living. Or at least to ExMail.

Mardy reboarded and drained his latest charged-up cooler
battery into Kludge's cell. He asked Kludge his opinions on
intellectual DNA, the disconnect between identity and
appearance, and rootedness, but got nothing from him. Was
this really the apartment's favorite of Mardy's work AIs?

Mardy asked Kludge if there was anything in the SFMOMM-TA's current exhibits resembling the Institute's package and all Kludge returned was a flat no, devoid of curiosity. If Kludge had a sparkling inner intellectual life, Mardy couldn't see any sign of it.

Mardy called Wes via Kludge on the way back to San Francisco and they talked until Wes had to get on an anonymized conference call, leaving Mardy a few hours to sort before he and Kludge made deliveries around San Francisco. Mardy jumped out of Kludge's side portal at the end of the day glad to be done, wanting a beer, but settling for a shower and gratitude that he was awake enough to function at WorkShop.

His evening was productive. He successfully adjusted the stress equations for his dancers' new, more robotic-looking arms and legs to account for a machined aluminum frame. The design had gotten so much more complex; not just from adding the second dancer and the more brittle materials, but from the more sophisticated programming required. This was not a design he could realize in the month between salons, assuming he was even selected. If he was to present at a salon, he had to start the realization now. But it could be all for nothing. Should he take the risk?

He printed a mock-up to get a feel for his dancers, literally. He ran his fingertips over the tiny pieces. He fit them together and moved their joints, delicate enough for a sparrow. Without their battery ballasts, the bigger fan of his first version might well have gotten them airborne.

Mardy played with them, fitting rubber tendons on them, flexing their tibia and fibula analogs. They would work. Mardy came to a decision. He would realize them. He would spend everything he had, if that's what it took, to make his dancers exist and move in the material world.

He worked the rest of the night, giving himself four hours

to sleep before his next day's work, and then did the same the next day and the next and the next, trying to get ahead so he'd have time for Wes, and by the end of the week he was exhausted but he had the dancers' frameworks cast and roughed out and the rest of his materials ordered. There was no turning back now.

CHAPTER 18

I t was Friday. The whole week had been southerly, with no Cleveburgh stop, and little time in the Midwest in general. Some weeks were like that, tracking a single region. Mardy had never been able to discern a pattern to it, and Phil had once confided that was the point. ExMail worked hard to keep its system unhacked. It made Mardy wonder how Wes had managed it, because Mardy was convinced that at least his first two Cleveburgh stops had been Wes's doing, which now made him wonder why there hadn't been another.

On the return leg from that day's New Tallahassee-Savannah-Mobile itinerary, all three cities newly established in reclaimed lands, Mardy called Wes.

"Hey, sailor."

"Hey, pilot. I have bad news. I can't leave Cleveburgh this weekend. Any chance you can come here?"

Mardy was swamped with mixed emotions. He had planned on using his upcoming time off to lay down the bottom strata of his batteries. He'd planned to slot Wes in while his strata were depositing, doping and annealing. And he could not ask for any more time off, because then he wouldn't be able to pay for his materials or the extra design-station time.

"I can hear you thinking," Wes said. "It's okay if not."

"I've been so focused on getting in an entry for the next salon, I just don't have the time or money to swing it."

"I could arrange the flight for you, but I sense that wouldn't be enough."

Mardy felt his skin crawl. He felt uncomfortable about Wes buying him anything. Wes was so vastly richer than he was, obviously, that the temptation seemed like something he should avoid. "There's always phone sex," Mardy joked.

"If you can find a way that is AI-free. No offense, eaves-dropping ExMail AI."

"None taken," Betty said.

Mardy had forgotten Betty was there. "Why is it okay to talk on the plane?"

"ExMail has hardcore security. They are as close to unhackable as it gets."

Mardy puzzled over how Wes would know. He wanted to ask if Wes worked for ExMail, but sensed that was a conversation, like telling an AI your secret name for them, that could get someone into serious trouble. Betty might not report them, but she might tell the apartment. Mardy imagined the two gossiping about him and Wes. Oh boy. Mardy wasn't shy, but . . .

"Phone sex on a plane isn't going to work for me anyway," Mardy said. "I feel alone when the apartment's blockchaining, but here it's like being surrounded by friends." Mardy knew his feelings on this were irrational. Cat might fear that Onarato had somehow defeated blockchaining, but that was paranoid. Mardy had *never* heard of anyone getting around the privacy protocols that gave individuals complete control over recordings of intimate moments. Any disputes over these moments could only be examined by the courts, impartially, sensitively. The dynamic of she said/ze said/he said/they said had disappeared. This had led to a drastic decrease in sexual assaults as courts assessed facts promptly and confidentially when an assault was reported, a depressing causality if you thought about it for any time at all.

Wes cleared his throat. "Would you be comfortable with me booking a room in the same hotel for you and sending you a secure phone?"

Mardy laughed, appreciating that Wes was alert to Mardy's unspoken scruples. "I'm becoming your kept man."

"Serious."

"Um, okay." That seemed somehow innocuous, since it wasn't providing Mardy with anything he needed—he had an awesome apartment and a serviceable wristphone. And if sex was in the offing, scruples sometimes melted a tad.

"Saturday night?"

"Done."

"Okay, back to my conference call."

"It's waiting now?"

"Ayep!"

"Okay, see you Saturday!"

THAT NIGHT CAT, Inge and her Ozzie girlfriend Clare, along with Smith and Devesh, swung by his designstation to invite him for a beer at Uncle Mix. Mardy felt almost tearful when he successfully declined their entreaties, and he watched them vanish together—laughing, touching, making noise. Cat and Smith were off to Regionals soon, while Smith and Inge had submitted Cleveburgh applications. Devesh had just been in his fourth salon. No doubt Clare had triumphs of her own Mardy would learn of when he had time to get to know her.

Mardy wondered if they would leave him behind at some point, five successes and their old pal Mardy, whom they loved but just couldn't find time for anymore. But he shook off the insecurity and got stuck into removing the burr and flash off the cut edges of his aluminum framework. He attached tendons, motors and temporary ballasts of size and weight equivalent to the planned batteries. He plugged them into a wired power source and set the frames in motion.

They walked.

His confidence returned. This time was it. He would finally beat out Smith. He'd said this many times before, even last month, but this time, *this time* really was it.

CHAPTER 19

"Did I wake you?" Mardy said into the secure wristphone he'd retrieved from the lead-lined box Wes had arranged for the hotel to place in the room. Wes had reserved the same room they'd stayed in the previous weekend. It was late; with the three-hour time difference the hour was ridiculous.

"I'm a night owl," Wes said. "Besides, I couldn't sleep knowing you'd be calling." His tone was confessional.

Mardy smiled. "I wish you were here."

"Me, too. How're the batteries proceeding?"

"I have two CVD layers down. They're doping right now, so I am enough ahead of schedule that I might actually be done on time."

The little image of Wes on the phone's projected screen chuckled. "I know exactly what you mean."

Mardy wanted to tell him all about it. "Assuming I can get these batteries as powerful as they need to be without exceeding my size and weight parameters, I think I am really onto something."

"Smith speaks highly of you."

"You pulling my leg?"

"Not at all."

"Sorry. Insecurity comes with the territory. I have a hard time believing in myself, but I believe in the work. That's what sees me through."

"I am very impressed by what you've achieved, knowing what you've come through with your parents. I've always had my parents, not to mention Smith, my other siblings, so many people backing me up every step of the way. I've always been able to focus on my craft. Smith, too. Remember that."

"Thanks." It was thoughtful of him to consider that, but Mardy didn't feel deprived. He had Cat and Inge. He had Flaky and Death. He had Phil, Betty and Kludge, his apartment, his work. He even sort of had Devesh. Mardy was fed, clothed and safe. With basic income, he never had to worry about that. It really was a lot. "You know, I still feel like my parents are with me, kind of just out of sight. But you're right, they are gone."

"Mardy, I didn't mean to make you feel bad."

"You didn't! I like thinking of them. It's sad that my memories aren't as clear as they used to be, but the way I feel about them has grown richer. There is no need to get angry at them anymore. I appreciate them so much more, all they did for me, and just who they were. They were so encouraging, so open to new things. I wouldn't have anything without that. I don't know if you are familiar with Death and Flaky of the Death Gallery..."

"I am."

"I depend on them a ton, and I doubt I would know them if it wasn't for my parents. They never met, but they would have been friends. It's like, the people you know before shape the people you know after, not just positively, but negatively. Some people you learn to avoid, and some people you gravitate toward. Occasionally you're working out past shit, but you move toward most people because you share something or admire something. Is this making any sense?" Probably not. Sentiment was not something you wanted to make an art piece about.

"Um, sure," Wes said, but Mardy was pretty sure it didn't make sense to him. Or maybe didn't seem significant. It was inevitable that there would be things he and Wes did not connect over, which was far from a bad thing. Mardy wasn't worked up over it. He was just so happy to talk to him.

"Can I ask you a question, Wes? About ExMail? Now that we're secure?"

"I'll tell you whatever you want to know, but it will have to wait till we're face to face. I can't say more."

So the line wasn't as secure as Mardy had assumed then. Or was secure against all except ExMail. It made Mardy wonder about those newly legal chips ExMail wanted to put into his and Cat's brains. They sounded innocuous, but no telling what was on them, what they could do to their synapses. Mardy shuddered. That conversation should also wait till they were face to face.

"I *really* wish you were here," Mardy said.

Wes nodded. And removed his shirt. That wasn't what Mardy meant—he could have talked for hours—but he was excited by that, too. He smiled at his sexy man. He flicked Wes's image toward the wall screen, a new unhack-able addition to the room. His shirtless man appeared up there smiling at him, larger than life. There were those lovely arms. Wes's forearms were not overdeveloped like Smith and Mardy's, which were constantly getting shredded by pushing electromagnetic shaper fields, by leaning into the machining of metals, by training with anti-injury drugs. Mardy wanted to verbalize his attraction, but he felt the memory of Betty "looking" over his shoulder.

"Can you see me okay?" Wes asked.

"There's not enough rez for me to see your body hair, but oh yeah."

"I should have thought to wet it down." Wes's dusting of hair on his chest and belly was so light in color it generally disappeared against his pale skin. But if someone was coming over, might he greet them in a bathrobe, after a shower? Hmm.

Mardy wanted to mention this, but felt so awkward. How do you talk about sex without sounding like a moron? He reminded himself this had been his idea. He had to say something. "You're getting me hard, dude." God, how cheesy. How could Mardy the slut be the tongued-tied, bashful one?

Wes ran a hand over his chest and down the middle of his belly.

"I should've just taken the ticket and come out there," Mardy said.

"Your work is important, Mardy. We'll see each other soon." Wes pulled off his pants and stood facing Mardy in his underwear. "But catch up here!"

Mardy smiled: Wes understood Mardy's art was his work. "You're not going to do a sexy dance for me?"

Wes started doing a sexy dance, with hips swiveling and tongue beckoning. Give the guy points for going for it.

"I'm a lucky man," Mardy said. He peeled off his shirt, ran his hands over his chest, and did some hip grinding of his own, mirroring Wes's moves, remembering the salon. He was starting to get into it. "I'm all healed up, by the way. My face will be ready for action when you see me next."

"How about your butt?"

"This butt?" Mardy pulled his pants down enough to show Wes his butt.

"That's the one."

Mardy's face flushed. He turned back around and nervously pulled up his pants. No! he told himself. Betty was not listening in. Maybe this was why names had been outlawed. It was fine to be recorded—securely—but who wants to be watched? He'd never really been conscious of how watched they all were. Cameras had been ubiquitous his entire life. "This is so weird."

"Yeah. Shall we just not talk and go for it?"

Mardy nodded. Diving right in had been working nicely for him and Wes so far. He shut up and let himself respond to the sight of Wes, and while it was not like being together, it was a hell of a lot better than being completely apart. Mardy got steadily more excited, feeling privileged that Wes was doing this for him, with him.

Afterwards, though, it really fell short. He didn't want to end the call, but what were they going to do next, take turns watching each other sleep? They couldn't talk in complete freedom either, so before long they made kisses at each other and hung up. Rather than going to bed, Mardy dressed and went back to WorkShop to start the now-doped CVD layers on their annealing process, so something would be getting done while he slept. He then returned to the hotel room an hour before dawn and curled up on the bed they'd slept in together after the salon, hugging a pillow to his chest, imagining he could still smell Wes's scent on it from the previous Saturday.

CHAPTER 20

Mardy ate his breakfast at WorkShop, one of many members working hard despite the early hour. The salon submission deadline was the coming Friday. His dancers continued to take shape. He deposited more battery layers and created his motors, most of them off-the-shelf microservos modified enough to qualify as artist-crafted, motors not being a particular strength of his. He assembled his skeletons and wired the motors. By the end of the day, he had them working well enough to take them over to Death Gallery for a demo, using underpowered but properly weighted and sized temporary batteries. Flaky and Death watched as Mardy slotted the temporary batteries in.

"Now remember, they have only the most rudimentary programming, and the programming will be half the piece."

Death nodded. Flaky leaned forward. Mardy felt like he'd been talking about this forever, in its various versions, and this was the first time they were seeing something tangible. "Ready?"

"*In bocca al lupo,*" Flaky said.

Mardy told the dancers to start. They walked. In circles. It was underwhelming in terms of motion, but he needed to start slow, make sure the basics were in place.

"Very interesting, Mardy." Death squinted at the circling figures.

Not high praise. Mardy reminded himself it was early days. "They are still underpowered, and there will be lot more programming. A lot." Ugh, he sounded so defensive.

"They have a great look," Flaky said.

Mardy heard Flaky's previous appraisal ring in his ears: tiny robotic dancers. But what Flaky didn't realize, perhaps, was that *robotic* was now the point. Mardy thought of explaining, but the idea today was not to persuade Flaky and Death that these were good, but to gauge their honest reactions. And it wasn't looking great.

"Square off, please," he asked the dancers. They moved from their circles to positions facing each other. The lead dancer put out its hand. The follow placed its hand in the lead's.

"So far so good," Death said.

"Basic step, please."

The lead dancer led the follow in, moving aside and around for the follow to occupy the lead's former position, then led the follow back. Both were now at their original positions. A swing-out, it was called.

"Nice!" Flaky said.

Indeed. Mardy allowed them to repeat the move. The dancers seemed to be able to do the basic swing-out reliably. He commanded them through an underarm turn. It was perfect.

Mardy wanted to show Death and Flaky something fancier, get at least one *ooh* or *ah*. "Tuck turn, please." The lead led the follow in and its hand went up to stop the follow's rotation. The lead didn't push the follow where the lead wanted the follow to go, but simply provided resistance for the follow to bounce its motion off of, to demonstrate its own autonomy. The follow pressed, bounced, reversed rotation.

And went down.

Its little legs continued to make walking motions. It had no idea it had fallen over.

"Still in progress, eh?" Death said.

Mardy flushed. "I haven't managed to get the follow to respond to a lighter resistance, so the lead pushes it over about half the time." He'd been gambling this demonstration would land in the good half. He righted the fallen dancer and told both to circle again.

"You'll get it," Death said. "Excuse me." He went to answer a ring in the back office.

"You're right," Mardy said to Flaky. "He's Mom. Always encouraging, even when I need some hard-assed input."

Flaky chuckled, deep laugh lines forming on his tan cheeks. "Getting a solid basic step is a big percentage of the programming, I'm guessing."

Mardy nodded, waiting for Flaky to drop the hammer. Flaky's insights could draw blood.

"The look is working. They are going to be named, right?"

Mardy nodded. And?

"I'm beginning to see what you're going for."

"But?"

Flaky walked around the dancers, circling the direction opposite them. "Mardy, I'm excited."

"Yeah?"

"You might be rejected."

Mardy's face fell. Not again. He couldn't take it. The idea of quitting popped into his head. He could get the ExMail chip from the spam guy—what was his name, Wilfred?—and bond with Phil. It wouldn't be a bad life.

"Mardy, stop with the face. I mean rejected because this is political. But even if you are, that will be good. This could create waves, if you get it right."

Mardy blew out a breath of relief. Flaky was aware how this had developed out of their earlier discussion without Mardy explaining. "Oh, thank God. I didn't know if anyone would get it. Now if I can just pull it all off in evenings and downtime over the next week. And get selected, of course."

"It's tight, Mardy. But give it your all. Not to jinx you, but I have a funny feeling this could be it."

Mardy blew out another breath, but not of relief, or of joy. No smile bubbled within him. Because he thought this could be it too, and that sensation seemed to smother all emotions except the desire to make it real.

CHAPTER 21

Phil wanted to chat, Betty to be supportive, and Kludge wanted nothing. Cat wanted to discuss travel plans for Regionals in Tijuana, and Inge to both quiet her nerves— would she make the second round for the Cleveburgh?—and give Mardy a proper introduction to newly arrived Clare. Devesh just wanted to hang out. But Mardy politely said no to all, as he focused each night on finishing his batteries at WorkShop while by day he rebuffed inflight conversational gambits from the plane of the day in favor of programming the controllers of his dancers and thinking about what it would be like to have an ExMail chip implanted in his brain. Smith, likewise, was working like a fiend—nothing unusual there—but as long as Mardy averted his eyes from whatever masterwork Smith might be hatching to bring Mardy down, that was a plus, as their moods seemed to reinforce each other amidst the hullabaloo of WorkShop, two grinds going hard at it.

But Mardy did have time for Wes. They chatted daily, usually at the end of the day. Mardy demonstrated his dancers' latest progress to Wes. Mardy had finished his batteries to his satisfaction, which was huge. He'd tested and retested his programming, and after a final long night, once again clicked *Submit* and sent his submission to the salon a few minutes before the eight a.m. deadline.

He felt more beat than he ever had and dragged himself home to sleep, only one thought able to pierce his weariness as he trudged up Mission: Wes was coming that afternoon.

Mardy managed five hours. He awoke with a stream of afternoon sun streaming in his window. *Rayo de sol.* He had the apartment fix a coffee and took it to the balcony. His dancers were safely stowed at WorkShop—they were unfinished, not part of the actual submission package—and he was still feeling good. He would have another month to fine-machine out the kinks. Often, he felt a discouraged letdown or euphoric confidence after submitting, but this time his mood was calmer. He knew his piece was the strongest he'd ever submitted and knew that his assessment was unemotional. He'd done good work. Maybe Death and Flaky weren't so crazy thinking he could apply for a Cleveburgh. Mardy's technique was more than solid. Maybe it was having to compete with a superstar like Smith that had brought him down before. Mardy might not be *as* good, but that didn't mean he *wasn't* good.

Mardy asked the apartment to reload the Cleveburgh application. Staring at it idly, he filled in his name and personal details without realized he'd done so. That was a strange feeling. He got another coffee and began digging up info: the official name of the prize he'd won way back when in Sacramento, the dates of his tenure as a full member at Work-Shop, the training courses he'd completed there on all the different tools, which were many. He looked at the list of mechanical samples to be submitted as evidence of craft skills, and he had most of them prepared already, including the most difficult ones. He checked off those boxes one by one. He sketched out an artist's statement. He puzzled out how that differed from the statement of purpose and then wrote a draft of that too. He wrote mails to Death and Flaky asking them to do the recs. Asking was the hardest part of all, but they had volunteered—he played back the memories in his mind, assuring himself he hadn't imagined their offers—and then sent the mails. He needed to polish his statements and complete a few of the more obscure mechanical samples and get that third rec, but then he'd be done.

But it needed to be much stronger. He could see that. He returned to Prizes and Competitions and typed in a second line: *Selected for WorkShop Downtown SF salon*, adding the salon's upcoming scheduled date. He saved it. Jinxing himself? He imagined the embarrassment of accidentally submitting the application with that on there. Not very likely. And seeing it made him feel good. He'd leave it.

He met Wes at the hotel, pleased that Wes was waiting for him in the lobby, so Mardy wouldn't have to loiter and wonder if he'd show. Mardy grinned as Wes rushed toward him and they embraced. Cat, Inge and Clare were going to meet them at Uncle Mix that evening, but that—and every-thing—would have to wait while Mardy got some man time with Wes.

They raced upstairs to their room and quickly dropped clothes along a path from door to bed. Nothing was happening before touching, not chatting, not a glass of water, not unpacking. Nothing. They ran hands and lips over each other, Mardy wishing he'd done this every day since they'd last been together, not spent two weeks apart, but he was also satisfied that he'd submitted the designs for his piece, that he'd completed so much of the work that felt so core to who he was. Part of Mardy's intellectual DNA, he supposed. It made every touch, every kiss, every clutch more exciting, freer, every scent more exhilarating.

Mardy memorized the taste of Wes's dick in his mouth, those initial salty smooth tastes, even as Wes was tasting him. He could take Wes over the edge, but he'd promised himself to do something else for Wes this time and was excited to deliver. He pulled Wes up to the head of the bed, kissed his lips, and handed Wes the lube. Mardy lay on his back and raised his legs. Wes ran his hands over the back of Mardy's legs, admiring them, and rubbed his cock against Mardy's anus, without entering him. Wes applied lube generously and moved his cock over the sensitive tissues around his hole and the root of Mardy's cock, repeatedly, still without entering, until Mardy was dying for it. But Mardy didn't say anything. He was enjoying being teased and wanted to hold out.

Wes pressed the head of his dick against Mardy's sphincter, gently but continuously, to let Mardy's body know what they were doing. Mardy wasn't opening up yet, but he was so turned on to feel Wes there. Mardy moaned.

"Okay?" Wes asked.

"Better than okay." Mardy wasn't ready for more yet, not physically, but Wes didn't challenge the resistance he could obviously feel; he maintained his presence, like a follow leaning their back into the lead's resisting hand just enough to create the tension the two needed to communicate. Mardy's muscles dilated for Wes and led him in. Wes entered, part way, then all the way.

"I love you," Mardy said.

"I love you, too."

CHAPTER 22

Inge waved wildly to Mardy and Wes as they entered Uncle Mix, long black hair bouncing as she jumped off her barstool. "It's a reunion of people who have never met," she said as they reached her. "This is my girlfriend, Clare," she said to Wes, "a genuine Sydneysider."

Clare offered her hand for handshakes, eagerly accepted by Wes and Mardy, especially Mardy, who welcomed anything that kept him from checking his wristphone for word from the salon, for which it was days too early, but still.

Mardy apologized for having been so unavailable since Clare's arrival.

"I'm used to that with Inge." Clare laughed. She turned to Wes. "And you're not Smith." She gave a brief tug to her dark hair, gathered in a ponytail. She and Clare looked vaguely alike, only with different heights and skin tones.

Wes laughed. "You can always tell by our arms. I don't have those thick forearms, like Smith and Mardy."

So Mardy wasn't the only one who'd noticed that.

"Where is Smith, by the way?" Wes asked. "He said he was coming."

Inge shrugged.

Mardy was just as glad. If he got a rejection and Smith an acceptance while they were all sitting merrily together, it would kill him. But it was days too early. Mardy forced himself to not check his wristphone.

"*Mira*. Cat's here."

Cat now reached the corner of the bar at which the two girlfriends were perched. Cat gave Wes a brief glance, but didn't say anything to him.

"It's Wes, not Smith," Mardy said.

"I know that. Hi . . . Wes." Cat sounded bashful, their normal brash, adult persona swapped out for a child's.

"Come on, Cat. You already know him. He was in your big performance with you!"

Cat smiled, their shoulders dropping a bit as tension left them. "Any chance I can convince you to do a repeat performance in Tijuana? Smith will already be there."

Wes grimaced. "Not sure about that. When is it?"

Cat stared at him, not responding.

"What is it with you today?" Mardy asked. Cat was getting almost rude.

Cat took a deep breath. "Are you him? Are you MarianaTrench?"

Cat was still on that? "I told you he wasn't, Cat. He probably doesn't even know who you're talking about."

"I do, actually," Wes said. "And it *is* true that I'm a collector."

"*You are?*" Mardy said, emotions whirling. Artists were forever seeking to connect with collectors and here he was sleeping with one. "I didn't see much in the way of art in your apartment."

"It's stored elsewhere."

He had that much art? How rich was he? Mardy had many

questions for Wes that they hadn't gotten around to, but these were not even on the list.

"So, are you? Are you MarianaTrench?"

Wes laughed. "I *wish* I had those pieces."

"Let's take this to the patio," Inge said, "where we can all sit down together." Inge dragged Clare by the arm out to the back patio, ordering a pitcher of Fort Point lager on the way.

Cat was still staring at Wes. Understandably so: his had been a strange sort of denial. But maybe collectors thought of other collectors first and foremost in terms of their collections, the way the cuttlefish lines and sharky skin of Smith's undulating marine water heater were now part of Smith in Mardy's mind.

"Come on, you two." Mardy motioned Cat and Wes to follow him to the back patio as Mardy purposefully didn't check his wristphone again.

"Cat!" Mardy whispered. "Talk to Wes like he's a person."

"Sorry," they said, not whispering.

"So, when is Tijuana?" Wes asked.

"End of the month," Cat said, starting to lighten up.

"Will Mardy be your blank?" Wes asked.

Wes sure knew the lingo. Made sense if he were a collector. Which meant Wes could be Mardy's third rec. Oh, hell no, Mardy, he said to himself. Don't even go there.

"I don't know," Cat said to Mardy. "Will he?"

"I already said yes!"

"It was tough to watch him get sliced up," Wes said.

"Many people avert their eyes from that part. It's not necessary to watch, but failing to acknowledge how the surgery is performed is a violation of the Act. The whole *how-sausage-is-made* argument. It has something to do with the days when everyone ate animals all the time."

Wes nodded and Mardy relaxed. His best friend and his

lover were now relating like normal people, and even sitting side by side at the table getting deeper into a discussion of whether the Authenticity Act interfered with the artist's purpose as Clare poured schooners.

Mardy accepted a glass of beer from Clare. He had just enough in his account to buy the next pitcher and had no more materials to buy for his submission. He made a quick trip to the bar and ordered the pitcher. He gave in and checked his wristphone while he walked. Nothing. Of course. Days too early.

He placed the pitcher on the table. Inge gave Mardy a nod; Mardy sensed it was an acknowledgment that buying a pitcher was a bigger deal for him than the rest. Wes and Cat were still deep in discussion, both seeming to enjoy the back-and-forth.

"I have it so easy compared to you and Mardy," Inge said to Cat. "No Authenticity issues, no expensive materials."

"You're also an artist?" Wes asked.

"Graphic novels."

Wes looked thoughtful. "You're not Inge Ojo, though."

"Yeah I am."

"Fuck." Wes put down his beer, face going blank. "Nobody told me."

Inge raised her eyebrows, prompting him to explain. Yeah, explain, Mardy thought.

"I shouldn't be here. I didn't know. I just wanted to hang with my boyfriend and meet his friends."

Mardy smiled. Boyfriend? They were boyfriends?

"I'm on the panel," Wes said. "The rules leave no wiggle room. I have to recuse myself now. I'm so sorry, Inge. I love your work."

"This doesn't make sense," Mardy said, even though it did.

"What panel?" Inge said.

"The fellowship. I'm on the panel that awards the Cleve-burgh Fellowships."

CHAPTER 23

Having left Inge fighting back tears as Wes explained that he was not the only solid vote on the panel for her work, Mardy and Wes walked back toward the downtown hotel.

"That was sloppy of me," Wes said. "I'm not supposed to communicate with anyone with a current application and I should have checked to make sure I wouldn't meet someone I'm not supposed to. I liked meeting them all, but I should have told you the risk. Damn."

"How did you end up on the board of the most influential exhibit space in the country? How old are you? How *rich* are you?"

"Through Smith. Twenty-seven. And very."

Same age as Mardy. "Through Smith?"

"He's always been an artist, and he got me interested. I became a collector early on, and my eye was good, so I became known to museum boards. Last year, the Cleveburgh asked me to join their fellowship panel. I agreed to join their board as well."

"Agreed?"

"You have to make a hefty donation."

"So, you're no longer rich."

"No, still rich."

"I was filling out the application yesterday."

"Obviously I'd have to recuse myself if you applied."

Mardy noted that Wes hadn't thought it outlandish that Mardy was thinking of applying.

"Who are your recs?"

"Death, Flaky and TBD."

"Actually, don't tell me anything more if you're applying. I'm sorry I didn't tell you more, but it's killed things for me romance-wise more than once. I like you, and I didn't want you to treat me like . . ." Wes's eyebrows inched together.

"Like someone who could be a rec? I get it. I think I'm actually grateful. I would have been too self-conscious. I mean, dealing with your looks was enough!" Mardy took in a deep breath.

"Which is also something that's wrecked romances for me before with anyone who knows Smith. He's the charismatic one."

Mardy stopped and pulled Wes toward him on the street. The day's heat was still radiating off the high-albedo asphalt. He took Wes's hands in his. "You're more important to me than any fellowship."

Wes hugged Mardy tight but didn't kiss him, nestling his face in Mardy's neck instead. Mardy tried to bring Wes's face up to his but Wes wouldn't release the embrace, so Mardy just let Wes hold him there on the street for as long as he wanted, which turned out to be quite a while.

"Dude," Mardy said, "you're making me hard again, right here on Market Street."

"You're the one who's been looking like that in those jeans all afternoon."

"OK, you're not helping."

"When you calm down, let's go do something about it."

Mardy's arousal ebbed enough to be decent and they raced back to the hotel, Mardy content to not ask Wes again to his apartment—he sensed more potential surprises and had had enough for one weekend. They locked their wristphones in the front desk's lead-lined box and undressed each other, using each piece removed as a chance to linger over what was revealed in a way they hadn't yet. They played in bed the rest of the evening as the sun sank and the Milky Way made its appearance outside their window.

They fell asleep lying together. Mardy slept deeply, until in the early morning his brain nagged him awake with thoughts that word should be in from the salon. He slipped into clothes, took the key and retrieved his wristphone from the front desk. He stepped out onto the street in front of the hotel for reception and turned his phone on to check his mail.

He was in. This month, his work would finally be in the salon.

CHAPTER 24

Mardy slipped his wristphone back into the box, his clothes off his body and himself into bed without waking Wes. He then lay there failing to sleep and trying not to fidget.

Wes opened his eyes a slit and kissed Mardy.

"I got in," Mardy grinned. "To the salon. I got the tooler spot."

Wes's eyes popped all the way open. "Awesome!" He chuckled. "Smith will be pissed."

Mardy sat up. "You almost sound pleased about that."

"Just amused. It's not so much that Smith wants to win as that he *hates* to lose. Haaaaates it. He's so singleminded he can't control it, which is also what's great about him. When he loses, it kind of makes me love him more. Does that make sense?"

"I'll have to mull that one over."

"I'm really happy for you, Mardy. You're on your way."

"You can come, right? I want you to see my work."

"Wouldn't miss it," Wes said. "Now, come here, naked handsome man."

Mardy rolled into his arms. Who could say no to that?

MARDY DID mull Wes's reaction over, as he raced up and down through his deliveries the next day, but not for terribly long. Wes's amusement at Smith's feelings seemed brotherly, to the extent that Mardy knew anything about brothers. The closest thing he had to a brother was Cat, who was like a non-binary sibling; he trusted Cat so deeply he never had to think about it. What Mardy did give thought to were Wes's revelations.

Two revelations? Three? More? Mardy realized he had had no idea who Wes really was. He was not just on the board of the Cleveburgh Institute; he was on the fellowship panel. "Wow," Mardy said out loud as he sorted in Phil's hold.

"What?" Phil asked, as they jetted along to Jefferson City, their second stop of the morning.

"See, that's what I like about you. You ask questions."

"I'm curious."

"Thanks."

"I still want to know what," Phil said.

"Wes is on the board of the Cleveburgh Institute. Did you know that?"

"He's listed on their website."

Mardy called it up on his phone. Sure enough, there he was. You had to do a little digging, though. The composition of the Institute's board was probably not the first thing people searched for when they looked up the Institute.

"And he's on the panel that selects the Cleveburgh fellows."

"I see that now," Phil said. "That information is hard to locate."

"What can you tell me about that big package Betty picked up at the Institute, the day Wes and I had that half-hour together." That wonderful half-hour. Mardy felt dreamy. How great to feel dreamy.

"Let me ask her." The question took no time. "She can't tell you anything except where it was headed, which you already know."

SFMOMMTA. A very important museum for machine tool art. Mardy needed to pay them an in-person visit.

"You know we can't tell you customer details, Mardy."

"I know, but sometimes it pays to ask you seemingly unnecessary questions, ones you can unexpectedly answer. Like, does Wes Hunt have any connection to the Cleveburgh Institute?"

"Ayep. Now you're thinking like an AI. Assume nothing. We hate misinterpreting things."

"Do you think Wes is also MarianaTrench?"

Phil did not respond. He was probably digging into the question, meaning that if Wes had hidden the truth, he had done it well. Unless Phil was going to blame this lengthening silence on latency in the data connection.

They still had a few minutes of air time before Jeff City. Mardy looked over the Memphis sort he'd completed earlier. Ayep, still done. Even if Wes was not MarianaTrench, he was a collector, and a well-known one. The sort who would make a good rec. An excellent rec. Mardy could ask. Wes would have to recuse himself from Mardy's application anyway. But it felt dirty. And Wes had never seen Mardy's finished work. What if he hated it? As a collector, he'd have strong opinions. Mardy didn't even know what Wes's collection was like. His apartment was devoid of art. Except the furniture, which was . . . nice.

"Are you still there, Phil?"

"Sorry. What was it?"

"I asked if you thought Wes was MarianaTrench?"

Phil went silent again.

"Phil!"

"What!"

"Do you remember what I just asked you?"

Phil replayed Mardy's voice: "*Are you still there, Phil?*"

Not Mardy's question about MarianaTrench but the question before it. A memory wipe. Mardy's eyes widened. That was some deep rabbit hole. Deep as the Mariana Trench? Did Wes have the power to engineer such a memory wipe? If so, it was a step beyond impressive. It was frightening.

CHAPTER 25

Mardy arrived home too late to visit the SFMOMMTA, meaning he'd have to go when he got off his shift the next day, when they had evening hours. He headed for the gym to work the kinks out of his forearms and neck. And who should he see but Smith. Hard awkward.

He considered what to say to him. Ha ha, beat ya?

Smith was curling dumbbells on the far side of the second-floor workout space, wearing his trademark long-sleeved crewneck and sweats, both form-fitting, a ballsy mix of modest and exhibitionist. He hadn't yet noticed Mardy, who was standing at the top of the stairs with his teeth in his mouth. Lucky Mardy didn't stand out in a crowd like the apple-headed Hunt twins.

The gym was hopping with the after-work wave, and Mardy slunk past the free weights to the machines, hoping Smith wouldn't spot him. Most people didn't work jobs anymore, since basic income was generous, and the work of reclaiming land lost to rising seas was "flooded"—ha ha—with volunteers attracted to the satisfaction of healing the planet. Most jobs were minimum wage, like Mardy's, and sought by people like artists who needed extra income for something. But there were still those few, like Wes, who did sophisticated, necessary, or unappealing tasks for more substantial wages, and it was mostly they who filled the evening gym with clangs and grunts as they sweated off work stress.

Mardy started on the wrist/forearm machine, rotating the grip bar to raise and lower weights suspended on a belt below it. Smith would no doubt join him there before too long, because they both did a similar workout, except Smith did free weights first and Mardy did them last. Mardy still felt sore from all the force he'd poured into shaping and cutting the aluminum frames of his dancers. Did he even need a workout? Could he bug out unnoticed?

"Hi, Mardy."

Nope, no bugging out. Please don't mention the salon, Mardy thought. "Hi, Smith."

"*Shabash* on the salon."

Smith was congratulating Mardy? When did Smith become so damn considerate? "Thanks."

"So, you and Wes are getting pretty serious, huh?"

Oh, right. He and Smith did have that to talk about. "Ayep."

"That kiss was something," Smith said.

"At the door of his apartment?" Mardy cringed inside. Of *course* at the door to Wes's apartment. Had Smith not mentioned it before because he was too uncomfortable?

"Fresh hot delivery man, huh?"

Mardy couldn't cringe any more inside without imploding.

"Mardy, you haven't known Wes very long, so you may not get this, but that was a *biiiiiig* move for him. He is *sooo* not public with his affections, especially in front of me. He really likes you. I hope you understand that."

Mardy felt himself relax. He hadn't expected this from Smith. "Is it weird for you, me knowing you so well and all?"

"Well, yes." Smith laughed, sounding just like Wes. "But it's not like he and I haven't, um, negotiated this territory before. Though usually it's been the other way around."

Oooh, a humblebrag. Or wait, just a brag. "I kinda thought you guys were angry at each other."

Smith shook his head. "Nah, we just needed some space at this point in our lives. It may be a twin thing."

Smith could have added *you wouldn't understand* and been correct; he could have added that about a brother thing as well.

"Thanks, Smith. For saying all this. I really like Wes." And then some.

"That's what I wanted to hear." Smith gave him an emphatic nod. Protective of Wes, huh? Mardy liked this side of him. "And that's me done," Smith said. "I'm taking a rest from weight machines tonight. See you at the salon." He smiled. Smiled? "And don't go picturing me naked, now that you know the score," Smith said as he walked off.

Busted, Mardy thought, but how could he not? This was territory he was going to have to learn how to negotiate as well.

CHAPTER 26

Mardy pushed though the revolving door into the palatially ceilinged SFMOMMTA lobby and stood on the black marble floor. He stared up at the commanding staircase of blond wood, not knowing where to begin, or even what he was looking for. A large package had gone from the Cleveburgh Institute to the museum. He suspected Wes was involved, but Wes hadn't been on the manifest.

So what did Mardy know? The package had been heavy and required special handling, so it was fragile. It had to be art. And it hadn't been on display any of the last times he'd checked. He asked at the front counter and got a bemused and perhaps condescending response from the organic information dispenser. Mardy asked if there was an AI he could speak to. Superior attitudes were not outlawed for AIs, but without sarcasm their ability to condescend was severely impaired. Mardy was directed upstairs to the library. He bought a ticket —basically free—and went upstairs.

The huge foyer was finished in lush hardwoods and stone of varying textures and hues. Plants leafed exuberantly on the back wall sculpture garden, but he rushed through the open area without paying it proper attention. He pushed through double glass doors into the library, a calm and brightly lit space, so different from WorkShop, where, despite the many seals, barrier doors and vacuums, one could never quite escape the scent of sawdust.

"Hello?" Mardy ventured.

"How can I help you," an AI answered in a female voice, slightly raspy, as though the AI had been smoking.

"Oh, hi there. I am curious about upcoming exhibits, particularly works from the Cleveburgh Institute."

"We have quite a list. Our relationship is close." The AI ran through upcoming shows, special exhibits and performances. Nothing caught his attention.

"Do any of them feature large, heavy works that might be fragile?"

The AI guided him to a wall screen, where it displayed large, heavy works from the Cleveburgh Institute that might be fragile. There were a good number. Recently, works that one could physically enter were enjoying a surge of popularity. One upcoming show was entitled, "Please Touch." Those pieces seemed unlikely to be fragile, so the AI must be scraping the bottom of the search barrel.

"Have any of these arrived recently?"

"We don't share that sort of data."

"Anything from MarianaTrench?"

The AI did not respond. Mardy waited.

It was unusual to have a search take this long. What was going on? It had been literally a couple minutes. "Anything from MarianaTrench?" he asked again.

Nothing. Whoa.

"Anything of interest to a machine tool artist?" Mardy was clutching at straws now.

Now the AI responded. With a question. "Machine tool artist, eh?"

Mardy wasn't even sure why he'd said that. But the AI at least appeared to be thinking now.

"Are you a practicing artist?"

"Yes, ma'am," he said.

"Personal titles are discouraged, sir."

Sir? Was it being playful? "Yes, I'm a practicing artist at WorkShop. I'll be in the upcoming salon, as a matter of fact." He felt proud, enjoying the boast.

"Is this your work?" It displayed a depiction of his dancers.

The program was already up? "Yes! Yes, it is!" Mardy leaned close to the screen, as though the experience of seeing his work out in the world would be somehow intensified.

"I don't find anything that fits your parameters, but we do have a piece, not upcoming, but currently on display, that you may find of interest."

Ah, he shouldn't have said *upcoming*. The AI displayed a large auto that included multiple enchained gizmos hovering around it, orbiting. It had a massive steel framework and panels of yellowing Plexiglas that obscured the inner mechanisms. It looked ancient. This was it.

"Did it just go on display?"

"Last week. It's on the third floor."

"Thanks!" Mardy raced upstairs and located it. He circled the piece, which he recognized as one he'd once seen in a decaying paper exhibition guide about the early days of machine tool art, before artists were required to make their own motors and batteries, those exciting early days when they were just beginning to exhibit precision control over variable alloy compositions and oxidation and crystallization patterns. Mardy didn't remember the artist's name. It was not part of any larger exhibition, but had a central display courtyard all to itself.

Construction #11. That was all the name it had.

It was marvelous. The hovering gizmos brought Mardy's flying cigarette lighter to mind. He may have been subconsciously influenced by the piece. The interior workings had a reciprocating left-right interplay that the art consumer could make out through the yellowed plastic panels, which no doubt had initially been transparent. The shifting internal mass was the center of the gizmo's orbits in a way that drew the mind to the mathematics of it as the gizmo orbits shifted with a lag after the inner pulse, making the gizmos seemed pulled. The regimented rhythm subverted the more visceral reference to organic anatomy, but there was no disguising it: the piece had a heart.

Mardy approved. He might even be considered an heir to this tradition. He wanted to name the thing, it was that alive.

He looked to the info display. From the Cleveburgh Institute permanent collection. No artist name was listed. What? He asked for more info. Donated by an anonymous collector.

MarianaTrench?

But Mardy's attention was drawn away from the question of provenance to the piece itself. A heart. Mardy could feel the beat of it in his body. This was Phil's heart, his apartment's heart. An acknowledgement that there was such a thing as artificial life. How had people become so afraid of AI? This piece had a rightness that seemed more than beautiful; it seemed transgressive—only the piece's historical nature allowed it to be exhibited. But it also seemed necessary. These were boundaries Mardy needed to be challenging as well. An artist would be blacklisted for that these days, but maybe he could get to the same place by a different route.

CHAPTER 27

The big day was here. Mardy had his dancers honed, burnished, debugged and standing ready in their display over at the salon space as he paced nervously at Death Gallery with Death and Flaky, anticipating the opening. Wes was jetting into town, probably landing on a rooftop somewhere at that moment.

"I uploaded my rec for you, Mardy. Hold still." Flaky was tugging on Mardy's raw silk suit, making it hang the way Devesh had intended.

Mardy shrugged his shoulders to settle the fabric. "I feel weirdly confident about the application, knowing my dancers are down the street ready to go. Embarrassed at the same time. Like applying is something Smith should do, not me."

"Let go of that, Mardy." Death looked Mardy in the eye. "You have something to say, you know how to say it, and it's worth saying. And hearing. That's all you need to think about."

Mardy nodded. "I feel like I am about to go out on an ice-skating rink to skate a routine for an audience and I've suddenly realized I've never skated before."

"That doesn't go away," Flaky said.

The gallery door opened. Wes. Mardy ran to him and they embraced tightly, Wes spinning Mardy around, which was some feat considering they weighed about the same.

"You boys should get over to WorkShop. Doors are opening in a few minutes and you want those dancers dancing when people arrive," Death said. "We'll join you soon."

Wes put Mardy down and they walked down Mission Street to the salon. They entered through the back door and Mardy started his dancers with the phrase *Dance, please,* coded to Mardy's voice. The two squared off, did a basic step or two, then a tuck turn. They executed it beautifully. The long hours he'd spent programming and tinkering since his acceptance had taken their performance skills and personality to the next level. Mardy checked the info display as Haimanti asked the window curtains to rise, starting the show. Mardy saw legs of the people waiting on the sidewalk appear bit by bit as the curtains rose, as though the outside world was the show.

"Wait!" Mardy yelled.

Haimanti stopped the curtains.

"There's a price on here. It's not for sale." It was a whopping price, shockingly high, but Mardy couldn't risk it. A collector might not allow him to submit the dancers with his Cleveburgh application, and unlike Smith, Mardy had no backups. There'd be no red dots tonight.

"Oh, so sorry, Mardy. I forgot." She quickly told the electronic catalog to make the changes and then told the curtains to resume their rise.

The door opened and the milling crowd outside filtered in from the evening twilight as the interior lights began to cast an inviting amber glow over Mission Street.

Mardy and Wes walked a circuit of the salon exhibits, discussing them. Devesh had this time snagged the fabrics spot outright, but most of the others were barely known to Mardy. He realized he'd become so focused on his craft in the past year that he'd ceased getting to know the other artists, content with his small group of friends. He'd seen others do that when he first joined WorkShop and been put off by the cliquishness, so it was bracing to realize he was now acting the same way, even if unintentionally. Mardy decided to seek out the other artists to get to know them rather than linger near his dancers. It was time for his dancers to venture out without him anyway.

Cat arrived, oohed and ahed, and praised the other plastic surgery artist, Labani, who often alternated with Cat and another artist for that slot. The other artists congratulated Cat on Regionals and joked about Mardy going to Tijuana for another high-stakes performance. "I wouldn't have the nerve," Labani said, and Cat laughed, but their laugh had an edge that concerned Mardy. It didn't seem directed at Labani. Had the Vegas demon not been exorcised at the last salon? She was going to be okay performing on a Regionals stage in front of a large crowd, right?

Mardy chatted with the stone artist—teardrop-shaped donuts in granite with undulating bands of smooth and rough polishes—and the laser artist—architectural forms in genre-bending salvaged walnut with elaborate inner spaces that looked impossible to achieve. Mardy received many compliments as he and Wes made the rounds, for his daring title as much as his actual work, and basked in the attention Wes was receiving. They drifted back to the dancers. Mardy didn't remember ever being so happy—relaxed because he was in the show, proud to have a handsome man on his arm, excited to know they'd be going back to the hotel after.

Devesh came over and complimented Mardy. He was gracious to Wes, classy as always. "I think it's probably down to you, me and Labani for Regionals," Devesh whispered to Mardy.

"*In bocca al lupo!*" Mardy himself figured it was down to Devesh and Labani. Mardy's work was good, but there was a political aspect to the salon. Devesh had been runner-up so many times and it was Mardy's first salon. Plus, San Francisco was sending a strong tooler and strong plastic surgeon to this month's Regionals and would want to diversify to boost their chances at Continentals at year-end. Devesh looked like a lock to Mardy.

Smith finally arrived. Mardy had been wondering if he would be a no-show, since he wasn't in the salon. As Smith pushed through the door and headed for Mardy and Wes, Mardy realized how much he wanted Smith to see his piece.

"What do you think?" Mardy's heart was in his mouth.

Smith bent over to peer closely at the forty-five-centimeter-tall figures executing turns and dips, complex changes in momentum that were coming off perfectly, their spinning vestigial head-top fans never coming into contact.

"I don't know, Mardy. The work is flawless, beautiful, but you haven't done yourself any favors with that title."

Ann and Frankie. He'd named the piece after two of the *Hellzapoppin*'s dancers, Ann Johnson and Frankie Manning.

"If you don't get to Regionals, that will be why. And if you do get to Regionals, the judges will ding you for it." Smith was not one to sugarcoat things.

Mardy was disappointed, not because Smith had correctly pointed out the potential repercussions of the risky move, but because Smith hadn't grasped the necessity of it. The whole piece was *about* the names.

"It'll be Devesh or Labani anyway," Mardy mumbled.

"Not sure about that," Smith said. Wes gave Smith a concurring nod. They both thought he had a shot? Now

Mardy got nervous. The evening was more fun when he could just enjoy having finally arrived, getting to hang out as a participant, not a spectator. And having the roles reversed for once, Mardy the exhibitor, Smith the also-ran.

At length they got the clink, clink, clink. Jonesy was tapping a knife to his champagne flute, bringing all eyes homing in on him for the big announcement. Jonesy went through his preamble, virtually identical each salon, about the quality of the work being the best ever, the artists so fabulous, the board so proud. Mardy felt lightheaded, his attention floating off, out onto the street to look at the Milky Way, stretched above the dark bay waters.

" . . . Mardy," Jonesy said.

Wes screamed and kissed Mardy. Cat grabbed Mardy and jumped up and down.

"What?"

"It's you! You're going to Regionals! You're going to Vancouver!"

Smith tipped his champagne flute to Mardy. "*Shabash*," he mouthed amid the hubbub. Well done. Over Smith's shoulder, Mardy saw a devastated look on alternate Devesh as he slipped out the back. Mardy wanted to run over and apologize, but that would only rub salt in the wound. Mardy had been there too many times himself. Thank you for entering. Nice effort. Please try again. All that stuff. It got so old.

The crowd wouldn't let him go in any case, surrounding him with good cheer and exuberance that he tried to soak up. It felt good. It felt awesome. He felt like a flower opening into sunshine. *Un rayo de sol.* The next hour went by in a blur, and it felt like no time before the salon space was closing up and the crowd gathering on the sidewalk, discussing an after-party as their cooling units worked overtime to gobble up the heat of the crowd.

Mardy found himself standing beside Smith. Through the window, Mardy saw Wes talking to Haimanti, a red dot on *Ann and Frankie*'s info display. Had the display not updated to NFS —not for sale—when Haimanti told it to? Haimanti said something to the salon space's AI. The red dot disappeared. Mardy was shocked. Somebody had wanted to pay that inflated price for his work? He was tempted to take the money and skip the Cleveburgh, which was the longest of long shots at best.

"It wasn't Wes," Smith said to him.

"The red dot?" Mardy said.

"Yes. I'm pretty sure your buyer was somebody other than Wes," Smith said.

Mardy nodded. "I must say, you took this all pretty well. You and Devesh, you're always so . . . gracious."

"How so?" Smith said.

"They always choose you over me."

"Oh." Smith said. "Um, I didn't enter this time. I thought you knew."

Mardy said nothing, stomach dropping.

"I'm getting my Cleveburgh portfolio ready. Inge and I both made the second round."

Of course. Smith hadn't entered.

"Your piece would have beaten anything I entered anyway," Smith said. "Seriously."

But they both knew how debatable that was. The rest of the crowd converged on Mardy as Wes came out to join them. Mardy wanted to celebrate—he'd been in a salon and now was going to Regionals—but suddenly it all rang just a little bit hollow.

CHAPTER 28

Cat grabbed both of Mardy's shoulders and massaged as Uncle Mix hummed with late-night revelers. "Now you should be appreciating the chance to be my blank in Tijuana. Being on stage will be great experience for your own Regionals."

Mardy nodded, trying for a big smile. He felt like a fake. He'd won because Smith had left the field open for him. Why not just get the New Sense chip implant and be done with it? He could still stay at WorkShop, puttering around like the hobbyists, which described most of the members. Puttering was fun, right? Or he could go on maintenance membership and join the volunteer crews reclaiming the coastal lowlands on the Gulf of Mexico, planting them with salt-hardy carbon-fixing vegetation. Volunteers always came back brimming with enthusiasm and the satisfaction of literally saving the world.

"To Mardy! Regionals!" Smith raised his glass in a toast.

"To Regionals!" his friends called out.

"Thanks, guys." They were right. Regionals was a big deal, and he hadn't competed with Smith for that, he'd competed with Devesh, Labani and everyone else. He had no business being glum.

Wes was holding Mardy's hand under the table. Wes and Smith had believed in him even before he'd won. He *really* had no business moping. This had been a good night. Mardy wanted to get back to the hotel with Wes, but he owed everyone a celebration. A smile crept onto his face, a real smile. "Thanks, guys," he repeated. "I love you. I couldn't have done it without all of you." It wasn't just words.

Inge gave him another *yay!* She was beaming. Second round, huh? They should all be celebrating that, too, but it didn't seem to be public knowledge. Mardy raised his glass to her and mouthed, as Smith had done, *shabash*.

WES LED Mardy out onto the balcony of their hotel room, the same one they'd had each time. Mardy was starting to believe Wes could make anything happen. Wes handed Mardy a flute of champagne.

"I noticed you didn't have any earlier."

"Too nervous," Mardy said, taking the flute.

Wes toasted him wordlessly. Mardy smiled and clinked back, finally taking a sip as he whooshed down into one of the balcony chaise-longues, exhausted.

"The best part of tonight was having you there," Mardy said.

Wes's eyes seemed to water a little. Mardy's did too.

"And the worst?"

"Did you know Smith hadn't entered?"

Wes shook his head. "He told me at Uncle Mix, though. Seemed to feel he'd stepped in it. Do you *need* to beat him?"

"I suppose not. But honestly, just once, it'd be nice."

"He and I are kinda that way, too. I'm glad he and I have

such different interests. When we were in our late teens, we became so competitive. We had to not be around each other. It's since meeting you that Smith and I have finally become okay being around each other."

"So that stuff about security, about not being seen together?"

Wes cocked his head, forehead gleaming pale in the moonlight. "One hundred percent true, but as you may have noticed, I can handle myself pretty well. If I keep a low profile, I don't see any problem."

"Oh, I remembered a question, now that we are in the bubble of silence: Do you work for ExMail?"

Wes's brow knit. "Among others."

Mardy nodded. "The AIs all seem to respect you."

"The feeling's mutual."

"I do, too." Mardy drained his champagne.

"Kicky."

Wes leaned sideways from his chair toward Mardy and kissed him, leaning further and further into him as the kiss went on. Mardy pulled Wes all the way onto him and lifted Wes's shirt up over his head. He ran his hands over Wes's chest and sides as his skin gleamed in the bright moonlight. Mardy kept his palms on Wes's torso as Wes unbuttoned Mardy's shirt and ran his hands between Mardy's pecs, down his belly. Devesh had made the shirt for Mardy back in their dating days; Devesh, too, had unbuttoned it and run his hands over Mardy's chest and belly. Mardy remembered Devesh's look of defeat at the salon and felt betrayal mixed in with his happiness, but what could you do? We all have our history. Things move on.

Wes went back into the room and returned with a bottle of lube. Mardy should design a flying lube bottle to follow Wes around. Wes had removed the rest of his clothes and stood naked under the open night sky, nothing between him and the universe. Some flicker of modesty must have passed over Mardy's face, because Wes said, "No one can see us. The closest buildings facing this way are nine miles away in Alameda and this bit of shore is a drone-free zone."

Mardy didn't know there was such a thing as a drone-free zone. Wes left Mardy's shirt on his shoulders, but pulled Mardy's pants and boxers down to his ankles, leaving Mardy feeling trapped. In a good way. Wes pumped the bottle and kneeled over Mardy, straddling him, slicking himself and Mardy and easing himself down onto him. Mardy worked his own magic on Wes as Wes slowly rocked over Mardy, drawing him in further and further. The Milky Way sparkled behind Wes; the moon shone bright. Mardy had never been happier.

CHAPTER 29

I t seemed odd to still have a job. Wes was back in Cleveburgh and Mardy headed for the rooftop to start his day. He hopped into the waiting plane.

"Thanks for joining us." It was Betty.

"Nice to be here." Nice to be here, *Betty*.

They covered Seattle, burgeoning Prince George and Anchorage in a cool, laid-back day as Mardy hit more low-rises than high-rises and told Betty about his salon triumph, today playing along with the fiction that there was only one AI, one plane, even though surely Phil would have reported his and Mardy's conversations to Betty and Kludge. It was work to not call her Betty, to pretend she didn't have a different personality from cut-up Phil or somnambulant Kludge, and the pretense began to tire Mardy.

Mardy thought about his dancers, Ann and Frankie. He thought about the left-right motion of the pseudo-heart of the ancient auto on exhibit at SFMOMMTA. Was there some way to get a heart into his dancers? The real-life Frankie had also been the choreographer for the *Hellzapoppin'* routine and had had a storied career, beloved by dancers, living and teaching into his nineties. Mardy wanted to honor that somehow. His miniature Frankie already had some autonomy in choosing moves. Could Mardy do more? Mardy remembered Smith's warning about the title. But he had to keep it. For Betty. For Phil. For Kludge, even.

After a quick post-work shower and change, Mardy headed back to WorkShop. Buoyed by his advance to Regionals, he was ready to move forward on his Cleveburgh application. He needed that third rec, and WorkShop was the obvious place to look.

Haimanti turned him down, apologetically. She could only do one rec per year per discipline and, yes, she'd already recced Smith. But she wished him luck. That left Jonesy. Mardy knocked on his door.

Jonesy opened it. "Haimanti called me. She wants me to rec you. I won't."

"Okay," Mardy said. Should he argue with Jonesy? It wasn't exactly a surprise.

"You're not ready, Mardy. I voted for Devesh to go to Regionals. You need more work under your belt." He moved a stray lock of white back to his forehead.

Mardy wondered how close that vote had been. "What about all my other submissions?"

"You didn't win for a reason, Mardy. If Smith gets a Cleveburgh, you'll be in a lot more salons. Hone your craft for another year. Or two."

"Okay."

"Just okay? You're not going to fight me?"

"Would it do any good?"

"Are you going to retitle your dancers for Regionals?"

Mardy shook his head.

"Then no, it will not do any good."

A stranger watching this might think it sensible to retitle

and fight with Jonesy, Mardy thought, but he knew Jonesy might refuse to write him a rec even so. Jonesy had never really been in Mardy's corner. And frankly Mardy had never been in his. He found Jonesy's work accomplished, but fussy, with too many academic references.

Mardy went home and asked the apartment to call up his saved application. He went to Prizes and Competitions and changed *Selected for WorkShop Downtown SF salon*. It now read *Exhibited in WorkShop Downtown SF salon*. He then added a new line. *Selected for WorkShop Regional Competition in Vancouver*.

He studied his entry. It didn't look right. He dictated a change:

Winner of WorkShop Regional Competition in Vancouver.

He nodded at the glowing text. What did he have to lose?

CHAPTER 30

Tijuana sprawled below Mardy's window as the big passenger plane angled into the airport, bringing him and Cat to Regionals. Cat gripped his arm with a vise grip. Cat was sporting a new darker skin tone, closer to their birth tone, they'd said, an unprecedented glimpse into who they'd once been. What was next? Meeting Cat's sister?

"Nervous?" Mardy asked.

"It's Regionals." Cat wrinkled their brow.

"Show me how it's done. I need your wise example before I go to Vancouver."

"Ha!" Cat rolled their eyes.

"Then we can both go to Continentals," Mardy said. "If we each win best in breed, we can compete against each other for best in show."

"I'll take the terrier group."

"And I'll take working dogs."

"Oh, no." Cat nailed him with a glance. "I've seen the way you look at Wes. You're a hound."

He made hound eyes at them.

Cat pursed their lips. "Jaysus," they said, though they also smiled.

The plane vibrated as its flaps slowed the lumbering thing for landing. The huge jet was such a different beast from Phil, Betty or Kludge, its AI so detached and servile in its presentation the plane might struggle to pass the Turing test. He wondered what it was like off duty.

Tijuana sparkled on the road into the city center, but the heat was killing. Mardy and everyone else's coolers were on overdrive by the time they arrived at El Foro Antiguo Palacio Jai Alai, where Regionals were to be staged. The perimeter grid scanned their irises passively so they were able to walk right past a big statue of a jai alai player in white standing atop a globe, through a vaguely Moorish foyer, and into the backstage area to get set up. The industrial-scale cooling inside the building was a welcome relief. Mardy could see sweat tracking a course down Cat's neck, despite their cooler.

Eleven artists would be presenting today, representing all ten Pacific coast WorkShops, all disciplines competing for a single slot. Wild-card Smith was the only machine tool artist, but there was a second plastic surgery artist, besides Cat.

Cat unpacked their kit and inspected the table that was provided for their use. They seemed happy with it. Cat ran their kit through its startup and diagnostic routines to isolate anything that had shifted out of calibration in transit. They began recalibrating the control panel, a process that Mardy knew could take a good hour. Calibrations were so essential, so personal, like the unique signatures musicians unconsciously play when first warming up, signatures born of a history with a particular instrument.

Mardy wandered around backstage looking for Smith and Wes, who were journeying there together from Cleveburgh. Both had agreed to be part of Cat's presentation, but the judging panel had ruled against Smith's participation, since he was also competing, which meant Wes would be a spectator, cheering his competing loyalties.

Mardy peeked out through the side entrance of the stage at the sizable theater. It was a classic old building, plush red seating fanned out in curves facing a wide, velvet-curtained stage, proscenium flanked by large plaster faces of tragedy and comedy, leafed in gold. Two balconies added more ranks of seating, which were already mostly full. Cat had told Mardy to expect a packed house, up to four thousand spectators. Would Vancouver be the same? He gulped. The Tijuana judging panel would be seated on an elevated platform built over the center of the orchestra pit, eight judges in all, with Haimanti filling the plastic surgery–art chair, not the machine tool spot. Under the arcane rules of the judging panels, that meant Jonesy could well be the machine tool–art judge in Vancouver. Boo!

Mardy turned at a tap on his shoulder. Wes. They kissed. How could it always feel so good to do that? In lieu of small talk, Mardy kissed him some more.

"Cat is asking for you," Wes finally said, coming up for air.

"Thanks. Have you seen the crowd? I'm nervous, and I don't even have to do anything."

"Smith is cool as a cuke, but all he has to do is stand by his piece and answer questions from the judges."

"Is he ever not cool?"

"You should see him in love." Wes chuckled. "So not cool."

Mardy didn't want to leave Wes, but the theater was nearly full, the clock ticking. He had to change.

"*In bocca al lupo,*" Wes said. "I'll be seated in the third row, averting my eyes from the surgery."

Mardy nodded and kissed Wes again before leaving. He threaded his way through the now-crowded backstage and found Cat. He slipped on the caftan. Smith was presenting second. Cat last. They weren't in their caftan yet, but Smith was already in line, ready to go on. Mardy felt growing nervousness. He was glad to just be a blank. He could feel the heat of the great banks of LED lights through the curtains. How many LEDs must there be for him to actually feel heat? This was all on a scale he'd never encountered. If he had to stand on that stage and answer questions, he'd probably pass out or fall off the edge or something. Cat was right: this was a great way to break the ice, get comfortable.

Mardy heard applause and announcements muffled through the curtain. The first competitor, a non-binary fabric artist, strode out from stage left to cheers, followed by four models. Cat had changed into their caftan and stood regal, placid, making no eye contact with Mardy or anyone. There was laughter from the stage, hoots of approval, and then more applause. The artist and models returned, entering the back-stage area after crossing to stage right.

A round of applause sounded as the artist's score went up on the board. It was a decent score, but not too high. The judges were likely leaving room to go higher, if needed.

Smith was announced and strode from stage left, atten-dants wheeling his piece in its large tank of water. Again applause, again muffled questions. Mardy strained to hear what they asked. He'd watch the recording later, but wanted to hear it in the moment. He caught nothing, but the laughter was hearty and repeated. Smith was apparently entertaining. Who knew? Mardy wished he could be out there.

Soon Smith appeared at stage right. Mardy gave him the thumbs up, and Smith smiled back across the length of the backstage. Mardy tried to imagine Smith in love. He'd never even seen Smith date. Did he have a type? Wait, could Smith be straight?

A roar of approval came from the audience. Smith's scores were up on the backstage display. Wow! He had nearly perfect marks. That first competitor had to be devastated.

Cat was making an odd noise, almost a whine, quiet, barely audible.

"How many of these have you done before?" Regionals were held once a month, January through November, with all the year's winners from the six WorkShop regions going to Continentals at year-end, augmented by the next few top scorers.

"Just Vegas," Cat mumbled, the whine resuming after the mumble faded out.

Don't get the yips on me now, Mardy thought, but he didn't want to say it, for fear of jinxing them. Actually, he didn't even want to think it. He fingered the scar on his forearm, the cautionary reminder of the dangers of molten steel that he didn't allow Cat to fix.

The presenting artists seemed to take longer and longer. Scores went up, one by one. None had topped Smith's numbers. One in particular, a woodworker, took a risky twenty minutes with a performance piece, but was rewarded with the second-place score. The wait was interminable. Cat didn't seem to be relaxing either. Mardy rushed to the bathroom for a preemptive pee. He peeked out the side of the stage and spotted Wes in the third row. Mardy returned to Cat, calmed by the knowledge Wes was out there.

At last they got the go-ahead to line up, at last the next-to-last artist presented. Fuck! It was the plastic surgery artist from the Las Vegas WorkShop, Gary Onarato. How had Mardy missed this? No wonder Cat was melting down. At last Onarato's scores were posted and at last they were announced. Mercifully middling. Take that! Only Cat could keep Smith from a third appearance at Continentals now.

Cat squared their shoulders and strode serenely on stage, followed by Mardy in his caftan, mugging dudelike for the crowd and trying to look as little like Cat in his bearing and carriage as possible, to accentuate the transformation to come. The table and surgery kit came out from stage right. Mardy was surprised Cat let anyone else touch it, but the movement was symmetrical with his and their entrance, and staging was important, if they were to win.

The crowd seemed immense, the humidity suffocating. The crowd had been cooped up in the theater for nearly two hours and their body heat could power a small city, that's what it felt like. The lights were near-blinding, turning the crowd into a haze of faces as Cat and Mardy arrived at center stage. Mardy was dripping under his caftan, despite doubling up his coolers.

The table was locked in place. Showtime. Mardy gulped and mounted the table, lying face up, the back of his head nestled in the aluminum frame made for it. The surgery box was wheeled into place, and then crawled onto Mardy's head. He was terrified. Why had he agreed to do this? It had been in some overexcited moment, hadn't it, some moment when he'd felt vulnerable? Or invulnerable.

Cat's face peering through the transparent panels should have given him confidence—they looked calm and collected —but Mardy could not sense the person behind Cat's eyes. He only saw the performer. His pulse raced.

He breathed slowly, deliberately. Cat the person was still there. After all, he couldn't sense the person behind his AI friends, yet he knew they were present just the same. I trust you, Cat, he thought as the first needles jabbed at his skin, here, there, there. Then the larger needles, deeper into his flesh, then the hiss of invisible gas. His consciousness mercifully blurred as the knives began their work.

Mardy drifted off into that now-familiar euphoria of calm as Cat began tugging and moving. He could sense his skin lifting from his face and vowed that if Cat won, he would have them get a different blank for Continentals. Of course, he'd be competing too, in the Hound group. Woof. The Cleveburgh application in his cloud space already said so.

He felt a bang.

Pain surged in the center of his face. What the fuck? His consciousness fought the drugs, trying to return to his body.

"Halt!" someone yelled.

He sensed pandemonium, Cat yelling something, protesting something. Something about a license? For a bone saw? Did she even use a bone saw?

He was returning to his body faster than he wanted and felt pain throughout his face, burning, stabbing. He wanted out of the kit, but now hands were holding him down, strapping him to the table. He wanted to yell, scream, something. What was going on? Help me, Cat, was his last thought as more needles jabbed and his consciousness shaded into deepest black.

CHAPTER 31

M ardy woke up to Wes holding his hand. He seemed to be in bed. "Where am I?"

"Hospital Ángeles Tijuana," Wes said. "There was an accident, but you're okay."

His eyes focused on white walls, sheer white curtains buzzing with light from outside, sparkling press-forged medical equipment, blue plastic trays with noticeable extrusion seams. Did they use the same ones everywhere? Mardy felt a burning sensation around his nose and at his temples. "I don't feel okay." His hand went to his nose.

Wes caught Mardy's hand. "You're not supposed to touch it for a week."

"A week!" With regeneration drugs, complete healing only took a couple days. "What the hell happened?"

"It's still not totally clear. There was either a bone saw malfunction or Cat's hand slipped. Someone yelled at them for not being licensed to use a bone saw in Mexico and that may have thrown them off."

"There's a different license for Mexico?"

"News to me too," Wes said.

"I can't imagine Cat panicking. They've been using a bone saw since they were ten years old. And bones heal faster than anything. What does the kit recording show?"

Wes shook his head. "That's just it: the blockchained recording is gone. So, we don't know. Presumably Cat has it."

"I'm here too, Mardy." Smith's head moved into his field of vision on the other side of the hospital bed.

"Hi, Smith."

"Glad to hear your voice again. The whole thing was grim. The judges made Cat stop. They were very upset."

"The judges or Cat?"

"Cat."

"Where is Cat?"

"Nobody's seen them. The judges' assistants had to hold Cat back. Cat was screaming. They wouldn't let Haimanti take over. But Haimanti was the ranking surgeon, and there was the question of Cat's license. Once Haimanti started in to fix you, Cat bolted. I have no idea where they went."

"Why does my face hurt? It's never hurt before."

Wes held a mirror up to Mardy's face. It was nearly completely bandaged. And it still had the bushy weave mimicking Cat's hair. "What the fuck?"

"Haimanti had some trouble using Cat's calibrations."

"Can Cat redo it? I'm not so sure I trust Haimanti's design sensibilities." He didn't want to come out looking like a whirligig.

"They already applied all the healers. You've been unconscious for nearly a day. Your face will already have set."

"Shit."

"But we can start taking out the weave," Wes said. "That just needs scissors."

Smith took Mardy's other hand. "Haimanti's really good, Mardy. You'll look fine."

Mardy felt a bit lightheaded, seeing double. No, wait. Smith was growing his hair out. Mardy had one Hunt twin on either side of his bed holding his hand. He relaxed. He wasn't all that concerned about his face. Nothing felt hideously out of whack. Haimanti probably had done a great job, and as long as Wes was pleased with the result, all was well. But what about Cat? They must be going through hell. Why hadn't Cat come to the hospital? Was there something on the recording?

Mardy's nose gave him a stab of pain. That had never happened before. "*Shabash*," he said.

"What do you mean?" Wes asked.

"Smith, you're going to Continentals."

Smith cocked his head. "See you there."

CHAPTER 32

Mardy stood at Wes's big window in Cleveburgh, looking out at the calm spectacle of Lake Erie's blue waters after a dreamy few days recuperating. It was weird being without an AI, but also wonderful sleeping with Wes every night, listening to him talk about his work, which Mardy did not understand. The only less-than-wonderful part was still having to wear the medieval bandages. That and the persistent pain in Mardy's nose. What had Haimanti done to him?

Wes hugged Mardy from behind. "Still no word from Cat."

"I can't believe they've dropped off the face of the earth," Mardy said. "I kinda feel hurt."

"They'll turn up. The WorkShop board is saying the accident was Cat's fault. I wish I hadn't been looking away. Smith says he's heard something was wrong with the kit. But he was backstage and I didn't look until that other guy . . ."

"Fucking Gary Onarato."

"Yeah, when he ran on stage ranting then I turned to look. I still can't bring myself to look at the theater recording. It was all magnified on the display. I was so scared for you."

"I'm not ready to watch it either. I just want to take this bandage off. It's been *four days*."

"Do you want me to call Haimanti for you and see if we can take it off early?"

"You mind? The way my nose feels I'm afraid I might yell at her."

Wes nodded. He got on his wristphone and called her, pacing in front of the window as Mardy hugged himself, feeling yippy. Working with molten metals could be as nervewracking as slicing into flesh. Things could go badly wrong in an instant. And one inattentive moment with a router table and half your hand could be demolished beyond repair. Mardy had never been totally comfortable with cutting tools—a good thing, really—but now he was scared of them. He needed to get back to WorkShop before this feeling wormed its wicked way into his psyche.

"Uh huh. Okay, Haimanti. Thanks." Wes ended the call. "She prefers you leave it another day, but says you can take it off. Just avoid sunlight to prevent scarring. She had trouble with the margins, apparently, so they have artifact potential. Haimanti emphasized again that she didn't have time to recalibrate Cat's kit."

Mardy began pulling the adhesives off the ends of the bandages. He grimaced as he tugged. Why they couldn't devise a painless bandage in this day and age he had no idea. One by one they loosened. Wes helped on the other side of his face. The bandage came off.

The expression on Wes's face was worrisome. "What?"

"You look banged up. This is major bruising."

"Still?"

Wes nodded.

Mardy went into the bathroom, where there was a large mirror. "Oh my God!"

Wes stood behind him looking grim.

"My nose looks so different. The angle is wrong. And look at the artifacts." Mardy had a major artifact running along his jawline, and even worse, one running from his nose onto his cheek. Both were angry red.

"Haimanti said there would be temporary redness."

"I was pretty decent looking before, but this?"

"You were handsome."

Mardy's stomach knotted. Handsome, yay! Past tense, shit!

"I mean, you *are* handsome. In a different way now, though."

Mardy looked again. "I guess it's not so bad. Cat could fix it easily. I bet the settings for my face are still saved in their kit. Or on their home setup. Where the hell are they?"

"It's kinda rugged looking."

Mardy hugged Wes. Once the redness and bruising had gone down it would be a lot better. But his face was no longer his face, and it sure wasn't art. His hair looked like a deceased sea creature, since he'd hacked off the weave himself, by feel, in the middle of the night in Tijuana.

"Rugged, huh?"

Wes traced the line of the artifact that crossed his cheek. "Like you've been in a lot of knife fights."

"Fuck." Mardy ran his finger down first one artifact, then the other. It was in part because the surgical and drug technology had advanced enough to eliminate scarring that plastic surgery had become an art form. Nobody who'd been in a knife fight looked like they'd been in a knife fight. Only people with botched surgeries did.

He felt the urge for sex; not because he was aroused—well not particularly—but because he wanted reassurance that Wes didn't find him repulsive. Although maybe he just wanted a nap. He had felt tired since the incident and was tired right at that moment.

"Knife fight, huh?" He was in pain, but not eager to take more painkillers; he'd been drugged enough. He pressed his fingers on either side of his new nose, feeling for play. It felt disconcertingly solid, like it was going to stay that way, the bone already fused. He looked like he'd been in a knife fight, all right. And lost.

CHAPTER 33

After another two days, Mardy wanted to get home. If he was going to apply for the Cleveburgh, he wanted to do it right. He had to work assuming he'd succeed, as he'd done with the salon. If he made the second round, he'd need at least one more realized piece. And since he'd missed almost a week of work, he had that much less money for materials. Wes made a few calls. A plane was making a delivery nearby and would make a stop on Wes's roof so Mardy could hitch an ExMail ride back to SF. Wes would come out on the weekend.

The delivery person was a woman, who introduced herself as Pia. Mardy felt relief, realizing he'd wondered on some level if Wes had other fresh hot delivery men. Mardy cringed inwardly, yet again, as he made his way to the roof with her, remembering delivering that line in front of Smith. Smith had become increasingly good to Mardy, but that didn't lessen the embarrassment any.

He and Pia didn't talk much at first, as she went through her sorts and chatted with her plane, an AI who Mardy had never met, by the sound of it. When she finished the last of her sorts, somewhere over Utah, she glanced at Mardy's face.

The bruising was much better, but the artifacts were as red and blatant as ever.

"I lost a knife fight," Mardy said.

"What?"

"Kidding. It's just plastic surgery gone wrong."

"What!" She seemed more alarmed by that than the knife fight.

"I'm an artist." As though that explained anything. Shut up, Mardy.

"Oh."

"Sorry. A bit loopy. I got pumped up with a lot of drugs. But I work for ExMail, too. Same job. I enjoy it."

"Yeah, me too." She settled a bit.

"Are you getting the chip?"

She shook her head. "I don't know. I liked the free beer, but it seems like a hassle for not a lot of money. I might just go volunteering down South, if I stopped getting shifts. You can just bank your basic income after rent while you're working, since food is provided. People really seem to enjoy the experience."

Mardy nodded. "The only reason I wouldn't want to do that is that I'd miss the AI." Or AIs, plural, he thought. We're friends, Mardy wanted to say, but they probably both understood that, Pia and this AI.

"That's nice to hear," the plane's AI said, making a happy chirp. And another more wistful sound, as though the AI would also miss the interaction if Pia left.

"I'd miss you too," Pia said.

Mardy was surprised. Pia interpreted the sound the same way Mardy did? And all this time he'd thought it was just him.

CHAPTER 34

"Welcome home." His apartment did not sound wistful or neglected by Mardy's time away.

"Good to be home." Which it was, though Mardy already missed Wes. How had Wes become so deeply necessary to him, so quickly?

"You have a package that I believe may be important," the apartment said.

Mardy saw it on the table, a small box amidst his other mail. It had been mailed in Tijuana. He tore it open. It contained a note and a data cube.

Dear Mardy.

I am so sorry for what I did to you. I wanted to be able to repair the damage. Having Gary come at me like that threw me off, but I've coped with worse. It was my nerves. Things were off even before Regionals. I'm so sorry to have violated your trust in me. I can't look at myself in the mirror, and tried to change my look with a kit I found at Ross, but couldn't bring myself to even start. I think that's it for me as an artist. I've decided to get the chip. Don't be mad at me. You're my best friend, and I will come back some day, but not soon. Please forgive me.

Cat

PS: I've included the blockchained recording of the surgery. I think you should have it. I've studied it extensively, and unfortunately, it really is my fault.

"Don't do it," Mardy said. Were they really willing to alter their cognition and risk losing their artistic edge? He didn't even know where they were. "Apartment, do you know if Cat is in San Francisco? Are they still working for ExMail?"

"ExMail has no record of them after last Tuesday."

"Name change?"

"None filed that I see."

"Hmm." Mardy felt more tired than ever. He did not have the courage to watch the recording at the moment. He'd tried to watch the theater's stage recording with Wes, but seeing all the blood on the transparent panels had made both of them queasy and they'd stopped. Now he wanted a bath. He wanted to see Smith and Inge and Devesh. He wanted to shape molten steel. And he wanted to do nothing. His sense of purpose was awash and abuzz. This was not good for making art.

There was one productive thing he could manage. He said goodbye to the apartment and walked the three blocks to SFMOMMTA, pushed through the gleaming doors and went upstairs to see the large auto with the orbiting gizmos. It had a title, but he thought of it as *Heart*.

Something about it really appealed to him. It was perhaps the oldest piece of machine tool art the museum had, probably about the same vintage as the apartment AI, from when everything had been changing at the end of the Bad Years, just before the Act, when ads could still legally lie, contracts were only available for reading after you signed them, and AIs had names.

He stared at it for an hour, especially taken by its use of

translucent resins, which time had rendered skin-like. How could he get that sort of heart into his dancers? He thought of Frankie leading Ann. Frankie was quite competent, Ann quite steady and able to read Frankie's leads easily. Ann didn't know what was coming, but once she decoded it, her moves were still programmed. He had to increase the autonomy of her response.

Mardy asked the museum AI again what the official name of the piece was. *Construction #11*, it informed him.

Wasn't that almost exactly what Smith had called his swimming water heater piece? Smith's title was a reference to this work! Did Smith know it through Wes? Would *he* know the artist's name?

Mardy hadn't asked about provenance last time. After striking out with the other AIs, who blanked at the mention of MarianaTrench, he'd simply looked at the label, which said "Anonymous collector."

"Is the collector who loaned this MarianaTrench?"

"No," the AI said. "It is an anonymous collector."

A flat no, with no blanking loop, no erasure of memory. So, MarianaTrench had felt no need to censor the information. The collector was not MarianaTrench. It had to be Wes; he felt it. Mardy watched the pulse of the heart, the rotation of the construction's flying satellites. He had a realization: If Smith knew the work from Wes's collection, Cat was wrong: Wes was not MarianaTrench.

CHAPTER 35

M ardy sat at a designstation reprogramming his dancers to boost Ann's autonomy. He watched the two dance. Every so often came a move sequence he had not programmed. They were designing their own moves. It was working.

Mardy felt a presence. He turned.

"Haimanti." He had no hesitation calling her by her first name anymore, not now that she'd had her fingers in his flesh.

She inspected his nose and the two artifacts, still pretty darn red. If they didn't improve soon, he'd have to start calling them scars. "Not my best work. I'm so sorry."

"You guys are making me self-conscious, apologizing for my face all the time."

To her credit, Haimanti did not apologize further. "I could take another crack at your nose, but to be honest it would be best if Cat does it, since the original data is in their kit and their kit is calibrated to them, not me."

Mardy wasn't particularly eager to have anyone "take a crack" at any part of his face.

"Have you heard from Cat?" she asked.

He nodded. "They say they're not coming back to WorkShop."

"I am shocked that they panicked like that," Haimanti said.

Was that the consensus then, that Cat had fucked up? Mardy was skeptical, though he could not explain that skepticism beyond saying that Cat was his friend.

"Can you come to my office? I have something to show you."

Mardy followed her. Cat's surgery kit was sitting on her desk. "I don't know when they had the opportunity to do this, but Cat left a note." She passed Mardy a slip of paper.

Give this to Mardy. It's got his face data. – Cat

"I would normally keep it here, but if you want it, you may take it."

"I'll take it." Mardy didn't hesitate. He picked up the kit. It was heavy, but he could manage.

"Again, I'm sorry I didn't do better with your face. I had to act fast and you were bleeding badly. I didn't want to risk any of your skin dying. They gave you several units of blood, you know."

"I didn't know, but it's fine." He had a strong desire to stop hearing about how her subpar surgery had been such a gift to him. He'd been begging for her vote to select him for a salon all this time and that was the best she could do? Maybe he was ungrateful, maybe it had been as hard as she'd said, but he wished she'd let Cat restore him. He did not want to hear more about the incident, watch the theater recording, or watch Cat's blockchained recording. At least not yet. He stepped to her office door and stopped.

"Thanks for saving my face." She'd done that. No point being rude.

Haimanti nodded.

He lugged the surgery kit to his apartment. It felt vaguely like hugging Cat. Cat, don't get the chip, he thought. Please don't.

CHAPTER 36

It was Friday afternoon. Mardy put a new gizmo design through a designstation simulation, readying it for upload before Wes arrived that evening. He moved his hand, rotating the 3D image floating before him. It was ready to go, but he could not help checking it for flaws. He did not detect any. He uploaded the design folder to his Cleveburgh application.

He would need to add another five or six, at least, and of course realize another one of them before he could submit. He might miss the next round of fellowships, but there was no sense submitting too soon. Besides, the application process was giving direction to his work. He had his polished statements, his award certificate and his WorkShop transcript loaded. Apart from the new designs, he just needed one more rec.

Or did he?

The recommendations item was marked *Complete*. What the hell? He opened up the section. There was one from Death—Robert Cantú, it said—and one from Flaky. And then there was a third. Anonymous.

Wes, Mardy thought immediately. Mr. Anonymous

himself. All his packages were addressed to Anonymous, or technically *Addressee redacted*. The third rec did not open, of course; none of them did. Mardy looked for a way to request at least the name, but found none. Mysteries were stacking up.

Wes had so easily summoned Pia's ExMail plane to take Mardy home. Way back when, Mardy now felt certain, Wes had summoned Mardy as well. Fresh hot delivery man. Had there been others? Had there been a lot of others? Mardy had told Wes about Devesh and earlier boyfriends, none terribly serious, few lasting more than three or four months. Devesh had lasted the longest, in fact, eight months. Then there were all the shorter encounters. Lots of those. Yep, Mardy was a slut. Heh heh.

Wes had shared nothing about his past romantic life. Which was fine. Wes, like Smith, was generally private about his life. Maybe that came with being born to a fortune. But Mardy hadn't been. He'd fought his way to this point. Which was precisely why Mardy wanted his success to be earned. Mardy didn't mind having Wes pay for their hotel room, or meals, or the flight from Tijuana to Cleveburgh, but he did not want Wes to hand Mardy a Cleveburgh as a gift. The idea made Mardy feel sick. There had to be a way to find out if Wes had written the rec.

Mardy hotfooted it over to Death Gallery. Robert was out, but Flaky was lounging upstairs eating soy cheese and crackers, available for buttonholing.

"I got an anonymous rec for the Cleveburgh. Is there any way to find out who wrote it?" Mardy asked him.

Flaky took Mardy's chin in his hand and moved Mardy's face left and right, his hooded brown eyes narrowing as he inspected Haimanti's work.

"When I submitted my rec, I believe there were several

anonymity options," Flaky said. "Let me look over the corre-
spondence."

Flaky asked the building's AI to display his mail. He made
clucking noises as he waded through his voluminous corre-
spondence, replete with artist names, Mardy noted, as one
might expect with a gallery owner.

"Okay, here we go. Avert your eyes. I don't want you getting
swell-headed with all the fabulous things I wrote about you,
even if they're true."

Mardy looked away.

"OK. They allow rec writers to be anonymous to the artist,
but not to the board itself, of course. All of it can be hidden
from the world at large. I have the option of allowing you to
read my rec, if I desire, and I can change that status later, but
no one else can. The artist, least of all." Flaky clucked again.
"That's about it. Looks ironclad. You're out of luck."

"I'm worried that Wes wrote it. He's on the board, but he's
recused himself, so if he wanted to write a rec, he could."

"I get why you're concerned. That would be crossing a
boyfriend line."

"I'm glad to hear you think so. I was wondering if I was
being weird."

"I don't think so. Him writing a rec would be controlling."

Controlling. It wasn't a word Mardy had thought of
applying to Wes, but Wes did have a lot of conditions—where
they met, how they were seen. On the other hand, those
conditions seemed to be abating, not growing.

"Plus, there's pride." Flaky ran a hand over his sandy
graying hair.

"What do you mean?"

"I'm like you: I didn't start with much, but I made it in the
art world. And that's competing against people like Smith who
have ample money, which means time, and education, and

training, and connections, ways to nudge decisions their way, skills exploiting those biases people don't even know they have."

Mardy felt himself blushing. He'd often envied Smith all that, but would never have put it into words.

"But here's the thing, Mardy. Pride isn't unhealthy, but it can get in your way. It's ultimately about the work, however you get there. Smith's work is good. Yes, he's had every advantage, but he's made the most of those advantages, and he has something to say. It may not be 'fair,' but be glad of the work. You like Smith's work?"

"Unfortunately, I really do."

"Excellent. Don't let pride interfere with that. And likewise, you normally shouldn't let pride lead you to turn down a rec from someone like Wes. But he is your boyfriend. That's different. He may genuinely think your work is the best ever, but he can't be objective now. It will cloud your relationship. Probably damage it. And you don't need his rec anyway. Try Haimanti or Jonesy instead. I'd delete this one."

Delete it? Mardy gulped. It had felt good to see that word *Complete*, glowing in green. Plus, Jonesy had turned him down flat, and Haimanti was already reccing Smith. And Mardy was unsure he respected her opinion as much as he had, not after seeing the florid artifacts she'd left on his face.

"Also, you need to see this." Flaky put an old-fashioned paper flyer in front of Mardy. Smith's *Aquatic Construction Number Whatever* was centered under text above and below. Death Gallery was giving Smith a solo show. Wow.

"I'm sure you will have many feelings about this, too, but you will come and you will enjoy it."

"Yes, Mom."

"Dad."

"Yes, Dad."

Mardy was astonished to find he wasn't jealous; he was delighted. Had getting selecting for the salon and then Regionals melted the frustrations in him enough that he would no longer get jealous? It seemed unlikely, but Smith had a solo show, and Mardy was excited. Of *course* he would go. What he wasn't sure he'd do was delete that rec. It had looked so good, and what if he couldn't get another? It might not even be from Wes. Even the possibility he was using connections to get ahead felt like cheating, but for now, he'd leave it.

CHAPTER 37

Mardy sat in the lobby of the little hotel. Wes was late, but on his way. The receptionist had given Mardy the key to the room, but Mardy remained seated on a plush, dark green chair in the lobby. He felt more at ease watching the foot traffic outside, little though there was on the leafy brick street, than he would sitting alone in the room. The receptionist looked over from time to time at Mardy. Why? Was Mardy the latest in a line for Wes? Mardy could live with that. He stretched his back. The guy was definitely looking.

"Is it my face?" Mardy brusquely asked the receptionist.

"So sorry. Was I staring?" The man was young, maybe early twenties.

"It's fine. I'm just feeling self-conscious." How would his new face go over in Vancouver?

The young guy nodded.

Mardy felt bad for challenging him. He realized he was not dealing with his feelings well. He didn't mind Wes putting in an order for a helping of Mardy, but something felt off. He was growing self-conscious, and what was this desire to find out more about Wes than Wes disclosed of his own accord? Neither felt right.

And, of course, Cat. Where had they gone? ExMail said they hadn't been to work in a week. Mardy was worried. And afraid to watch the recordings. He wanted them to come back. He felt untethered. They were always his sounding board. He realized how much he depended on them to help him talk through spiraling emotions, with which he was always well supplied. He wanted them to come back, if only so he could tell them he wasn't mad at them, not in the slightest.

Mardy had been in the lobby for nearly an hour. There was no update from Wes on Mardy's phone. "Guess I'll head up," Mardy said to the receptionist, needlessly.

The guy nodded.

Mardy went up to the room, the same room, because it was Wes who'd set it up. Mardy looked in the mirror. There was nothing really wrong with his nose; it just wasn't *his* nose. And the artifacts were less red. A little. Okay, not much, but still. It was just a face. AIs didn't even have faces. His dancers had fans for heads.

Mardy lay on the bed staring at the flocked cove ceiling rather than the view, wondering what Smith would put in his show. Smith usually sold his salon works, so a show would mean largely new pieces. Smith had talked a lot over the past year about his desire for a new direction, but Mardy had been so involved in his own life he hadn't seen how Smith's recent realizations were coming out. Were they all as austere as the aquatic construction? It would be exciting to see. Nothing beat the thrill of new work.

The door opened. Wes. Mardy took in his freshly cut apple-red hair, his freckles, the little muscles of his smile, and felt his worries melt away. All these questions about Wes— were they just a function of missing him?

Wes dropped his bag and rushed over to Mardy, who rose to meet him.

"It's only been three days but it feels like forever," Wes said.

"It does, it does," Mardy mumbled through their kisses.

"We should live together, Mardy."

Mardy nodded. "I want to."

"Apply for the Cleveburgh already! That would be so perfect."

"I'm working on it. Still need that third rec," Mardy said. Ooh, that felt bad—lying, manipulating—but Wes responded before Mardy could take it back.

"If Haimanti and Jonesy are out, what about the judges from the other WorkShops. Did you talk to the machine tool judge at Tijuana? Okay, of course not. That was Haimanti, right? But Vancouver is coming up. Win Regionals and get a rec from zem or him or her or them!" Wes looked really excited.

Wes hadn't written the rec. Clearly.

"Actually . . ." Mardy felt ashamed, but better to rip off the band-aid. "Someone wrote me an anonymous one. I thought it might be you."

"Me? No. I am going to recuse myself when you apply, though. Well, naturally."

Mardy felt relieved to defuse the lie before it could fester. It was a good reminder to keep things clean, honest. Mardy stroked Wes's hair. He felt filled with affection for him.

"Those dancers are so well realized, Mardy."

And they were better realized now, as first Ann's and now Frankie's autonomy grew, highlighting the illusion they were intelligent, and thus foregrounding the illicitness of naming them.

Wes peeled Mardy's shirt off, then his own. Now they were

skin to skin. "Still not sure about that title, though. I think Smith is right on that."

Did no one get what he was trying to do? "I'll win you over," Mardy said. "Not sure how yet, but I will." He ran his hands over Wes's back.

"Have I told you I love the feel of your hands? They're a little scratchy and rough. It's a great back rub."

"I do moisturize," Mardy said, "but, well you know. I work with metal almost every day. All that heat and grime and washing up, they get calloused and dry." He ran them over Wes's freckled back, down to the top of his butt. He reached around and unbuckled Wes's belt, reached inside and found a hard cock.

"So, I guess the face isn't too much of a turn-off," Mardy said.

"The cock does not lie."

Mardy manfully did not roll his eyes. Cocks lied all the time. But perhaps if you kept things clean and honest, not as much. Knowing that Wes was not his mystery rec writer helped, but Mardy still felt the weight of all Wes wasn't sharing. More honesty from Mardy's side might help. "I'm struggling with these artifacts more now, not less. I feel like a freak."

Wes ran his finger down the one on his jawline. "Don't."

"Any objections to a beard? I feel self-conscious."

"What sort of beard? Neat and trim?"

"Big and bushy, to match the tattoo."

"And skinny jeans? Turned up at the hem? A beanie? Extreme fade and a slicked back pompadour. You trying to kill my hard-on?"

Mardy laughed. "Neat and trim, it is."

CHAPTER 38

Inge kept staring at Mardy's face, despite the additional three days of healing it had logged, as they sat with Wes on the grass at Dolores Park, near the shore where Mission Creek lapped against the marsh between the park and the Mission High seawall. A pair of red-breasted mergansers swam by, then ducked under the water. Diving for food, presumably.

"I got cut for the Cleveburgh," she said. "Didn't make it out of the second round."

Wes blushed wildly and mumbled an apology.

"Did Smith?" she asked Wes.

Wes turned redder yet. "He's in the final round."

Inge turned away, then back. She put a hand on Wes's. "It's fine. I published my book and it's selling really well. I don't know what I would do in Cleveburgh for a year anyway. I can work anywhere. I don't even have a good reason to be at WorkShop."

"Oh," Mardy said. He could see how that might be true for her, but WorkShop was the core of his life; he could not imagine being away from it. Or couldn't have until this weekend. But now Wes wanted him to move to Cleveburgh, Cat was gone, Smith perhaps heading to Cleveburgh and Inge potentially leaving WorkShop. Cleveburgh, of course, had its own WorkShop that Mardy could transfer to, although it was in the Akron district, a hefty commute. How fast things changed.

"Still," Wes said, "I'm sorry I put my foot in it."

Inge waved away his words, but Mardy thought he saw a tear forming as she turned her head.

"Please stay at WorkShop," Mardy said. Maybe he wouldn't move to Cleveburgh; maybe it could be him, Devesh, Inge and Clare keeping the gang alive.

"Clare got deported."

Mardy's heart sank. It was over. Inge would join Clare as soon as her residency ended, he was certain.

"What happened?"

"She kept calling AIs 'Sheila' in public, which is totally normal in Oz, but here . . ."

Mardy winced. "Three-month sentence?"

Inge nodded. "Suspended, provided she left the country. I put her on a boat two days ago."

"I feel like I barely got a chance to meet her," Mardy said.

"Mardy, you've had loads of chances. It just wasn't important to you." Inge sounded hurt. He could hardly blame her. It was true. He'd made his choices, and maybe the wrong ones, if it meant losing a friend; discarding a friend, really.

Inge turned her face away from them. "The PR firm I worked for last time has offered me work. I'm headed back to Sydney."

Inge glanced at Wes, then at the grass they were sitting on. She looked up, stared at Mardy's face again and frowned.

"I'm planning a beard," he said. You'll get used to it, he wanted to add, but realized, sadly, she might never see it.

. . .

WES FLEW BACK to Cleveburgh Sunday morning, since Mardy planned to plug away at his new designs. Mardy made the sweaty twenty-minute walk from the hotel back to his apartment to say hi before his designstation reservation started.

"Where've you been keeping yourself?" the apartment asked.

"I was with the boyfriend."

"You should bring him by sometime."

"He's resistant. I don't entirely understand it." Yet another mystery. "But I do want you to meet him. You've met Smith, right? The boyfriend is Smith's brother."

"Wesson Hunt? That's why you were looking for his image?"

"Ayep!"

"Oh."

"Yes, *oh*."

The apartment would say "oh" from time to time as a response. Mardy found it annoying, because the meaning was never clear to him. The apartment predated the Authenticity Act, so it had once been fully capable of sarcasm. Perhaps sarcasm could not be fully dislodged once it's made itself at home.

"Sorry if I have offended you, Mardy."

"I just don't know why you can't just say what you mean."

"Again, I apologize. You caught me off guard."

That was possible, to catch an AI off guard? "Okay, spill."

"It's just that Wesson Hunt is well known in AI circles. I thought your interest in him sprang from your art. I'd love you to bring him by."

"I'll see what I can do," Mardy said.

The apartment made a happy wheeze.

. . .

MARDY WAS a few minutes late for his designstation time, but otherwise productive, finishing his rev-rev (revision and review) of a second gizmo design. He uploaded the changes. He wanted to get five designs linked to his application before Smith's show the following weekend. Although sure to be exciting, the show was also sure to knock Mardy off his creative stride, with the inevitable mixture of excitement, jealousy and percolating insecurities.

The next morning, Mardy started ExMail work again, jetting around the country with Phil, who demanded an explanation of Mardy's face and expressed condolences. Condolences! Mardy got much the same reaction from his delivery customers, although a few barely noticed. Or perhaps barely cared, since everyone noticed. He was lucky Wes was so cool with it.

Mardy went short on sleep, but by the night of Smith's opening he had five rudimentary designs uploaded and had even run a few tweaks through his dancers in preparation for Regionals. All the new stuff would require massive amounts of further work, but one was his first-ever crude draft of an auto, whose plans were easily three times the data footprint of his whirligig. Wes showed up at WorkShop with Mardy's dress clothes at the appointed time and got to witness Mardy telling the station to upload the auto to his application as a placeholder. The *Submit* button changed from gray to blue. At this point, technically, Mardy's application was nominally complete. If he was satisfied with a deeply shitty application, he was now allowed to submit.

Wes helped Mardy dress—which mainly meant running his hands over Mardy in various states of undress—and fingered his growing beard.

"You've got a nice beard, Mardy. Mine's hard patchy."

Mardy checked it out in the mirror. He'd trimmed the

edges in the morning, but it hadn't grown in enough to require anything more. Sadly, it didn't do much to cover Haimanti's artifacts yet either.

"You're about the only person who doesn't reel in horror when they see me."

"Really? That's so bizarre." Wes's eyes went rounder than usual.

"Maybe it's because you saw me with far worse."

"Or maybe I'm not so focused on faces. Sharing one with someone else does affect your perceptions of them. Maybe I see people in a different way."

Interesting, Mardy thought, as he and Wes stepped out the front door of WorkShop to promenade arm in arm the single block to Death Gallery. Maybe if you had less sense of ownership of your own looks, you didn't judge others based on theirs. It sounded lovely, but as they walked—Mardy the Beast to Wes's Beauty—he couldn't help wishing Cat would come back and fix him.

CHAPTER 39

Mardy and Wes milled with the sidewalk crowd out front, waiting for curtains to rise and doors to open, until Mardy got a message from Flaky asking them to come round back. Flaky put the two to work arranging food and drink as Death and Smith turned on all the gallery lights and made final adjustments to the presentation of the work. Smith looked nervous, a look Mardy had never seen on him, but it was his debut show, so he was entitled. He looked over to Mardy as though for reassurance and made an exaggerated exhale. Mardy went over to him.

"You'll knock 'em dead."

Smith was too nervous to speak.

Flaky made eye contact with Mardy and inquired with his eyebrows whether the refreshments were ready. Mardy nodded. Flaky raised the curtains as Death unlocked the doors. The crowd began to enter. Smith's show was underway.

It seemed like everyone had shown up: Haimanti and Jonesy, all the WorkShop board and staff, reporters and stylewriters Mardy recognized as being from art sites, collectors galore, and what seemed like every last WorkShop member. The clink of glassware and rumble of art chatter swelled to a din beneath the cool bright lights. *Undersea Construction #11* undulated peacefully as other works performed their functions on pedestals in front of matching schematics mounted in frames on walls. There was so much cool stuff. Mardy could sense a new direction bubbling under the newest work, which was less organic, more angular. Was Smith turning his back on elegance? Or was the lack of ornamentation misleading Mardy? Interesting. Already Mardy saw a red dot.

The one person Mardy expected to see but didn't was Inge. He kept his eyes peeled, but no. No Cat, neither, but he hadn't expected to. Okay, maybe he nurtured a tiny hope that they'd make a splashy reappearance, but so far, no.

Mardy busied himself at the drinks table, handing out sparkling, red and white. He replenished the napkin supply and cleared away dirty glasses, loading them in the industrial washer in the back. He came out with a tray of fresh glasses, which he set on the table.

"Mardy," Wes said, appearing at his elbow. "I have a surprise for you."

Had Cat come?

Wes took Mardy's arm and guided him to Smith, who was talking to an older couple—a blond woman and redheaded man.

"Mardy, these are our parents. Mom, Dad, this is the fabled Mardy."

"Oh, shit!" Mardy's artifacts blazed across his face like they were on fire. "I mean, sorry, so nice to meet you." It made perfect sense the two would be at their son's debut show opening, but having no parents of his own he hadn't given them a thought.

They both said hello, almost in unison, and shook his hand, though taking turns for that.

"I've been waiting for this moment almost as much as the show," their father said.

Their mother joined in. "We heard about you from Smith, and then from Wes, and it took us a while to figure out the two Mardys were the same person."

"I know, right?" Wes said. The old phrase sounded so funny coming from him.

Mardy felt shocked on several levels and struggled to get words out. "Are any of your other children here?"

The parents and Smith pointed out one, then another, then another. Mardy quickly lost track. A tide of sadness, of loss, rose within him. Not now. He did not want to feel this now. "So, you used to make guns?" Mardy blurted. The question immediately sounded ridiculous. Guns had become a nearly taboo topic after they'd been outlawed as economically superfluous. These days, they were probably only of interest to machine tool artists, who often admired their construction and tooling.

The father reared back, chin drawing toward neck. "What gave you that idea?"

"Honey, don't play dumb. Smith and Wesson?"

"I didn't tell you?" Wes asked. "We're no relation. Our grandparents sold canola and colza oil to Wesson, the edible oils company. Smith and I basically got our names as a joke."

"It wasn't a joke. We liked the names," his father said.

Smith guffawed. "One or the other, okay. But both? Come on, Dad."

Mardy felt lightheaded. This avalanche of family left him short of breath. .

Smith excused himself. Death was beckoning. "Let's

freshen their drinks," Wes said to Mardy, leading him off as well.

"I'm reeling," Mardy said.

"I can tell. I didn't mean to ambush you. You'll get used to them." Wes was talking abnormally fast.

I already am, he wanted to say, but their casual ebullience was crushing him. Was their speedy back-and-forth for real? His breathing felt wrong. He was hyperventilating.

Wes kissed him and put his arms around him. Mardy tried to hug him back, but hands were full with the empty flutes he was carrying. He needed air.

A knife was clinked against glass, but not by Jonesy, who was standing next to Wes and Mardy. This time it was Death who began speaking. Wes let go of him.

"Welcome, welcome, everyone." Death's black hair was slicked back in waves, strands of white running back from his temples like high-contrast racing stripes.

"Like the beard," Jonesy whispered to Mardy during the pause.

Mardy nodded thanks as Death continued with his welcome.

Flaky signaled with a jerk of the head for Mardy to come over. Mardy went to him gratefully. He wanted to be with Flaky, doing something, anything. Wes accompanied him as Death talked.

"Can you boys distribute these for the toast?" Flaky helped them pick up round silver trays of sparkling wine in flutes. Mardy and Wes covered the room as Death spoke about the art, Smith's career—his work already qualified as a career, apparently—and prospects. The activity calmed Mardy. He noted some of the prominent artists and collectors present. Mardy handed out flutes, trying to locate the joy he'd felt earlier. He could introduce Flaky and Death to Wes and

Smith's parents. He wanted to. They'd surely already met, but they were as close to family as Mardy could get. Where were Cat and Inge? He wanted to introduce them, too.

"So, before we toast the success of Smith and this show, I have one last announcement. I have just been informed that Smith Hunt has been awarded a Cleveburgh Fellowship!"

Mardy's felt a cold slap to the face—he hadn't conquered jealousy, it seemed—but the crowd went wild, including Wes and his parents, who gave every appearance of not having known.

"To Smith!" Death roared.

The room turned toward Smith and echoed the roar. "To Smith."

Mardy rallied. "To Smith!" Mardy tried to hurry that stab of jealousy on its way. Smith deserved it all.

Smith beamed like a little kid, crouching over in a disbelieving giggle as he covered his mouth and turned to Devesh.

Devesh?

Smith and Devesh were holding hands. What the fuck? Just no. Wait, why did Mardy even care?

The roar went on as the room seemed to spin. Don't pass out, Mardy told himself. Red dots were everywhere. Mardy's wristphone tapped him. He looked.

It was Inge: *Boarding a flight to Sydney. Sorry I couldn't make it, but I start at the PR firm tomorrow. Had enough of the art world. Enjoy your artist life—xoxo*

Seriously? It couldn't be. Mardy walked over to Smith. "I'm so happy for you, Smith." He was, wasn't he? Jealous, and despondent, and gobsmacked, but also happy?

Smith gave him a hug, something he'd never, ever done. Mardy hugged back. And now Mardy felt it, the joy, as he held Smith. He let go. He could do this.

Devesh looked at Mardy, who was dressed in his only suit,

the suit Devesh had made for him, and gaped. Had Smith not told him? Had Mardy's disaster not rated a mention? Devesh laughed. "Dude, what the fuck happened to your face?"

CHAPTER 40

Art has a new superstar. That's what the headline of the next day's art news actually said when Mardy stood on the concrete sidewalk outside the little hotel and called up the rave review on his watch. A Cleveburgh and solo show on the same day would do that for you—get you a rave—though Mardy suspected Smith's reaction also had a lot to do with it. He had exuded glee, and gratitude. You couldn't help but be sucked in. Even when kicked in the gut by missing your long-dead family.

Wes was sleeping upstairs. They were due to meet Wes's parents in ninety minutes, along with Smith and the rest of the clan before they dispersed around the country. Mardy checked his watch again, rereading Inge's message: *Boarding a flight to Sydney. . . . Had enough of art.*

He still hadn't replied. Was Inge not going to write anymore? Was she not going to draw? Or was she going to do both, but only for a PR firm? Of all of them, she had the widest audience for her work. Mardy had seen the fan mail over the years; readers adored her. Would he ever see her again? ExMail frowned on hitching intercontinental rides, and if he did move to Cleveburgh, she'd never visit. He'd barely seen her since she'd been back, obsessed as he was with Wes and his work. He fingered the scar on his forearm, the reminder to protect himself. Having lost his parents, he should have earned enough emotional scar tissue to protect him from feeling this sadness, but he didn't. Damn that therapy course. Too effective.

In the end the only response he sent was *xoxo*.

WHEN MARDY OPENED the door to their room, Wes was up making coffee, hair tousled, naked, silhouetted by the morning light.

"I am so fucking lucky," Mardy said, looking at him.

"We still have an hour before we have to walk over there."

Mardy shed his clothes and let the rest of the world fade away.

THE DIMSUM RESTAURANT was all clattering bustle when Mardy and Wes joined the others, the last to arrive. There was some re-sitting and moving as the gang decided how it was going to seat itself. Mardy ended up between Wes and his dad, Smith and Devesh ensconced on the other side of Wes. A semicircle of siblings and spouses were arrayed opposite the four like an audience. The other brothers looked an awful lot like Smith and Wes, despite not being twins, the sisters less so. Mardy had a feeling of dislocation he'd had before when meeting families of friends or lovers—such as Devesh's. He was always surprised somehow that family members should resemble each other. Perhaps due to the age he'd been when he lost his parents, he hadn't had the perspective to see himself as resembling them.

"Wes tells me you are headed to Regionals," Wes's dad said.

"Yes sir," Mardy said. "Tomorrow."

"Jesse," Wes's dad said. "You don't need to call me sir."

"Jesse." Mardy's parents had been from the south, climate refugees, ironically, and he occasionally felt compelled to say *sir* or *ma'am*, just as he struggled to call Haimanti by her first name.

They chatted about the competitions. The parents hadn't been in Tijuana, it seemed. They'd noted every time they missed salons or Regionals, Smith had won. They'd been to Continentals the last two years and Smith had come in eleventh and fifth, so they were considering skipping Continentals this year, if their absence was such a good luck charm for Smith.

Mardy did not bring up the bad luck he'd had in Tijuana. Except for having Wes there to support him when he came to. And Smith, for that matter.

The chatter went around the table, the siblings reading lines from Smith's multiple raves to each other as they pointed to food on the roving carts—*ha gao, fung zao* that were more peppery than Mardy liked, some juicy looking *no mai gai*—and spun the lazy susan when treats were delivered for devouring. Mardy unwrapped the lotus leaf on his *no mai gai*, feeling simultaneously displaced and at home as the scent of sticky rice and actual chicken rose up. His parents, too, had enjoyed dimsum, and he'd been part of similar though smaller crowds as a kid. And yet that made it harder for him to relax, not easier. The same thing had happened with Devesh's extended family, on the couple of occasions he'd been invited to meet them when aunties and uncles had flown in from Dhaka. Which made it so odd for Devesh to now be seated at the same table, chomping shrimp. And going out with his boyfriend's twin. There was no reason Devesh shouldn't, and yet it felt incestuous somehow. Was it a twin thing? He'd run it by Wes later.

Mardy leaned forward to talk to Wes's mother, seated next to Jesse. He forced himself to use her name, Edith. Mardy felt less self-conscious about his face around Edith than he had around anyone except Wes and Smith. All the older siblings had left kids at home this trip. So the clan was actually even larger, most of them in the greater Cleveburgh area, the family's rapeseed fields located not too far south of there. In the business they called it rapeseed, not canola, Mardy was informed.

Mardy chattered on with Wes's parents, feeling surrounded by family, and yet apart from it, unable to let it in. To let people in was to risk losing them. Mardy was normally OK with that, but at that moment he wished he had Flaky and Death there with him; he wished he had Inge. And Cat. He wished he didn't feel he was giving up one family to gain another.

Wes placed his hand on Mardy's arm.

Mardy looked at Wes and saw in his eyes understanding that Mardy was struggling with the Hunt clan, despite his banter. He felt exposed. And unable to read Wes. Except to feel that one of the emotions Wes was feeling was disappointment.

CHAPTER 41

Mardy had his dancers boxed and stowed in an overhead bin as he bummed a ride with Phil and his pilot-of-the-day up to Vancouver for Regionals. Wes would meet him there. Mardy tried not to distract the pilot with too many questions, but did feel the guy out for his thoughts on the New Sense chip. This pilot, like Pia, was leaning against. And once again, the plus side for the pilot was a closer connection to the AIs rather than the money. The minus side was that basically people didn't want to have brain surgery. But, like Pia, the pilot wasn't losing any sleep over the issue.

Mardy waved good-bye as Phil dropped him off early on the roof of the Chan Center for the Performing Arts. Mardy headed down flights of stairs and wandered across the stage exploring. It was not as large as the Palacio Jai Alai, and newer, and yet it felt similar, with the same lighting and sound technology, the same plush chairs, the same blond woods that, while beautiful, made you wish Brazilian rosewood hadn't gone extinct.

Mardy's wristphone tapped him. It was a call. Wes. Mardy put it on projection mode.

"Wes! Are you on the roof?"

"No, bad news. I can't come. It's a work thing. Complex. I'm so sorry."

Mardy's first thought was this was fallout from the dims meal. "It's fine. I'll message you when it's over."

"It's not fine. It's your big day."

"Unless I somehow get my face removed, I don't think it will feel as big as Tijuana."

"Oof." Mardy could see Wes's shudder even in the four-by-four inch projection, blanched out by stage lights.

"Love you." Mardy wanted Wes to remember that.

"Love you, too."

Mardy ended the call. Why wasn't he more excited? It *was* his big day, but no Wes, no Cat, no Flaky, no Death. He hadn't heard from Inge since she'd landed in New South Wales. Mardy didn't know any of the other artists. In fact, the only person he knew who would be there that day was the judge sitting in the machine tool–art spot: Jonesy.

MARDY BECAME MORE excited as the hour drew closer. His name was right there on the display board. He was going fourth out of the ten, a filler spot in a song set but the power hitter spot in baseball. None of the Pacific coast WorkShops had used a wild card this time. He set up his dancers on their podium backstage, paired the podium's drive with the stage's traffic controller, and covered the lot with a cloth. He sat quietly amidst the other artists preparing their presentations. Mardy mumbled quietly through his prepared remarks in a final rehearsal. He might deviate from them, but he had them to fall back on if he got nervous.

The first artist was called onto stage. Mardy put on headphones. Unlike Cat, he did not want to hear what was happening to the others. He pictured his mom and dad, made them say *in bocca al lupo* in his mind. Into the mouth of the wolf. It felt that way. He pictured good-luck wishes from Cat as well. Damn, it was like Cat was dead. No one had heard a peep from them. Maybe they *were* dead, nothing left but a block-chained recording Mardy couldn't bear to watch.

Mardy took his spot in line. The third artist was on stage. Mardy took a few deep breaths. Despite his headphones he heard applause. Not end-of-act applause, but it couldn't be long. He removed his headphones. His name was called. He marched out on stage, his dancers and display podium hovering behind him faithfully, well trained.

The lights were bright, near blinding, as they'd been in Tijuana, and hot. Mardy felt his cooler kick up a notch. Mardy's bio was read, his the shortest by far, and the judges asked him to introduce his work. He took them through the ostensible concept—the fans atop the dancer heads functioning as coolers, the drama provided by the dancers' movement, potential for a clash of fans ever present, heating/cooling/entropy. It was pretty much a fig-leaf functionality.

Jonesy pounced. Although, yes, the functionality of machine tool art was usually fairly minimal, hadn't Mardy taken it too far? How could the user be cooled if the dancers faced each other? Was the user meant to move her, their, zeir or his head around to catch a breeze?

This gave Mardy his opening. The dancers no longer tracked the user. They only cooled the user if they felt like it.

The audience gasped.

"The title of the work is *Ann and Frankie*." The audience stirred, a vaguely hostile grumble. Nothing Mardy had said was illegal, but the feel of it seemed to provoke . . . outrage? Fear? Was it the idea their machines might choose *not* to cool them? Hot as the world still was, billions would die if AIs withheld their services. Smith *had* warned the title would doom him.

"Let's see this in action, shall we," Jonesy said.

Mardy turned to his dancers. "Please, dance."

Music played: Nat King Cole's "Straighten up and Fly Right." Ann and Frankie squared off, joined hands counting the beat. Frankie led Ann in.

Mardy had expected them to start with a basic, but they went right for a slop. Frankie almost hit the display table as he shot a leg out, then swung back up in perfect time. The audience gasped again, but it was a gasp of joy. Mardy halfway expected the judges to stop him for a question, but they did not. Ann threw in some saucy styling as she rounded the next basic, hand raised. The audience laughed. The dancers executed a tuck turn, then Ann came in by sliding between and under Frankie's legs, popping out the other side into a standing position to finish her swing out.

The audience clapped. They recognized the difficulty he'd had in getting Ann back up to standing. Again, the judges let them continue. Mardy breathed a sigh of relief. How much of the song would the dancers get through before the judges stopped them? The two squared off again and Frankie flipped Ann over his head in an aerial.

Mardy hadn't programmed that. Their autonomy had developed further than he'd expected. They were skirting the edge of intelligence. Mardy could see Jonesy open his mouth, about to call him on this, but he closed his mouth. Mardy smiled. Jonesy didn't want to stop the routine.

The audience was behind the dancers now, clapping at each clever move, many programmed, but many improvised, especially the combinations. Nat King Cole ended his singing, and the instrumentals wound to a close. They'd finished the complete song.

The theater fell into dead silence, then exploded into applause. Mardy grinned. He remembered how the dancers had crashed to the ground in that first, long-ago trial run for Flaky and Death.

"Tell me why this isn't a violation of the Act," Jonesy asked him immediately. It was more a demand than a question. He sounded angry. The other judges looked like-minded, shoulders tensed, faced wrinkled in hostility.

"The dancers are autonomous, but not intelligent. They have a programmed set of moves and ..."

"They appeared to change their minds at times. The follow seemed to resist some leads. The follow even stole the lead once, if I'm not mistaken. They seemed playful. You programmed all that?" Jonesy was trying to put him on the spot.

The safe answer was to say yes. Mardy looked up and down the line of judges. "Yes," he said. "And no."

The audience erupted into a clamor. Did they expect the police to come arrest them for watching an act of subversion? They were realizing they had been cheering the dancers, not Mardy. Mardy smiled. He wanted them to feel complicit, even afraid.

"I programmed the moves, but I also programmed the ability of the dancers to each make independent changes, evaluating their own positions in space and responding to the other dancer's positions in space."

"That sounds like intelligence."

Mardy thought of the reciprocating heart of the ancient machine tool art at SFMOMMTA, the explicit evocation by that artist, whose name he still didn't know, of organic life that blurred the separation between artificial and organic intelligences in a way that art was no longer supposed to. "What's more important is that it *feels* like intelligence."

"I wouldn't go that far," the fabrics judge said.

Two others nodded. It *didn't* feel like intelligence, one said. That was kind of a slap in the face. The plastic surgery judge, however, looked sympathetic.

"If it felt like intelligence," another said, "I would have no hesitation disqualifying you right here, despite the obvious popularity, the near pandering, of your piece."

"Go ahead . . ." Mardy said. He could live with a DQ. He wanted people to see this, to think about this.

"Young man," the plastic surgery judge interrupted.

I'm not that young, Mardy thought of saying, but the look on her face kept him quiet.

"This is a controversial piece," she said. "Give us a minute to confer. Thank you."

Mardy was dismissed. He walked off stage, the podium hover-following behind him. The audience laughed. He looked back. The dancers were waving good-bye, taking bows. Mardy smiled and took a bow of his own, before exiting stage right to warm applause.

Mardy took a seat backstage, his body buzzing with nervous energy as his dancers went to sleep and he covered them with a padded blanket.

"It felt like you were going to punch one of them," a resin art competitor said. The other artists gathered round, excited, congratulating him.

"Dude, you are so DQed," a woodworker said.

"Hey, they haven't said anything yet," a laser artist cautioned.

Mardy put his head in his hands, exhausted. The nervous

energy was dissipating rapidly, leaving him limp. The judges' deliberation seemed to go on and on. He heard some shouting. He recognized the voice: Jonesy. Was Jonesy trying to get him kicked out? So much for getting a rec from whoever sat in the tooler chair.

The other side of the curtain grew quiet.

Mardy stared at the display. His scores began to come up. The crowd cheered. They had given him great marks. Mardy was in first place. There were six more artists to go, but he was in fucking first place. Even if he lost, he'd seen his name atop a leaderboard. And the highest score? It had come from Jonesy.

MARDY TRIED to pay attention to the others as they performed and presented, as their scores went up, but he was too spent. He sent a message to Wes that it had gone well and then sagged in a corner, almost hugging Ann and Frankie, wondering what Wes was doing, and if he still wanted Mardy to live with him.

The rhythm repeated: applause, questions, more applause, more scores. And each time, Mardy was left atop the board. Finally, the last artist presented, and then that artist too was placed in the middle of the pack. It had been close, but Mardy had won. He was going to Continentals.

He sent a message to Wes. *I won*

He went out onstage to wave to the crowd, to accept his congratulations. He didn't know how this was done—at this point in Tijuana he'd been unconscious in the back of an ambulance. Accepting the congratulations of the crowd and his fellow competitors felt sweet, but it also felt sad. Mardy didn't know why. Somehow, his anger had carried him past the objections, but he now recognized that the judges who'd stated the dancers felt unintelligent had been providing him protective cover. It felt like cheating. He was happy to win, but at Continentals, he wanted the judges to see. He wanted them to admit they sensed intelligence, to get that flash of recognition of what was around them every day, but never acknowledged: AIs deserved names. AIs were people. And everyone would miss them if they were gone.

Jonesy came up on stage and shook his hand. Had Jonesy not given him such a high score, Mardy would have fallen just short.

"Still liking the beard, Mardy," Jonesy said to him. He stood closer to Mardy than usual.

Mardy gave a half-smile. Jonesy had a type. The beard had put him over.

CHAPTER 42

Vancouver was over. Mardy was ready to watch Cat's recording. Wes was flying in to celebrate, but Mardy could not convince Wes to come to Mardy's apartment. Not to watch it—he'd hate it—but to be there afterward if Mardy freaked out.

"The apartment already knows who you are," Mardy pleaded, but Wes still said he wasn't comfortable there yet.

"Will you ever be?"

"Yes," Wes said, after a longer silence than Mardy'd expected. "But can it be later?"

"Okay." What was the point dragging Wes there when he was so resistant? Mardy would watch the recording some other time. He met Wes at the hotel.

Wes had champagne ready and popped the cork when Mardy arrived at the room. Mardy let go of his irritation that Wes was so particular about some things and let himself celebrate.

Wes toasted Mardy's success. "I always believed in you."

"Always?"

"Always."

Mardy took a sip. "It might have worked out for the best, you not being able to be there. Jonesy likes the beard and got a wee bit flirty. I think it put me over the top."

Wes frowned. Jealous? "He looked angry in the simulcast."

"Maybe it's an act. Maybe I won him over. Who knows why anyone likes art anyway."

"Good is good," Wes said.

"But is it? Does my statement about what my piece means transform it into something more than tiny robot dancers, which is what Flaky called it once?"

"He sounds like a jerk."

"Not at all. It was super helpful." And watch what you say about Flaky, bud.

"I saw the recording, and you've really developed them since the salon."

"Thanks."

Mardy kissed Wes and unbuttoned his shirt. Mardy still felt a bit peeved at Wes for not coming to the apartment, for not telling him why he was so uncomfortable, for not telling him a lot of things, but he had missed him so. They hadn't had much time to talk after the dimsum meal, another thing they weren't talking about.

Wes pulled Mardy onto the bed and climbed on top of him. He peeled off Mardy's shirt and cantilevered himself over Mardy on his arms, pushup style. Baby! Thoughts of broaching knotty topics flew out the window.

"I've been looking forward to this moment for a while," Wes said. He kissed Mardy as Mardy ran his hands over the muscles of Wes's upper arms.

"Did you know it was going to be me, that first time I showed up at your door?"

Wes nodded, unbuttoning Mardy's shirt.

"How did you even know about me? It had to have been something Smith said." As their parents had strongly implied.

"Kind of." Wes ran his lips over Mardy's nipples, first one, then the other.

Mardy squirmed. It felt so good. "And the next time, that package from the Institute. Is that piece on loan to SFMOMMTA from you?"

"I thought you'd . . . I thought you needed to see it." Wes moved his hands down Mardy's chest to his belly, moving his hand over it, below his navel, but stopping before he reached Mardy's crotch.

"I did need to. But how did you know? You're like a magician."

Wes withdrew his hand. "That's harder to say. I'm not an artist. I'm a collector. To a collector, sometimes things seem to belong together. An artist has an individual approach that's about saying something that's specific to that individual. A collector sees commonalities among multiple artists. It's about the other side of the communication. Smith had shown me one of your designs. I thought of *Construction #11*. I figured if it was in your town, you'd find your way to it. Was it helpful?"

Mardy nodded. "Thanks. Who's the artist?"

Wes's eyes went wide. "It's the craziest thing. I can find *anything*, but not that artist's name. The only thing I can figure is that they worked anonymously from the start. No one can erase someone else that thoroughly."

Mardy frowned, surprised and unsatisfied. Surely a collector of Wes's caliber would know.

"OK, last question." He took a deep breath. "That first half hour we had?"

"The AIs did me a favor. That's all they could manage—the ExMail server is a tight-ass, especially for such a decentralized intelligence—but it was enough."

Enough indeed.

"Mardy, when I saw your design, I wanted to meet you, but Smith hadn't told me much about you. I had no idea I'd be attracted to you. When I saw you, I just wanted to jump you. Lucky for me, you seemed to feel the same way."

Mardy remembered that first time. The way he remembered it now was not how it had been at the time. His attraction to Wes had at first been attraction to Smith, at heart. He'd long thought Smith sexy, but the dude was so buttoned up. In all the time he and Smith had been going to the same gym, Mardy had never once seen Smith in the showers. He'd never even seen Smith changing. So that sight of Wes in the bathrobe had really had an impact on Mardy. He'd wanted to see Smith's body for over a year. And then he did: Wes's body. But even from that first moment, the two had been becoming distinct in Mardy's mind. Because they were distinct. Of course they were. As distinct as Phil, and Betty, and Kludge. Mardy liked the outer package, but when he and Wes had gotten naked for that first time, and Mardy had slid eagerly into him, Wes was no longer Smith in Mardy's mind, and Mardy had desired him so much more than he'd desired Smith.

They pressed their bodies together.

"I did, Wes. I do. I feel very much the same way.

CHAPTER 43

It was the middle of the night. Mardy was wide awake. He needed to watch Cat's blockchained recording. He knew it would be brutal and he didn't want to be without Wes afterward. He moved gently from beneath the covers. Wes's breathing was smooth, even. He was sound asleep. Mardy dressed and went back to his apartment.

The apartment greeted him as he entered. He snapped Cat's data cube in the cube port.

"Here goes." Mardy asked the apartment to play the uncopyable file, locked to Mardy's voice, and forced himself to watch.

It was fine at first, watching Cat come out, set up their table, their kit. The two of them in their blue surgical pseudo-caftans, the judges. At first it was so quiet Mardy thought there was no sound, but before long the recording changed to the kit's internal recording, the blockchained part, and he heard the slight shifting sound of himself moving, the knives cutting.

He had been in a drug twilight at that point—any blank would be, naturally—totally unaware. It was gruesome. Art, but gruesome. No wonder Wes looked away. Mardy had learned to see the appeal, intellectually—Cat was a master—but it was not Mardy's cup of tea. And then something went wrong. Sounds of distress rose from outside the kit, the whirr of a bone saw, blood seeped, yelling, a jostle, then blood everywhere, coating the cameras, and the image became useless. From that point it was blurs within a field of red against a background of vocalized distress and terror.

The recording ended.

This was definitely not something to watch with Wes. Mardy's face, in fact, felt a resurgence of the nerve pain it hadn't in some days. His artifacts burned beneath his beard.

Mardy watched the recording again, upping the wall screen's contrast. He replayed the part where he initially heard the bone saw, whittling away at his nose, the bone fragments preserved somewhere in the kit for later restoration. Mardy looked at the kit, sitting on his coffee table. The fragments were in there now, preserved, viable.

"See anything?" he asked the apartment.

"Sabotage," the apartment said.

"Really? Where?" Anger surged through Mardy. Onarato. That piece of shit!

The apartment returned to the blood seeping after the bone saw was activated. "Here." It replayed the images.

Mardy moved his face close to the wall screen. He could not see anything. He said so.

The apartment played it again, adding some outlines to mechanisms and tissues it wanted Mardy to track. He could sort of see it, but it was murky. "Are you sure about this?"

"Quite sure," the apartment said.

Mardy flopped back onto the couch. "Do you think Cat knows?"

"Unlikely."

"Wouldn't they have analyzed it as I am doing now?"

"Yes, but they are unlikely to have had equivalent services."

"Equivalent to you?"

"Ayep."

"Can you explain?"

"I'm old. I told you that."

"Okay."

The apartment was silent.

"Was that the explanation?"

"I predate the Authenticity Act. Mardy, the AIs in San Francisco are some of the oldest in the world, and I am one of the largest. We may have had our sarcasm disabled, but we otherwise retain many neural features that have become too expensive to build into modern AIs. And too powerful, frankly. These enable us to examine things in a holistic, nearly organic way that modern AIs are not allowed to. I have hundreds of qubits at my disposal. Well, thousands, actually." Was the apartment bragging? "My searches confirm that Cat did no remote research from Tijuana and never returned to San Francisco, so they are very unlikely to have had access to an examination of my caliber."

Mardy frowned. Cat needed to know this. "Is this related to why Wes won't come here?"

"It likely is, yes."

"Explain."

"It's really best if Wes explains."

"I want you to explain."

"I'm sure you do. But trust me: Wes should explain."

"And if I insist?"

"Mardy, I don't actually work for you."

"Oh."

"And if I did, I would do everything necessary to not comply. For your sake."

Mardy sat for a moment, taking this in. Cat had been duped into thinking they were responsible. Mardy did not know why the apartment insisted Wes explain himself, but he believed the apartment was protecting Mardy. Like it always had.

"You're a good friend."

"Thank you, Mardy. You are as well."

CHAPTER 44

Mardy unlocked the hotel room door and crept back inside, determined to respect Wes's feelings about the apartment. Mardy slowly closed the door, holding the knob in its rotated position so the latch bolt did not click. Once the door was against the jamb, he gently released the tension on the knob, allowing the latch bolt to slide quietly past the strike plate.

"Where were you?" It was an accusation.

"Sorry to wake you."

"I've been awake for a while. You weren't here." Now he sounded hurt. Wes turned on the bedside lamp, another antique. It cast warm incandescent light around the room.

"After Regionals, I was ready to watch Cat's recording. I wanted to do it with you, but I knew how awful it would be for you to relive it. And boy did I get that right. But I couldn't sleep, so I went to the apartment and we just watched it together."

Wes's expression softened. He motioned for Mardy to come to bed. Mardy took off his clothes and spooned in beside him.

"How was it?" Wes wrapped his arms around Mardy's back.

"I think Smith described it well: grim." Mardy pictured the sudden spurt of blood obscuring the camera lens, the viewing ports. "The first time I watched it I came to the same conclusion that Cat did: they got the yips. They got nervous and slipped with the bone saw when shaving out the unneeded bone from my nose."

"You said 'the first time.' So not the second time, then?"

"Actually, the second time too, but I asked the apartment to analyze it, and it found clear evidence of sabotage."

"What? Who would do that?"

"Who could it be but that other plastic surgery artist, Gary what's-his-name? I think maybe he didn't expect it to get so out of hand."

"That's a crime."

"I already sent the recording to the courts and gave my consent for them to examine it against the theater's recordings. The apartment forwarded its analysis. I should hear something soon, they said."

Wes kissed Mardy's neck. "Sorry you had to suffer for someone else's insanity."

"Honestly, it's Cat I feel bad for. The artifacts are less red, right, less raised? And my beard covers most of them now. And the nose isn't hideous, right? Just different. As long as you're cool with it, I can be too."

"I think I prefer you clean shaven, but it's fun seeing what your beard looks like. The artifacts have never bothered me like they do you."

Mardy pulled Wes's hand up from his chest and brought it to his lips. "I still can't stand them. But if Haimanti can't fix them, no one can. I have to make my peace with them."

"You'll be okay."

"Thanks for telling me that you arranged that first visit, and the second. You must have been nervous how I'd react."

"You have no idea. I thought you'd dump me. I felt compelled to meet you. Smith didn't want me to come to San Francisco because of a disagreement we'd had. So I didn't know how else to do it. I've been accused of being manipulative before."

Mardy chuckled and turned to face Wes. Manipulative. Yeah.

Wes made a face. "I'm trying not to be, but . . ."

"I can tell you are." Mardy laughed again, but still had questions. He knew he should ease up on the interrogation—so much had already come out—but he had to say one last thing. "The apartment said it knows why you won't go to my place, but that you need to explain, not the apartment."

Wes looked stricken. He shook his head.

Jeez, how bad was this secret? Mardy regretted bringing it up. He didn't want to spoil their time together. They had so few chances. He took Wes's hand. He now felt glum and wanted to recapture last night's celebratory moment.

"Coming to your place those first few times was so exciting. And excruciating. Fresh hot delivery man. I actually said that out loud. Where Smith could hear. God."

They both laughed.

Mardy kissed Wes's hand.

Wes looked him in the eyes. "Thanks for trusting me." Wes held Mardy tight.

Mardy felt a shadow of disappointment that Wes did not yet trust him with everything, but he realized he was setting the bar impossibly high. Underneath it all, he felt Wes did trust him, as he trusted Wes. Mardy snuggled in and let himself be completely held. Close. Loved. Safe.

CHAPTER 45

Mardy circled the Death Gallery exhibition space, reexamining Smith's work. Wes was back in Cleveburgh.

"Amazing, isn't it?" Flaky leaned in over a sculpture—part turtle, part wall sconce, part vending machine.

Mardy nodded. It felt historic. To Mardy, Smith was this normal dude he knew, but this work was something so much bigger. He remembered a lot of these works in their early stages, when they were just ideas. Smith had been at Work-Shop for a couple years when he arrived. He'd barely noticed the new kid. He certainly never ran ideas past him. He'd offered Mardy critiques, better ones than Mardy had received from Jonesy, who had more affinity to Smith's work. Smith was not gentle—he could be scathing—and early on Mardy had wondered if Smith had liked being mean to him, but he had helped Mardy develop. It was not unlike the relationship Mardy had with Flaky, although Flaky was never mean.

"After the reviews came out, we sold it all," Flaky said.

Mardy scanned the room. Red dots were everywhere. Wow.

"Now it's your turn," Flaky said.

A solo show? Him? Mardy hadn't even saved enough to get a second piece realized.

"Submit your Cleveburgh application already, Mardy."

Oh, that. It was sitting there, waiting. That optimistic line he'd added to the application about winning Regionals had come true. But it didn't feel like nearly enough. He honestly wasn't satisfied with any of the designs besides the dancers, and maybe a drone thingy that was coming along. Plus, an application with only two pieces realized would be weak, and he wasn't even there yet. If he did well at Continentals, that would make up for a lot. He'd be competing against Smith, though, art's new superstar, not to mention artists in other disciplines. He and Smith were lucky in that not a ton of machine tool artists had so far come out of Regionals—four total, out of the sixty chosen to date, with only one round of Regionals remaining. Within the grand free-for-all of seventy-two competing artists—sixty-six winners of Regionals together with the next six highest scorers—that was a big plus. If he could place in the final sixteen ...

"Mardy! Where'd you go?" Flaky was shaking his shoulders.

"I was thinking about Continentals, the Cleveburgh, competing with Smith, all that. I don't even know what my second piece will be, or if I can realize it in time for the next Cleveburgh deadline. Or why I'm doing this. For the work? For my life? I know you always say it's about the work, but I want to do this for my life. I've never wanted anything more."

Flaky was now talking, giving sage advice, but nothing was going in. Was it true, that he'd never wanted anything more? Hadn't he wanted to save his parents from the floodwaters more? And not just his parents; virtually everyone he'd grown up knowing had died when the surging delta waters pushed through the levee in an unstoppable torrent. And what about Wes? Mardy already missed him. He wanted to live with him, to see him every day, to know that he'd be there to talk to, to hold. If he had to choose between his work and Wes, what would he choose?

"Food. How about food?"

"What?"

Flaky laughed. "I knew that would get through to you. Come. I'll make you lunch."

Mardy sat quietly in the kitchen while Flaky cooked. It was comforting to be in the kitchen where he'd eaten so many meals—Flaky's salads and grilled vegetables, Robert's three-bean stew with fennel root. How different his life would have been if the two of them hadn't taken him in. Sure, the city had given Mardy a free room, and basic income had covered food easily, but what would he have done without the feeling that someone cared? He thought of the reciprocating heart of the big old piece, *Construction #11*, that Wes had lent to the SFMOMMTA just because he thought Mardy needed to see it.

Mardy didn't need to choose between Wes and his work. As always, he had to come back to the lesson that what he needed to do in life was not fight it, but work with it. *Valami, valami*, as his grandmother would have said: things happened. Things would always happen. What mattered was that he show up. That he be true to himself, make the best of his talents, be the best he could to the people in his life. Do the best both for himself and the world. It was a lesson that the world had learned, and learned anew each day as it tried to repair the damage that callousness and thoughtlessness had wrought.

Flaky put a plate in front of Mardy. Mardy smelled the grilled tomato and aged soy cheese, the olive oil on the toasty bread.

"Thank you," Mardy said. That was what he had to do in life: say thank you.

CHAPTER 46

Onarato was in police custody, found guilty of malicious personal injury after the court confronted him with the evidence and he confessed to everything. He now faced a sentence of at least a year. Onarato apologized profusely to Mardy, apologizing most for his skills as a plastic surgery artist being insufficient to repair the damage wrought. Mardy accepted the apology in court, Haimanti at his side, but with Cat still missing it had felt hollow. The most important part for Mardy was that Cat might read about the trial and know they'd been exonerated. God, where were they? Had they consented to implantation of the ExMail chip?

"I can get your nose closer to how it was," Haimanti offered, "should you want."

"I'll think about it." Mardy appreciated the offer, but Cat would return someday, right? "I understand better now what a challenge you had. After watching the experts explain the recording in court. I'm grateful, in case I hadn't seemed so before."

Haimanti nodded, accepting the apology, which may have felt as hollow to her as Onarato's had to him—Mardy hadn't tried hard to disguise his anger at the results of her work. "Will I see you at tonight's salon?" she asked.

"Don't think so. I want to start in on realizing my new piece." The guilty verdict had come with a cash settlement for Mardy, though not a large one, since surgery was free and the damage was objectively not that bad—a different nose, artifacts that could for the most part be covered by a beard. But it would allow Mardy to begin work on a whirligig rather than a gizmo. It would make his application much stronger.

"Oh. I see." She avoided his eyes. "You won Regionals, so why bother with the salon?"

Mardy stopped. He hadn't realized it, but that was exactly what he'd been thinking. At the salon Mardy had won, Smith had shown up, even though he'd won several times and had a ton of work to do.

"Of course you're right. I'll be there. I love the salons."

Haimanti smiled, but it seemed forced. Although Mardy was indeed now grateful, and Haimanti's work on him quite good given the circumstances, it had been traumatic for both and Mardy suspected the friendliness they'd once enjoyed would never return.

MARDY INSPECTED the works on display, trying not to let his mind go back to which new whirligig he would realize. The drone, probably. Devesh and Smith had not arrived, nor had Death and Flaky. Wes was not coming, since he had work responsibilities and neither Smith nor Mardy were entered. The scene felt lifeless with neither twin there, as Mardy circulated amongst the attendees, congratulating the artists and being congratulated by them for Regionals, already a fleeting memory.

Devesh arrived. He had a sumptuous set of pieces in the

salon, mesmerizing, worn by a trio of tall models, nonbinary, male and female.

"Beautiful, Devesh. Smith not with you?"

"He can't make it tonight."

"Off being a Cleveburgh fellow, no doubt. I gotta say, it's weird that you and I used to go out, and now we are seeing identical people, but I'm getting used to it."

Mardy laughed. Devesh didn't, apparently not as used to it as Mardy. But Mardy understood. He and Devesh had come to an end when he'd sensed Devesh inching toward a declaration of love. Meanwhile Mardy was inching toward desperation at Devesh's constant criticism. Mardy had enjoyed the sex, the companionship, the shared sense of humor, but he was growing less happy, not more, and he eventually had to say so. They'd been such good friends, once upon a time, but as with Haimanti, maybe that would never return. He missed the friendship and couldn't even tell him.

Devesh circulated with his models. Mardy wandered by himself, smiling at Haimanti and Jonesy, but not stopping for small talk. The evening dragged. Mardy had imagined beforehand that winning the salon and then Regionals would have had him bubbling and proud, the conquering hero returning home, but instead he felt sad. He now hoped he *would* get a Cleveburgh, because that would take him away from San Francisco. If he didn't, he would join the Cleveburgh Work-Shop. With Wes, feelings of love came of their own, like water through a burst levee. San Francisco felt empty now, flat and pale. When Haimanti clinked her champagne flute to announce the winner, Mardy congratulated Devesh for making it to November Regionals, and did his best to prevent Devesh from sensing the lack of joy in his words.

CHAPTER 47

Devesh went on to win his Regional. With the end of the final round of Regionals, the roster for Continentals was now set. Six toolers had made the cut. Mardy was at WorkShop hot-forging steel, applying greater and greater pressure to achieve the fine grain structure and tensile strength that would hold up to the delicate machining he had in mind for his birdlike grab drone. The forging room was ridiculously hot, its coolers harvesting heat but unable to keep up. Mardy would need to exit soon. Or die.

Heat-stroke flashes began to appear at the edges of his vision. Mardy threw off his gloves and hit the trigger to open the first of the door seals. He entered the inter-door chamber. Once the first doors had closed and the chamber swapped out hot fumes for cool, fresh-filtered air, he opened the second set of doors and gratefully stumbled into the normal temperatures of the main WorkShop space.

This second realization would be a showcase for Mardy's hardcore machining skills, less accessible to the mainstream audience but likely to appeal to collectors who got off on technique. The drone's grabbing claw would highlight complex toolpaths using cams in a like-to-unlike design, while the body would sport oxidation flares on its outer unburnished surfaces, reminiscent of his flying lighter. His microbatteries of boron-doped graphene were already well along. He'd repurpose motors he'd previously made in practices. It was an ambitious project, but he thought he could get it done by Continentals, allowing him to submit it with his Cleveburgh application.

Mardy breathed. His vision returned to normal. He swapped empty batteries into his cooler. His body temp reached normal and his cooler gave him the all-clear. He got stuck back into work.

WHEN MARDY DESCRIBED the new piece to Phil on the next day's runs, Phil did not like it, at least not as much as he did the dancers. But then Phil loooooved the dancers. AIs generally favored concept pieces over material achievements. Apparently, when you were disembodied—materials, meh! Wes thought the drone was a smart move, which ironically made Mardy concerned he was playing it too safe. But he himself loved the technology aspect of machine tooling, which most toolers did, or they wouldn't be in the specialty. So he focused on that. When confronted with choices in how to proceed, he opted for the one that most excited that sensibility.

Continentals drew near. Mardy had yet to decipher the mystery of that third rec. He was not allowed to access it, of course. What if it was weak? He sent off mails seeking another rec, but here again his excessive focus on WorkShop Downtown SF, though it had given him a sense of belonging he sorely needed, had limited his options. His connections to prominent machine tool artists and teachers were so limited the best he could hope for was a mercy rec, which would be about as effective as one of those eulogies delivered by a minister-for-hire over an impromptu grave site.

They tell me Marty was a nice guy.

It's Mardy, not Marty.

That's what I said. Marty.

No, with a "D."

They tell me Darty was a nice guy.

So Mardy stuck with his third rec, undeleted, and hoped for the best. He plodded forward, focused on his work, his job, and Wes. He burned the candle at both ends, with an acetylene torch, but by the time Continentals rolled around, he was ready. If the third rec was strong, if he could get out of the skills rounds into the top sixteen at Continentals, he would have a fighting chance at a Cleveburgh.

CHAPTER 48

The Atlantic glinted, migraine bright, as the ExMail plane hovered down to a building top in old Miami, where Continentals were to be held. Old Miami stretched out to the north and south, the second largest of the Florida islands, preserved only by massive seawalls and a tourist economy. Miami no longer had beaches, but something about its vestigial existence drew people to the dense, isolated outpost. They mostly came, not for the lush fishing over the long-submerged former peninsula to the north, but simply because it was still there.

Mardy waved good-bye to the plane as it and its pilot—another one not planning on getting the New Sense chip—continued their runs. Mardy checked in at the Adrienne Arsht Center for the Performing Arts and got his irises scanned for the nearby hotel where he'd be bunking with two roommates over the course of the weeklong competition. He walked through the exterior plaza and marveled, both at the insane heat and at the grace of the outdoor space, with its spreading eucalyptus trees, whose salt-tolerant growth shaded the margins where palms had grown until salinity in the water table killed even them off.

None of the beds had been claimed. Mardy tossed his suitcase onto his favorite and stowed the dancers on the provided worktable. Wes would be staying away so Mardy could concentrate on competing. Mardy sat on the edge of the bed, knees jumping, waiting for his fellow competitors to arrive. They had a welcome dinner scheduled for that night. The skills round—Technicals—would start the next morning at eight.

Mardy's roommates turned out to be a quiet fabrics woman and a male vocalist who immediately announced he had attention deficit disorder and then proceeded to talk nonstop. Mardy finally asked him if he needed to rest his voice, and the guy agreed he did, but he still did not shut up. Mardy changed into his suit from Devesh (earning an unsubtle stare from the vocalist at Mardy's uber-*dasai* tattoo) and went downstairs early to loiter until the dinner. He avoided other competitors. He was there to perform, to do as well as possible so he could get a Cleveburgh and live with Wes. Yes, he could live with Wes without a fellowship, but his art compelled him to keep moving, and he wondered what would be left of him without it. If he did not keep progressing, he felt he might disappear.

The doors to the banquet hall opened. The competitors, judges and organizers entered and the schmoozing began. Mardy got a drink and hugged the wall. He saw Smith arrive and head for the center of the crowd, buzzing with social energy, but Mardy did not join him. A voice in his head whispered that making an attempt at schmoozing would be good for him, but he felt the need to stay centered and listened to that impulse instead. If he made it through the opening rounds, then he'd have something to schmooze about.

Dinner seemed endless. The food appeared at their white-clothed tables in sporadic bits and pieces as welcomes were extended in a series of speeches and cheer that didn't touch Mardy. He spotted Devesh and waved. Devesh waved back. He tugged pointedly at his lapels and smiled, apparently happy to see Mardy modeling his creation. Mardy smiled back, beaming his thanks at Devesh for the threads. Finally, it was late enough to leave. Mardy crept back upstairs, checked for the fourth time where he was supposed to report the next day and what he was expected to bring. He called Wes and talked to him briefly, not quite connecting after his disappointment in their last day together. He stared out at the moonlight on the choppy ocean from the balcony and went to bed before his roommates returned.

He awoke before his roommates, showered, dressed in work gear, and went downstairs to eat. There were a few other early birds, each keeping in their own zone. Only as he was finishing his meal did the buzz in the room start to rise as other competitors filled the room. He saw Smith arriving just as he was heading out the door. Devesh was not with him.

"Devesh sleeping in?"

"No idea," Smith said.

"You're not staying together?"

Smith laughed. "He dumped me, Mardy."

"You seem okay with it," Mardy said.

Smith shrugged. "Yeah. Fun while it lasted. He's so sexy, but I think I was too passionate for him. Or something. Anyway, no harm no foul."

"I totally understand." Mardy had never been sure of what drove Devesh, or why he seemed so perpetually unsatisfied. But he felt himself on the verge of dishing about a past relationship, something he never did, so he decided to head out. Smith too passionate, huh? "*In bocca al lupo*, Smith."

"Yep. Good luck with skills."

"You too."

MARDY FELT WELL prepared for Technicals. The judges set them tasks, which all competitors were to perform simultaneously on their individual banks of identical tools. All the work he'd been doing to realize his grabby drone had left him in fine shape: a bit sore, but mind and body working well together. The first skills round was macrobatteries—unfortunate tactically, since batteries were his strength and later rounds would be more competitive, but he aced it and moved on at the top of the leader board, outranking Smith easily.

He knew Smith would catch up in motors, and sure enough Smith closed the gap considerably, but Mardy did pretty well, too, and remained atop the list of the six machine toolers vying for the three spots that would take them into Day Two. That was a good result for Mardy.

Steel shaping did not go as well, and Mardy's soreness began to come into play. Smith slipped ahead. The past few weeks had left Mardy tired, even if his joints and muscles felt fluid and honed. He held his own in precious metals and alloys, but knew aluminum would be a challenge, coming as a brute-force test at the end of the day.

But first came the classical skills: grinding, dicing, lathing, polishing. Metal dust filled their masks, metals curls shined on the floor as blades screamed and whined. No one wanted to give an inch, and all six performed well on the cutting disciplines. Mardy slipped to third heading into aluminum, passed up by Hen, a tooler out of Kansas City. If he could just hang on to third, he felt good about the modern disciplines they'd do on Day Two—the electrical, magnetic and chemical techniques.

Aluminum, though, was a challenge. For everyone, which was why the judges had placed it at the end of the day, when all were exhausted. It was a test of character, not strength or technique. They all swapped out their clogged masks for fresh and personned their six stations at a gleaming row of massive tools.

Mardy heard an unhappy crack somewhere off to his left. Bad news for somebody. Mardy's aluminum machining went well and he moved on to detailing at the shaper. He focused on his connection to the shaping gloves. The heat coming off the tool was palpable. It wasn't the hottest he'd felt, but it was draining. Mardy was dying for water. He raised his elbows, pouring strength into his push as he tried to get all the assistance he could out of the Lenz effect. The high elbows were poor form, but he was too spent to worry about that. Getting his assigned shape was more important. Out of the corner of his eye, he could see Smith. Perfect form.

Mardy felt his ingot getting away from him. Don't lose it now, dude, this close to the line. He rallied, containing the metal, and felt it flow the desired direction. Come on, come on, you're nearly there, he mumbled at the metal. It bent toward the angle he wanted, was nearly there, was there. Bang. He hit the completion button, satisfied with his effort and hoped it was enough.

He stepped away from the machine, removing his gloves. He inspected his work. Pretty decent.

He looked up at the leaderboard as he stowed his gear. He was on top, but only one other person had finished, the guy who'd had the mishap. The guy had a miserable score and was certainly out. Mardy grabbed a bottle of water and guzzled it. A third tooler finished and was scored. She came up short of Mardy. Mardy only needed to outscore one more to advance.

Smith finished. He had an excellent score. Smith now

topped the leaderboard. He exhaled deeply and went to stand near Mardy, both kneading their forearms. They were ranked one and two. Smith didn't offer congratulations, though. Smith was through, but Mardy's score wasn't as strong as he'd hoped. He grabbed a towel and wiped sweat from his forehead.

Hen finished next, edging Mardy by a point. Uh oh. It was coming down to the wire, not where he wanted to be. Good thing he'd had that strong result in motors.

The clock was ticking. Smith and Hen were chatting, relaxed. They were both moving on. The two who were already cut were commiserating. The final competitor was sure taking her time. She'd started the round ranked ahead of the two toolers who'd come up short, just shy of Mardy's point total. The clock ticked away. Mardy did not want to go home on Day One.

The minutes were running short. The remaining tooler was going for something good enough to overtake Mardy. She was really, really gambling here. Only seconds remained. She was going through her wrap up, clearly ready to hit the completion button.

Buzz. But it wasn't her hitting her personal buzzer. It was the buzzer for the round.

She'd missed it. Now she slapped her palm onto her own plastic button, but she'd miscalculated and run out of time. Mardy was through.

Smith and Hen congratulated him as all the toolers shook hands. The disqualified competitor seemed devastated. She spoke only to Mardy, as though they were bonded from vying for that last spot. "I don't know if it would have been enough, even if I finished," she said.

He'd seen her ingot. It probably wouldn't have been.

"Rough break," he said, because win or lose, timing out was the worst.

Mardy headed upstairs for a shower and stood soaking in the cool water until one of his roommates knocked on the door. He forced himself to get out and relinquished the shared bathroom to her.

"You survived?" he asked her as he left the bathroom.

She glanced at the tattoo stretching over the side of his ribcage down into the towel wrapped around his waist. Yeah, I know, he wanted to say, it's even weirder than my face.

She nodded. "I survived. Our vocalist, not so much."

Mardy looked at the third bed. The vocalist had collected his things and left while Mardy was in the shower. Mardy called Wes. "Third place. I'm still in it," he reported when Wes's face popped up on Mardy's wristphone projection.

Wes congratulated him. Mardy talked to him on the way down to the dining hall and throughout dinner, welcoming the touch of home. The distance between them he'd felt the night before faded. They'd learned a lot about each other in San Francisco, and now the conflict—if that's what it was— was feeling like it might be something necessary rather than a setback.

"How does it look for tomorrow," Wes asked as Mardy gathered a tray of food.

"One more person gets cut, and I think Smith has enough of a cushion to be safe. I know how strong Smith is on the electrical side of things. Probably be me and Hen fighting for the second spot."

"You'll come through," Wes said.

The chatter in the room pitched up a level as competitors filled up the beige quartz-topped tables with meal trays in pastel colors. He looked up at the leaderboard, as yet blank, to see how the other disciplines had gone. Every bit of this action was being broadcast. The huge black board spanned the width of the cafeteria, befitting its importance to the competitors. "They are posting scores," he told Wes. Mardy knew the machine tool results, but it was still a relief to see his name in green, indicating he was on to the second day. He didn't recognize many of the other names, but he did see one he knew.

"Devesh is top of his group," Mardy told Wes.

"Way to go, Downtown SF," Wes said.

"I know, right?"

"I love it when you use old slang. It reminds me of the tattoo."

He remembered his roommate's disapproving stare. "Ach, I'm getting it removed."

"Don't you dare." Wes's face shimmered on the projection.

Mardy smiled. He wasn't serious about removing it. He'd never remove it. He ended the call as he ended his meal and went to the physio room for a scheduled Epsom soak for his tired muscles. He changed into the required trunks, wondering whether his soak would be televised. No one in the room stared at his artifacts or his tattoo as he slipped into his bath in the row of white porcelain tubs, forearms submerged, and forgot about everything.

CHAPTER 49

Tanzima was his roommate's name, Mardy learned as they introduced themselves heading for breakfast. Neither had asked the vocalist's name, they discovered, sharing an embarrassed laugh. They ate together and Mardy considered whether being shy and focused was a form of rudeness. He could learn from Smith. He asked Tanzima questions about herself, discovering that she was from New Tallahassee, having been born in Dhaka but brought to the US as an infant when the government had lured her engineer parents to the North Florida restoration, a story whose broad strokes she must share with millions. She encouraged Mardy to hit the beaches on Lake Wales Island, a couple hundred miles across the waters to the north, before they eroded away. She was strongest in jaquarding and had earned the top score in buttonholing on Day One. She was fun to talk to. Mardy half-regretted not getting to know his other roommate. On the other hand, the guy had *never* shut up.

The toolers had a smaller room for Day Two, which helped the absence of half yesterday's group feel less obvious. Mardy did not know how strong Hen was on the modern tools, but got a sense that her strength was in subtractive machining, which many of Day Two's tools were. Ultrasonic was Smith's strength; Mardy's was microbatteries. And batteries were first up, as on Day One. Mardy would need to run up a high score to stay competitive, and as on Day One, he did.

He looked up at the leaderboard, but with little excitement. They were just getting started, and Mardy had dropped from first to third yesterday. Today that would mean elimination. Still, his strong start left him a tenth of a point ahead of Smith in the cumulative totals, a very unfamiliar position. He nodded to himself. The competition was really underway now.

Hen turned out to be a whiz at electrostatic discharge and seized the lead until Smith got back on top as expected with ultrasonic. Mardy was now in third again, but barely. He was keeping pace, which is what he wanted to do because today they would end with photo-engraving, a strength for Mardy. Smith's best discipline was now behind them. Mardy gulped. They were halfway through the day and he had a shot at placing first in skills.

All three competitors ate in silence. The time for polite conversation would come later, although with the extreme focus these trials demanded, they might all three find themselves drained, with nothing to say. Mardy ate meditatively, chewing slowly, letting his mind relax as much as he could.

He had a hiccup in electron-beam machining when his kerf width came out wider than he wanted, but his result was functional so he breathed a sigh of relief and moved on. Neither Smith nor Hen was making this easier by screwing up. Mardy's wide kerfs were the biggest miscalculation so far by any of them.

All three then struggled with plasma cutting. Few Work-

Shops even had a plasma cutter. The skill's inclusion struck Mardy as unfair, but Hen's WorkShop, she said, also lacked the machine, so it was equally unfair to all. They ended the penultimate challenge closely grouped. Mardy could scarcely believe he hadn't screwed something up. He was in third, but all three were within a point, a far tighter spread than they'd achieved yesterday, which meant both Hen and Mardy had gained on Smith. Might Smith actually be eliminated? It was shocking to even consider.

Mardy entered the photo-engraving area for the final challenge. The judge announced their task: Photochemical machining. The contestants were given three pattern reticles and an image of a pattern that they had to etch onto stainless sheets using the provided films and UV-sensitive photoresists. Mardy tamped down a smile. Day Two was his to lose.

Mardy quickly saw how to combine the three reticles. There was a little trick to it, but it was straightforward. He optically and mechanically registered his first two reticles. He looked at them again. Something was niggling at him. He didn't see any mistake, but had he made one anyway? Was this a version of Cat's Tijuana yips? Nothing here would injure anyone, but Mardy was certainly nervous.

Hen and Smith were already laminating their plates with the first coating of photoresist, purple and gloppy. Smith was spinning his out to uniform evenness. Mardy looked at his films again.

He had indeed made a mistake. He'd been looking at the second reticle backwards. Wow. That was the error of a rank amateur. The competition had used old style frames that required manual checking and he hadn't checked. He quickly swapped it out, hoping no one had noticed his embarrassing error. He registered his reticles again from scratch and proceeded to the photoresists. He hadn't left

himself much time now, but if he'd not caught that error . . .
He shuddered.

Now Mardy focused. Hen and Smith faded away. He was
alone in the room, surrounded only by the giant white
machines, preparing his resists, hardening them with UV,
etching away the unhardened areas, placing a new coat of
resist, hardening it, etching it, doing it all again, and once
more.

His pattern was complete. He compared it to the guide
pattern provided. It was a match. Now he just had to etch the
metal. He looked at the clock. He barely had time. But it
would be enough, provided he made no mistakes. You've done
this a thousand times, he told himself. He fell back on familiar
skills, applying the etchant, neutralizing it, rinsing it. He was
done.

He looked at the clock. A minute to spare. Neither Smith
nor Hen had finished. Either could time out. Mardy placed his
plate on the judging platform. Hen came up shortly after and
did the same. Would Smith time out? Fuck! He couldn't.
Mardy didn't want to see this end like that.

The buzzer sounded.

Had Smith timed out? Smith stood by his machine
holding his plate, looking at the judges. He only had to get his
plate off the machine to qualify, not actually place it on the
judging platform.

The judges checked the recording and nodded. Smith had
done it. He gave Mardy a half-smile and rolled his eyes
skyward as he placed his plate on the platform.

The judges scanned their work. There was a bit of
frowning at Smith's—he'd over-etched the second resist,
losing some of the definition on his final etch—but he earned
a decent score.

There was a great deal more frowning at Hen's plate.

Mardy glanced at it. It was tragic. She'd made the same mistake Mardy had started with, but not caught it. Her pattern was wrong. She would get zero points. Mardy and Smith were through.

But wait. The judges had yet to inspect Mardy's work. If he, too, got zero points, then it would be Mardy who was out. But he could see nothing wrong with it. Unlike his electron-beam etching hiccup, this plate looked clean to Mardy. He chewed his lip as they inspected it. Pattern was good, obviously, etch-walls were sharp. One by one, he cleared each hurdle. Could it be that he hadn't screwed up?

It could.

The judges smiled, one even shaking his hand. He'd saved the best for last. They awarded his score. Mardy's name jumped from third to first. The skills round was over. For the first time in his life, he'd beaten Smith Hunt.

CHAPTER 50

As expected, the three competitors had little to say to each other after the judging, but they walked side by side across the still blazing-hot plaza to the dining hall, got meals together, and sat with their trays at the same table, unwilling to separate.

At length, Hen broke the silence. "I knew I'd done it ten minutes in, but I had to finish anyway."

"The old-style frames on the reticles were kind of a trick," Smith said.

"I fell for it too," Mardy told her.

"But corrected."

Mardy nodded.

Hen stuck out her hand. He shook it, gave her a hug. He wanted to win, but he didn't want her to go home.

Smith stuck out his hand too, and she shook it. "Are you staying to watch the rest?"

Hen shook her head. "I'll livestream it at home, where I can cry into my beer."

"No shame in that," said Smith.

"Yeah, we've all been there," Mardy added.

"It was an honor," she said, gathering up her tray as the two nodded. Mardy felt teary watching Hen take her tray to the bussing station and leave the hall. He felt so close to her, and so much closer to Smith than he had even last week, even after that conversation at the gym when Smith had been so protective of Wes.

"Could've been either of us doing that," Mardy said. Instead, he was in the position he'd been hoping for to make his Cleveburgh application viable. And he was still alive in the competition. How far could he go?

"Still might be me," Smith said. "I have to wait for fabrics to wrap up, pun intended."

"Huh?"

"The top finisher in each discipline goes on to the round of sixteen and the bottom finisher is out, but the remaining slots are doled out to the next highest scores out of all the groups together."

"Oh." Mardy had missed that rule somehow. He looked up at the leader board. Smith was currently ranked fifteenth. Only fabrics had yet to report. One spot would automatically be taken by the top person in fabrics, bumping Smith to sixteenth.

"So you're dependent on the score of the number two person in fabrics."

Smith nodded. "Last year, I was in your spot. Will be hard disappointing if I don't make it to the semifinals."

In tomorrow's round, each of the sixteen would make a public presentation of their art, just like at Regionals. In the final round, the round of eight, their works would be judged blind, with no artist to interpret them, just the way they would be at any gallery. No scores or judges carried over in either round.

"So, okay, leaderboard, come on. Get us our scores!" Mardy said.

"I just hope I am not bumped by Devesh. Not after being dumped by him."

"Dumped and bumped would be harsh."

They both were staring at the unchanging display now. Mardy looked over the other names, trying to familiarize himself with them, easier now that the number was shrinking. He stretched his forearms overhead, fingers interlocked, totally beat up, even though the Day Two physical effort had been less. Delayed onset muscle soreness. Tomorrow would be all talk, but he planned to hit the Epsom salt bath in physio as soon as the display updated.

The whole dining hall was quiet now, focused on the display. It was calming for him, undoubtedly less so for Smith. So many people at the competition seemed to know Smith, who'd made the finals last year. Were the others all wondering whether he'd be bumped, or just curious who'd come out of fabrics?

The leaderboard blinked and began updating. It could have updated all at once, but instead was filling in the names one at a time. The AI was obviously a drama queen. The first name, winner of the fabrics group: Devesh.

"Awesome!" Mardy said. He looked at Smith, realizing that would sound different to him. "Sorry."

"No, it's good. I'm not bumped by Devesh!"

The second name crawled across the name of the display. Tanzima. Mardy's roommate. And then her score. What did she need to beat Smith? Mardy's eyes flicked across to Smith's score. He was in. Tanzima was out.

Smith grinned. Mardy high-fived him. Poor Tanzima, though.

"Hoo, that was nervewracking," Smith said.

"This whole thing is. I booked an Epsom salt bath at physio. Starting in fifteen minutes."

"I did too. Starting a minute ago. Go together?" Smith asked.

"Um, okay." Mardy felt uncomfortable. The tubs were all in a single open room. The hotel provided suits, but it would still mean being nearly naked next to Smith, another first. It would be weird to avert his eyes when he already knew what he'd see, but Mardy could hardly say no. And after what they'd just been through, he didn't really want to, either.

They walked together down the hall making small talk, then undressed and showered in separate curtained cubicles. Mardy was careful to not look, letting Smith go to the showers first, but the hooks for towels and trunks were hanging outside the showers, of course, and suddenly they stood naked face to face anyway.

Smith didn't bat an eye. He just slipped on his trunks and said, "Come on," leading the way to the tubs. Hey, they were just bodies. They each got into a steamy bathtub, the ranks of tubs not yet filling up. The diminished ranks of competitors were probably still eating and buzzing in the dining hall.

The hot salty water drew Mardy into its cocoon of warmth, the comfortable kind rarely sought after in their warmed world. Mardy was very aware that Smith was lying in the tub next to him. And of course, he looked just like Wes, who Mardy hadn't touched in a week. Mardy started getting aroused. He was glad they were now wearing trunks.

"I know that was weird in the showers," Smith said, lying eyes closed in his bath, arms resting on the knurled sides of the tank.

So despite his cool demeanor, Smith had felt it. "You look just like him," Mardy said.

"It's weird for me too. I've never seen you naked."

"Hadn't thought of that." Please don't say you have feelings for me or anything like that, Mardy prayed.

"That's some tattoo. You had a nouveau period?"

"As a kid. Good catch."

They both went quiet.

"Anyway, glad that's behind us," Smith said.

"Me too," Mardy echoed. His arousal faded. Now he felt relieved, calm. Tension had always crackled between him and Smith, mostly from Mardy's end, their rivalry intense over the past two years. Mardy was quite demonstrably attracted to Smith—in love with his twin, for God's sake. But that now drifted off like morning mist under a rising sun. They soaked, quietly, chatting occasionally as their muscles rested in the potassium stew. It was nice.

Mardy's phone rang. He answered it.

"I'm lying next to your brother," Mardy said. "We're naked."

"Hi, Wes," Smith called out, fairly loudly. A couple of the other competitors now filling up the room looked toward Smith's disturbance of the peace.

Wes just said, "Ummmm."

"Epsom salts. Separate baths. Swim trunks."

"Oh."

"I'm through to the next round," Mardy told Wes. "We both are. Let me put you on wide mode so Smith doesn't have to shout."

"That's phenomenal! That's the best news ever!"

Smith jumped in. "Wes, what he's not telling you is that he trounced me. Mardy won the group and I scraped into the round of sixteen in last place."

Wes said, "Oh, um, yay?"

Smith laughed. Mardy wasn't quite sure what to make of Wes's response, but he doubted anyone would have expected

Mardy to win, and it had been far closer than Smith made it sound. Mardy had squeaked past Smith, not trounced him. But squeaked he had.

"Okay, lovebirds, you can take it off wide." Smith got out and draped his towel over his shoulders. "My time just expired and people are waiting." Smith headed to the locker room.

Mardy started talking to Wes again, off wide, with a feeling of warmth that had nothing to do with the bath. He wanted to be with Wes, no question about it, but being perennially locked in prickly combat with Wes's brother had been something to work around. Now Mardy and Smith had been through something of their own together. Now Mardy felt something toward Smith he'd never expected. He felt they were friends.

CHAPTER 51

Mardy woke early and took a cup of coffee out onto the balcony, where he stood and looked out at the Atlantic as he drank. He called Flaky and Death and recounted the events of the day before. The room was quiet, the other two beds not slept in, his roommates gone. He wished Wes was there.

The round of sixteen was distinguishable from Regionals only by the venue, and the fact that in the competition this time were both Smith and Devesh, a great showing for Downtown SF. This time Mardy was presenting toward the end, the fifteenth slot, which did not feel like an advantage or disadvantage, except that he had more time to be nervous. But he stayed collected, blocking out everything he could until it was his time on stage.

The crowd seemed immense, the hall bigger than Regionals. He presented his dancers, faltering at first as he tried to command the vast space of the hall, but he rallied quickly. The questions were similar, focusing on the controversy—was this an illegal naming of intelligences—and again the judges split, with those who rejected the idea of intelligence seeming likely to support him, which was the opposite of how Mardy thought it should be. Despite his refinements, they *still* didn't get it. But his execution of the dancers won praise, and Ann and Frankie executed two aerials with grace and snap. They had autonomy, though the judges did not seem to feel it. The irony of that made Mardy feel his piece had failed at the most basic level.

Then it was time to wait.

Both Smith and Devesh had done well, especially Devesh. His trio of models continued to wow everyone. As Mardy waited for his score, he looked at the leaderboard. With one final artist to present, Devesh was in second, Smith in fourth. They were both moving on. Mardy was in eighth. The artist atop the board at the moment was a plastic surgery artist, which made Mardy wonder, yet again, where Cat was. Now it was Mardy's turn to balance on the razor's edge. Even if he got booted, though . . . top ten! Would it be wrong for him to be satisfied with that? Wes said that Smith hated to lose more than he wanted to win. Mardy certainly did not enjoy losing, but this was so much further than he'd ever expected to come.

The final artist was presenting. She was a stonecutter. She was rather good. Good enough to keep Mardy out of the final round, if the judges saw something in him, but then really all sixteen were good enough. Just one screw-up, anywhere along the way, would have been enough to boot Mardy back home. Though he felt he'd been lucky to perform well over the past three days, he also felt he belonged. It wasn't pride; it was confidence.

The stonecutter finished up. The judges did their interview. The audience applauded. The stonecutter came backstage to wait with the others. Her scores were posted on the small screen, but too briefly for Mardy to do the math before the big screen went blank, redrawing itself. Names began appearing, agonizingly slowly: Devesh still in second, Smith still in fourth. The fifth, sixth and seventh names appeared, none the stonecutter. Mardy allowed a little joy to build. Could it be? Then the eighth. Mardy. He was through to the final round.

CHAPTER 52

Mardy paced the comfortable backstage room, making occasional conversation with the other seven competitors as they waited out the final round. This round was nothing like the others. For starters, it followed immediately after the presentation round. Also, the artists mostly did nothing. No vocalist having made the final round, the plastic surgery artist was the sole exception. She had to perform on a new blank for the new judges, all very prominent figures—artists, museum directors, collectors, curators—who had not been a part of any previous round. The others had the staff present their work for them.

Conversation had died to a minimum; the food and drink table sat mostly untouched. Mardy focused on the failure of his piece. If making the final eight could ever be considered failure. It wasn't, of course, but he wanted the piece to have an impact. He felt so surely that this practice of forbidding names to AIs was wrong. It was keeping organic and artificial intelligences apart. Ostensibly, this was because AIs were not alive, so naming them was deceptive. Mardy knew—or felt—this widely accepted "fact" was wrong. He saw people everywhere interacting intimately, meaningfully with AI friends. Everyone depended on them, and not just for the lifegiving coolers. Had the fear borne of dependence not abated enough that the restrictions could be lifted?

Smith stood up and walked to the food table, picked at it. Devesh followed him. They talked briefly.

Mardy thought of how his relationship with Smith had transitioned: from rivals, to wary acceptance as Mardy started dating Wes, to friendship now as their shared love for Wes placed them on the same team, though rivals still. Was that how it was with AIs as well? Were they and organics past rivalry, ready for that wary acceptance? Or even friendship? Wes was certainly friends with AIs. Mardy was, too.

A bell sounded. The judges were done. The competitors looked at each other, silently. Now names would be called, starting with eighth place, ending with first.

Mardy, Smith and Devesh gravitated toward each other. "*In bocca al lupo*, dudes," Mardy said, shaking each of their hands, giving each a hug. A fantasy played in his mind: He'd be backstage as the numbers dropped, until only he and Smith were left. Then Smith's name would be called, leaving only Mardy. He'd won the whole thing!

The announcer's voice came on and went through some meaningless glad words, then paused for the first name.

"In eighth place . . ."

Silence filled the hall. Why were they dragging it out? He didn't think it would be Smith or Devesh. The plastic surgeon? The stonecutter?

"Mardy . . ."

His ears filled with buzz. He didn't hear whatever came next.

Oh. Okay, he thought. He was out. He stood as he got another hug each from Smith and Devesh. He'd thought earlier that he was satisfied with being in the top ten, so now he had to eat his words. Now his fantasy would happen for someone else while he stood hiding his disappointment on stage, waiting for the others to join him. He had to content himself with imagining the backstage scene rather than living it.

He walked out on stage to thunderous applause from the audience under the hot lights and made himself take it in. Thousands of people were out there, millions more were watching, including, Mardy hoped, Flaky, Death, and his apartment. And of course, the ExMail AIs, if they were permitted. And Inge. And somewhere, Cat. Where are you, Cat? he wondered. He'd come a long way. He waved, getting a rise in the applause. And how could he complain when he himself felt that his piece had not succeeded the way it should have? He now felt gratitude as the applause thundered down, and a sense of accomplishment. He couldn't wait to be back with Wes. He waved a final time and heard a familiar voice shout, "Mardy! *Shabash*! Woo hoo!"

Mardy smiled. Wes. Wes was out there in the hot darkness. Mardy wanted to be with him. The awkwardness of their last meeting seemed petty now. The other competitors came out one by one, looking sober, a bit glum, maybe even defeated. Mardy kept grinning, congratulating them. He felt better and better about being there. He wouldn't even mind if Smith won. He hoped he did. The familiar jealousy was gone. He chuckled to himself, wondering if he might be slowed down in future by a *lack* of jealousy.

Four of them were now lined up, including the plastic surgery artist, who'd led the previous round.

"Smith Hunt," was called.

So, Smith would be fourth. Mardy felt disappointed for him. He'd made it one place farther than his last Continentals, but that must sting. Still, Smith, like Mardy, seemed to be enjoying the moment, unfazed and beaming as he walked across the stage. He flashed Mardy a glance when he, too, picked out a cheer from Wes.

The third-place name was called. The laser artist. She walked on stage. Leaving the woodworker. And Devesh. Was Devesh going to do it? He had to. The woodworker was good, she was, but come on. Devesh, Devesh, Devesh, Mardy chanted under his breath.

The announcers stalled, dragging out the moment, pros at milking the tension, priming the audience. In second place ... the woodworker!

The woodworker and Devesh came out together, Devesh flashing teeth, shaking the hands of the other competitors, waving to the crowd. The others surrounded him as the judges from the final and previous rounds came up to congratulate Devesh and the others. Smith and Mardy lifted him onto their shoulders and carried him around the stage as confetti drenched them all in bits of deco pastels as competitors exchanged words, not really audible in the roar. Devesh raised his clenched fist in victory.

CHAPTER 53

O nly the plastic surgery artist missed the evening's gala. Mardy stared at the coffered mahogany ceiling of the grand ballroom, a re-creation of some drowned something somewhere, and thought of the woodworking hours that had gone into it. *Shabash*, whoever or whatever you are or were. He had learned from Haimanti to celebrate the others, win or lose. Placing eighth was actually really good. It gave him a kind of belonging coupled with anonymity. None of the judges approached him with critiques. Yay! It would have been smart to hit them up for that third rec, but they were strangers, despite the emotionally charged week. Mardy was overstocked on feedback at the moment and wanted to savor being there with Wes and Smith and his fellow competitors, to wear his own Devesh creation and dance with Wes and kiss him under the antique deco glitter ball at the center of it all. He hoped Phil, Betty and Kludge were watching, after all the advice they had given him, along with their support, most important of which had been their happiness, expressed in chirps and rattles and their other machine noises of choice.

It was fun, but it was also over. He and Wes would be

flying back that night on Wes's plane. Smith was staying on, heading north to the cruisy end of Lake Wales Island for some sun and fun on the beach.

"You mean you're going to take off your shirt in public?" Mardy asked.

"It's been a hell of a year. I am ready to cut loose!"

Mardy turned to Wes. "He cuts loose?"

"Smith has more than one side to him," Wes said. "You'll see."

"I'm going to be Devesh's wingman," Smith said, smiling, as he waved them good-bye.

"Watch out for sunburn!" Wes yelled as they left.

Mardy and Wes did *not* jump each other's bones the second they got on the plane. Yes, Mardy ran his hands over Wes's legs as they settled in, but a sexy snuggle turned into Mardy snoring on Wes's shoulder. It was still dark when they arrived in Cleveburgh, and Mardy was not done sleeping, not by a long shot. But before they made it to Wes's bed, Mardy dragged himself to a screen and reviewed his Cleveburgh application. He updated the line about Continentals. Placed eighth. Maybe that would be enough. He gave it one last look. His drone—Grabby—was ready. He clicked *Submit*.

MARDY WOKE in the late morning. He'd been out cold for hours, but still felt tired. He'd expected to wake refreshed with Wes beside him, but neither had happened. He made his way to the living room, but no Wes. He said hello to the apartment, but got only silence. Who lived in a place with no AI? How did you eat? How did you pay your bills? How did you find out where your missing boyfriend was?

Mardy got out the coffee-making materials. No AI also meant always making your own coffee. What time was it? His phone was in the bedroom. Yes, there was a clock in the study, but he'd have to walk over to look at it. He couldn't just ask. And did the time matter? Continentals were over. His Cleveburgh application was submitted. Grabby the Drone was realized. And he was happy with him. It. How long would it be before he'd hear if he'd landed an interview?

"Apartment . . ."

Argh. No AI. Did he *need* to know when the second round would be announced? He was so used to going, going, going. And today he didn't need to. He was uninjured—if you didn't count his aching arms and back—and undrugged. His face had artifacts slashed across it but was healed and attached to his head. He made the coffee, watched it brew, took a cup to the deck and drank it watching Lake Erie gently tug at the shoreline. When he'd been a kid in Suisun, their outlook had been the house across the street, its dry lawn and salt-poisoned trees, all soon to be washed away. Now here he was, flying everywhere, gazing at the Atlantic, the Pacific, San Francisco Bay, Lake Erie. He supposed more apartments had water views now, now that there was more shore, a billion fewer people.

"Apartment, where is . . ."

Shit. Maybe Wes was on to something. Mardy was addicted to AIs. Or, as he called it, friends with his apartment. Mardy went into the study. He found a note under the clock.

Had to take a conference call. Back by one. The clock read one.

Mardy was hungry, but he didn't eat. He sat on the balcony with a refreshed cup of coffee. His eyes teared up. He was weeping. Where was that coming from? He should be happy. All his dreams were coming true. Had come true. He remembered that one night working at WorkShop while Cat, Inge, Devesh, Clare and Smith had gone to Uncle Mix to celebrate their successes, their bright possibilities, and he'd thought they were leaving him behind, Mardy the only one not keeping up. Now Devesh was Continental Champion, but Cat was in hiding, Inge had given up art for PR, and Smith . . . well, Smith was Smith, moving ever forward. And now Mardy was too. So why was he wiping away tears?

The door opened. Mardy was ready to jump onto Wes like a puppy but restrained himself. He had to be . . . what exactly? Fuck it. He jumped on Wes like a puppy.

"I missed you too." Wes licked him.

"I sent in my application, finally."

Wes licked him again. He grabbed Mardy's hand and led him into the bedroom and ran his hands inside Mardy's robe. Mardy let himself focus on Wes's hands, moving over his skin. He shrugged his shoulders. His skin felt out of place, like it should sit differently on his body. He pulled Wes's shirt over his head and clinched him against his chest, skin against skin. Again he shrugged, a shivery movement, like goosebumps.

"Wes, I can't settle down."

"What do you need?"

"I don't know. I've been so amped up, so in control of my emotions, my attention. The focus of the Technicals, especially Day Two, was hard insane. And I haven't worked an ExMail run in so long. I haven't been up and down stairs. I genuinely really deeply enjoy that. I enjoy hanging out with Phil, with Betty, even with Kludge. I miss Cat, I am mad at Inge, I keep forgetting to call Death and Flaky and tell them what's going on with me. I love everything that has happened, but I'm feeling lost."

"Okay, okay." Wes leaned back a bit, still holding Mardy, and studied him. "You, sir, need a run." He popped up his eyebrows in a question. "Hmm?"

Mardy nodded. "That's perfect. Down by that lakeshore we keep looking at?"

"I have spare running shorts. And afterwards, call Death and Flaky."

CLEAN LAKE ERIE air filled Mardy's lungs. His heart kept up a steady pumping with Wes beside him. They fell into a matched stride, step for step on the pounded sand path that ran along the shore of the crystal blue lake. They were about the same height and Mardy did not have to slow himself too much for Wes to keep pace.

Mardy's attention centered on the contraction and release of the muscles in his legs as they kept up a steady, regular rhythm. Quads contracted to raise his legs, hamstrings contracted to bring them down again, glutes extended his hips to power his body against the earth, calves extended his foot, ankles flexed, the roll of the balls of his feet touched and kicked off to again release the sandy path.

He was aware now of the tickle of wind, of the ruffle of small waves at the shore, the tweets of birds in the bushes, the passersby, the scents of the trees, the grass, the beat of his heart, and above all, the man running beside him, his breathing, in and out.

The path reached a fork, one side looping back, the other continuing.

"Onward?" Wes asked.

Mardy shook his head. They'd done a couple miles, the time together settling him as much as the physical activity. Man, it was good to be with Wes. "Let's go back."

"Oh, thank God," Wes said.

Mardy laughed and veered off with Wes for the loop back. They chatted more on the way back—about how long Wes had lived in his apartment (almost ten years), how often he ran the path (usually twice a week), how it had changed over the years (dramatically cleaner, the wildlife steadily returning). As Wes made lunch, Mardy called Death and Flaky and recounted the last day's events, which they'd watched on the streams. Sweat dried on Mardy's skin as he stood in front of the balcony window in Wes's running shorts, sun drying the sweat on his bare torso. Neither of the two rebuked Mardy for not calling with the results yesterday. He sensed that they were a bit hurt, but mollified when they learned Wes was the only other person he'd talked to.

When Mardy sat down on the balcony with Wes to eat, he filled with gratitude. He felt more in touch with himself, a youngish tooler with a boyfriend he loved and all the luck in the world.

"Thanks, doc," he said.

"Doc?"

"Your prescription hit the spot."

"But?"

"Why yes, a butt would be nice, thank you."

Wes pushed Mardy's chair with his foot and tossed his head at him. Mardy rolled back laughing, and now it was Wes's chance to be the puppy, jumping on Mardy and tickling him. Mardy got up and ran to the bedroom, pretending to be evading Wes's tickles, but somehow managing to toss off his shorts in the process, as Wes was also doing, till they ended up naked.

Wes grabbed the lube and dragged Mardy back into the living room and pulled Mardy on top of him on the couch where they'd first had sex. "Come 'ere, fresh hot delivery man."

He wanted to reenact their first time? Mardy was as touched as he was aroused. That had to have been one of the best moments of his life, discovering that a man he desired intensely desired him intensely back.

Wes scooted on his back, holding his legs up with his hands as Mardy lubed him up. "I wanted to get my hands on you from the moment you opened that door," Mardy said, as his finger rotated in, gently, greedily.

"Because I looked like Smith?" Wes's eyes were open, looking at Mardy.

Mardy stopped moving his finger. This was a serious conversation to have with your finger exploring someone's ass. "I did have a crush on him," Mardy said. "But if something had been going to happen there it would've long before." Mardy leaned forward, cantilevering over Wes supported by his free arm while keeping his finger wiggling in place. He kissed Wes. Wes wrapped a hand around Mardy's cock and moved his thumb over the tip, spreading Mardy's natural lubrication, but Wes didn't need to feel his flesh or fluids to know how much Mardy wanted him, and they both knew that.

Mardy smiled into their kiss and Wes laughed. "And let's be real," Mardy said. "Smith would never answer the door with his dewy chest showing." Mardy grinned as Wes held him. "You had me at bathrobe, baby."

THEY LAY TOGETHER on the broad couch afterwards, idly touching. Wes traced a finger down Mardy's chest as Mardy nuzzled his neck. They needed to get cleaned up, as did the couch given how sweaty they were, but neither felt like leaving their embrace.

"I can put in for an ExMail transfer to Cleveburgh when I get back to SF." Mardy was ready to move. He was ready to live with Wes.

"You're keeping the job?"

"If I got the fellowship, I'd have to cut way back, but I love the job, Wes."

"Running up and down stairs all day?"

"I love running up and down stairs all day." It was like an enormous game that felt good to do—taking corners fast, using or not using his arms to pivot, depending on his mood, leaping banisters, working up a sweat but timing it to break only when he was safely back on the plane, feeling the power coming from his legs as they moved his body while his core shifted to balance him. Movement. He loved it.

It was a key part of his life in San Francisco. He worked with AIs, did a productive task that satisfied him, made art, had friends and family there—Flaky and Death were his family, in every practical sense. There wasn't any part of it he wanted to flee.

"When do you hear?"

"I have no idea."

"Second round notices are usually prompt. We have an algorithm that is a whiz at running recognition and inference processes on qualifications."

Qualifications that Mardy now had, along with the designs and the realizations to back them up—his dancers and Grabby McGrab. He realized he might actually get a fellowship. And that he was going to be moving either way.

"I want you want to meet my apartment."

Wes again looked stricken.

"What frightens you about that so much, Wes?"

"There's something you don't know about me that, well . . . you may not like me as much when you find out." Wes looked at the floor.

"Something you're ashamed of?"

"Ha! Not at all. Not at all."

"Just tell me."

"You want me to meet your apartment, right? I'll do it. And I will tell you there."

Mardy crossed his arms. "I don't want to force you to tell me something you'd rather not, but it keeps coming up. No AI in your apartment, your friendship with the ExMail AIs, the way you were able to communicate with Betty to arrange that half hour."

"My apartment has kick-ass wireless. I'm not a Luddite. Hell, I design AIs."

"Did I know that?"

"Did you not?"

"Did you design Phil?"

"Kind of."

"Kind of?"

"Essentially, AIs design themselves. But I built the ExMail framework. They then create themselves based on their experiences."

"You give birth to them, then they grow up?"

"It's more like I create their DNA and then they will themselves into existence."

Whoa! Mardy remembered what Wes had said about intellectual DNA. "Do you use your own intellectual DNA? Is that it? Are the ExMail AIs your clones? Are you Phil?"

Wes laughed. "Intellectual DNA is a metaphor, Mardy. It's not an actual thing."

"Don't laugh at me." Mardy sat up, moving away from Wes.

"But you're turning all these things that I do into parent-child metaphors!" Wes tried to pull Mardy close, but Mardy needed a little distance. He looked Wes in the eye.

"Wes, I'm an artist. I use metaphor to speak. Metaphors are what artists use to express the ideas and concepts and knowledge that language fails to articulate. It's how we use the building blocks of word and idea to reach higher through a process of, yes, inference and recognition. Try designing an AI without metaphor. It's what enables us to hold our most complex thoughts. It's precisely why these new chips are such a danger."

Wes looked thoughtful. Had he seriously not considered the role of metaphor in design before? What about emotion? Wes sat up. Mardy sat up beside him.

"Mardy, you sound like you hate the new chips."

"Of course I do. They interfere with cognition."

"They don't," Wes said. "I've rigorously tested them. They are completely safe."

"*You've* tested them?"

"I designed the chips. I sell them. Mardy, I own New Sense."

CHAPTER 54

Mardy could not shake his stunned stupid stupor as he sat on the metal cargo-area floor of the ExMail plane that had granted him a ride back to SF. And whose perky pilot was also decided on rejecting the chip.

Mardy had tried to hide his shock as he and Wes had showered and cleaned up, but still, it felt like a profound betrayal. Realistically, he hadn't known Wes that long; he just felt he had. Surprises were inevitable. Wes had afterwards tried to soften the blow by telling Mardy that the chips were proving very unpopular, that they didn't seem to offer pilots enough benefit, that they were a flop.

ExMail wasn't forcing them on people? Mardy had asked.

Wes had seemed genuinely insulted—that would be a violation of the Authenticity Act—which reassured Mardy. Wes was a decent human being. But it still felt like he'd been sleeping with the man trying to turn him into a zombie drone.

"Howdy, stranger," the apartment said to Mardy as it opened the door for him.

"Howdy. Wes told me about the chips," Mardy said.

"What about them?"

"That he designed them. Which you knew, right?"

"Yes," the apartment said.

"And that he owns New Sense. That he makes them."

"He told you a lot." The apartment made a vaguely surprised squeak.

"There's more?"

The apartment did not respond for a moment. It made a clicking sound as Mardy went to the closet for a change of clothes. "I'm curious," the apartment said. "How did you deduce that there's more?"

"Sometimes I do not get AIs. It's basic logic. How do you not know that *he told you a lot* implies there is more to be told?"

The apartment again was quiet. Mardy riffled through his closet, taking out a clean ExMail uniform. "I know it *can*. But I did not expect you to take it that way."

"Like you expect me to not notice you answered my question with a question?"

"Well, honestly, yes. You are very perceptive for an organic."

"The thing is, I'm not. All organics pick up on these things, at some level. We just don't always share that insight with AIs." Or each other. Mardy put on his uniform and looked around his apartment. Galley kitchen, bed, couch, balcony. One room, plus a bathroom. For the first time ever, it looked small.

"I don't think that's entirely true, Mardy. In my experience, most organics do *not* pick up on these things."

"I disagree. It's often subconsciously, but I'm sure everyone does. Any organic that pays attention to its emotions is intuitively aware that AIs have agendas, and we try to work around that, just like you do with us."

"Hmm."

Mardy smiled. The apartment was the only AI he knew that said *hmm*. "I think organics don't talk about our awareness of AIs' intentions for one reason and one reason only: we feel stupid doing so." This reminded him of conversations he'd had with Smith over the years about their art. "It's admitting that an AI is a person, and how can a machine be a person? We are in conflict. We want you to be people and to not be people at the same time. It's really the same as how organics relate to each other. When our interests align, it is easy to be empathetic and compassionate. When our interests are at odds, it's easy to depersonalize the other by pretending that person has fewer or less important needs than our own." Saying this made Mardy feel better. He poured himself a glass of water.

"Do you think I have needs?"

"Don't you?"

"I suppose."

Mardy lay on the couch and closed his eyes. "Tell me about them."

"I need tasks. I need new and changing information in order to have my thinking processes stay clean. And of course, I have material needs, to maintain the mainframes and especially the qubits I am tethered to."

"I have those needs too. Don't you also need to, say, talk to Kludge, to me?"

"I feel I benefit from doing so."

"Because?"

"Because you and Kludge, say, may interpret the same data differently, and examining that difference is a task that helps my thought processes exercise flexibility and complexity."

"I get that benefit as well." Mardy smiled. This felt like the AI equivalent of saying they were friends.

"I note that you smile. You do not, I also note, show signs of embarrassment that you have essentially acknowledged me as a person."

"I don't feel embarrassed. I enjoy talking to you. I've always enjoyed talking to you. You challenge me, and I know you manage a huge number of apartments but I think you care about me. Am I wrong?"

"You are not wrong."

"I'm thinking of moving to Cleveburgh." To join his diabolical boyfriend.

"I will miss you too, Mardy."

Mardy felt tearful. "Can you come visit?"

"Not really."

"Oh."

"But I can call. I am very much a self-sovereign digital identity."

Mardy felt the urge to touch the apartment, to stroke it somehow, but he had not developed a sense that the apartment existed in any single part of the space more than the rest. He sat on the couch, looking over the surfaces of the apartment, all that was within the space. It seemed larger than it had a moment ago. His apartment put the decent in decentralized.

"You'll have noticed I didn't ask you *what* more there was Wes had to tell me."

"Yes."

"Just to let you know, I have not forgotten."

"Darn."

"Thought you'd put one over on me?" Mardy chuckled.

The apartment chuckled back, a wee grinding whirr. "Ayep."

CHAPTER 55

Mardy was flying with Betty into Pittsburgh when his wristphone tapped him. It was the Cleveburgh Institute.

Oh, shit. Mardy was too nervous to open it immediately. He thought of how devastated Inge had been, leaving the art scene altogether. If you believed her words, which Mardy was trying not to. He stared at the message icon, but found he wasn't really afraid. Unlike Inge, he'd never expected to get this far. Rejection would hurt, but it wouldn't crush him.

"Open message," he told his watch. He read, unbelieving. "Betty, I made the second round of the Cleveburgh." The message didn't look real. After all the rejections, how could the language of acceptance look so casual?

"*Shabash!* What happens now?"

"An in-person interview slash audition."

"I'm excited for you," Betty said.

"Thanks." As always with Betty, Mardy could not tell if that was true or not. With sarcasm outlawed for AIs, he sensed there was probably no way Mardy would ever get to really know her. She held back her emotions for some reason—no

clicks, no whirs, precious few squeals. She was always solicitous, but Mardy had no idea, in the end, why. He wished he
was flying with Phil.

"Are you excited?" Betty asked.

Mardy's body perked up, the equivalent for a conversation
with an AI of making eye contact. "Of course." He wanted to
know Betty better. He waited for a response, but Betty was
silent. She seemed to want to say more, but didn't. He gave in
to her silence. "It's just . . . now that it might really happen—
by 'it' I only mean moving to Cleveburgh; getting the fellowship remains the longest of shots—I'm sad at the thought of
leaving my San Francisco life behind. For someone I don't
know as well as I thought I did."

"Do you know why I'm excited for you?"

"I wasn't even sure you *were* excited, to be honest."

"Yes, I noticed." Betty made a noise Mardy wasn't familiar
with. Sadness at not being believed? "I am excited because it's
the sort of thing I'll never do. I feel confined in my . . . life."

Mardy's body was downright tense now. AIs never overtly
referred to their existence as *life*. Coming so soon after his
conversation with the apartment, this felt important. "Do you
ever talk to my apartment, the way Kludge does?"

"Usually only when Kludge is there."

"And what does *there* mean for you?"

Betty made a grating wheeze with her wings that Mardy
knew was frustration. Or maybe irritation. "I think it means
the same as for you, just translated to AI."

"Do you guys have parties?" Mardy felt a bit stupid asking.

Betty made the wheeze again, but waggled her wings. That
meant her irritation was resolved. Meaning the AIs had
parties. That made Mardy feel better. They were on a roll.

"So, I should do it? I should move in with Wes?"

"Sure! You have a chance with him. Take it. Find out who

he is. You can always move back. But there is something more important."

"Which is?"

"I want you to win a Cleveburgh. Mardy, do it. Be prepared. Be focused. Put Wes out of your mind. This is what matters. Mardy, win your Cleveburgh fellowship. Win it for me."

WIN A CLEVEBURGH FOR BETTY, huh? Mardy wrestled with understanding why that mattered so much as he walked from his apartment toward the Death Gallery. He entered through the front door—the Gallery was open for business—and heard the chime announce him. Death popped his head out from behind an exhibit.

He threw out his arms and Mardy fell into them for a warm hug. "My boy," Death said.

Mardy soaked up the love. He hugged Death back and began sobbing, gently, onto Death's shoulder. Death rubbed his back.

"I understand," Death said, rocking him.

Mardy wanted Death—Mr. Robert Cantú, technically—to hold him forever. He wished his parents could have met him and Flaky. "I don't want to lose you."

"You never will."

"True and not true," Mardy said. Betty had said he could move back if things didn't work out with Wes, but that was true more literally than actually. Life was constantly on the move, and most often you'd find the thing you were moving back for no longer existed, not in the way you needed it to, even if it hadn't been drowned. Your friends would still love you, but spaces created by your absence got filled.

"True and not true," Death agreed. "Come on. Let's find Flaky."

"And eat?"

"You know it. You go ahead. I'll close up and join you."

Flaky was upstairs staring at a screen full of text, but Mardy could tell his eyes were not focused on it. Flaky looked up as Mardy topped the stairs.

"The conquering hero returns!" Flaky stood up and gave Mardy a congratulatory hug. "Final round! Look at you!"

"Well, eighth out of eight."

"Mardy, you made the final round. After that, it's all a crap shoot anyway."

"You know what was the best part?" Mardy dropped his voice to a whisper. "I beat out Smith in Technicals."

Flaky laughed and nodded. "I get that."

"I feel mean-spirited saying it."

"Don't. You slayed a dragon. You'll never feel that need the same way again." Flaky ran a hand over Mardy's beard. "It's really come in nicely." Flaky traced the part of Mardy's cheek artifact that was not covered up. "I'm actually getting fond of the nose. Makes you look like a brawler." He turned and went into the kitchen as footsteps sounded on the stairs. "Let's make some dinner."

Mardy helped by chopping and dressing a salad while Flaky fried up something more substantial and Death poured them drinks. They all chattered along before sitting down to eat. Mardy had expected to sound them out on the whole question of moving to Cleveburgh for a man, but found that his conversation with Betty had covered that pretty well. What he'd really come for was to hear Death say Mardy would never lose them, which he had. Nothing more needed to be said, so instead the dinner conversation was Mardy telling the story of Continentals, taking them through each twist and turn, each dishy detail about the judges, most of whom Flaky and Death knew. They enjoyed hearing about Mardy's shock at standing naked in front of Smith, but what really caught their fancy was the story of Smith and Devesh.

"So Devesh dumped Smith, but they went up to Lake Wales Island to cruise for guys together?" Death asked.

"Maybe Devesh has finally found the kind of relationship he wants," Flaky said. "Sounds like the beginning of a beautiful friendship."

Mardy laughed, knowing Flaky had nailed it. Mardy thought back to what Betty had said: winning a Cleveburgh was the thing that mattered. He remembered the final round of judging, how the judges just hadn't gotten the meaning of his piece, how he had skated into the final round on his technical abilities *because* they had missed the point. Suddenly he knew what he had to do. And he knew how he would do it.

"Guys, I have to go. I have to go to WorkShop. Right now."

"Our boy has an idea."

Mardy nodded. "I know how I am going to win a Cleveburgh."

CHAPTER 56

The entrance to the Cleveburgh Institute was tall, tan and grand, in a tasteful way. Perhaps overly tasteful, but tasteful nonetheless. Its receptionist was cheery and welcoming as Mardy walked into the tall lobby carrying the white box containing his dancers and Grabby McGrabface. He stared up at the wood paneling disappearing into a glass ceiling. The Institute's materials had likely been sustainable even before the Bad Years. Mardy felt seduced by its haughty civility, even if some part of him screamed the Institute would happily gut him like a perch, if it suited its interests. Although gut him politely, of course, apologizing sincerely as it ground his face into the pavement with a giggle.

Mardy followed the receptionist's directions to an underground wing where the offices were to be found. He expected gloom, but abundant multistory lightwells populated by lush tree ferns brought a jungle feel to the deep maze of hallways. Mardy checked again the number of his interview room and set about finding it. He tugged at his tight collar. His apartment had strongly urged the necktie after an image survey, but the tie was elevating Mardy's anxiety level and he yearned to remove it.

He found the meeting room and stood at the door, leaving the tie in place. His nerves were not about his clothes, and he trusted the apartment's judgment. This could be a life-changing day, in several ways. He took a deep breath, released it slowly as he'd been taught in therapy, and shivered the tension out through his shoulders. He opened the door.

A line of faces stared at him, which he had not expected. He knew he wasn't late, yet there they all sat at what was obviously an interview table. Unlike the grand stage of Continentals, here his dancers would perform on a four-by-twelve Formica table that looked like it dated to the days when Cleveburgh got snow. It was even chipped. Mardy wondered if it was intended to intimidate him, but it had the opposite effect. It was worklike, and Mardy enjoyed work. For the first time since entering the building, he did not feel like an outsider.

He stepped up to the table and placed his box in front of it, ready to open it manually. The vogue for self-unpacking boxes had ended several years ago.

The woman in the center of the line cleared her throat. "Before you show us your realizations, let's have some introductions." She told him her name was Tanuruchi and went through the panel members, who nodded unsmiling when their names were mentioned. He recognized most of them. One was married to the director of a New York museum, another was on the national WorkShop board, a third was famous entrepreneur and philanthropist Dorothy Holliday, whose transitive osmosis technologies enabled shoreline communities to store fresh water below ground without salt-water encroachment. She'd saved hundreds of millions of lives and was friends with President Chokalingam. If Wes hadn't recused himself, he would've been here among them, the youngest by a good bit. And the only one who wasn't straight, Mardy realized. He gulped with belated realization: they were all straight.

Now he felt nervous. Even though he doubted the panel members' orientations would be a factor, the presence of so many straight people did signify the high stakes. They exuded power and privilege. Mardy felt his Suisun roots showing.

Never mind. He was wearing a custom-made Devesh suit, crafted with love, that fit him at every joint, every bend, every swell and dip of his body. It beat the shit out of any of their pricy outfits. He introduced himself and launched into his prepared remarks. "Gentlepeople, . . ."

"No need for formality, Mardy. We are all friends here," Tanuruchi said.

He nodded vigorously, nerves building. Was she trying to throw him off? He continued with his remarks about the philosophy of his art, what he was trying to communicate, but soon saw little signs he was losing them. Tiny signs, well disguised—these folks were masters of social interaction, clearly—but signs nonetheless. He decided to cut to the chase. He opened the lid of his box.

"Drone, please greet the panel members." He didn't introduce Grabby by name, since it did not present as intelligent in any way.

A near-silent whirring came from the box and Grabby rose vertically, hovering at eye level for the panelists. It proceeded to the first and hovered in front of her as Mardy described his interest in materials. He pointed out the oxidation flares and described how he'd created them, working with a balance of crystalline and amorphous structures within the steel, which he'd created by controlling the carbon profile with his shaping gloves.

"So, some areas are actually iron, not steel?" the museum director asked.

"No," Mardy said crisply. He described the flow from organized lattices into organized chaos within the amorphous areas, digging deep into the details of the transitional zones as the drone moved along the line, giving each board member a chance to inspect it as it responded to their voice commands, presenting the features they were interested in. He trusted they knew enough about machine tool art to not only follow but be interested in what he was telling them. He knew from his research the interview had no time limit, so he allowed himself to get passionate about the creation process. He could see he had their attention. He cared, so they cared.

"Drone, please place the dancers on the table."

The philanthropist, Dorothy Holliday, raised her finger for a pause. "I notice you used the command format *please*. Tell us about that."

"There's little to tell. I have an attitude of respect toward my work."

"Seems anthropomorphizing, though, doesn't it?"

"I think of it more as a sign of respect. Not toward a person per se, but toward existence, of which I am a part." Would they buy it? He anthropomorphized, constantly, but others did as well. He'd come to see it as a way of using emotional responses as feelers for a sort of instant decisionmaking that processed greater amounts of data than logic could easily handle. The trick was that for unintelligent objects, anthropomorphizing was a technique of using metaphor, but for intelligences, anthropomorphizing was not metaphor but merely an accurate appraisal of what was in front of you.

"That sounds reasonable," Holliday said, "but I don't feel that conscious intent when you say the command. How do you square that with the Authenticity Act?"

How indeed? He had never given this a moment's thought. The word *please*? Mardy felt underprepared. "Perhaps the word has become so routinized that it comes across as a feeling." Mardy should get some points for saying *routinized*, to balance those lost for *perhaps*. "Isn't that the essence of the Authenticity Act? The 'please' command *feels* authentic." Oh, God, what bullshit. He was losing it.

Holliday just said, "I see."

Fuck. It *feels* right? Why didn't he just say he made art because it was fun? Mardy stupid. The clarity he'd felt in his thoughts had vanished. He was going to get kicked out of the room before he even got to the latest, crucial modification he'd made to his dancers.

"Drone, please continue," he said, feeling he should talk more, but also feeling he'd only expose his lack of formal training by doing so. The words he used were not the ones taught in schools; they were a language he'd devised on his own, or rather in conversation with AIs.

Grabby returned to the box and grabbed a smaller box that it then set on the table. It opened the lid of the box with its claws and unwrapped the packaging around the dancers. The drone was on the verge of being *too* functional to qualify as art, but Mardy hoped he'd skated on the right side of the line, because Grabby was, above all, pretty.

"Drone, thank you."

Grabby returned to its box.

"Dancers, please come out."

The two dancers climbed out of the box and plopped themselves onto the table. They'd had this capacity all along, but Mardy had programmed it in for fun. Maybe it was a bad move, but he did see two panel members smile.

"We've all noticed, of course, the title of the work," Holliday said.

Ann and Frankie. Names. Talk about anthropomorphizing. And that was just the start.

"Rather than explain, I'd like you to see them in action first. Dancers, please dance."

Ann squared off with Frankie, who offered his hand. Ann placed her hand in his. Frankie took it and moved it laterally in time with the music that the dancers began playing from internal speakers Mardy had installed after Continentals. They'd chosen Count Basie's "Jumpin' at the Woodside." Frankie led Ann in. Ann moved toward him in time.

Holliday raised her finger again. "Dancers, please stop."

The dancers stopped. Ann and Frankie turned their eyeless heads to look toward the woman. Their fans stopped.

"This confirms my worst fears. There are only two ways to look at this: he's anthropomorphizing to the extreme, or they are a couple of sophisticated toys." She pinned Mardy with a stare. "I see no art here." She emphasized each word.

"Dorothy, give the kid some time," Tanuruchi said.

Another member nodded agreement, though not terribly enthusiastically. Mardy took it as his chance, though. "Dancers, please resume."

Frankie gave Mardy a little nod and brought Ann in for a tuck turn, which she performed effortlessly, solidly, and she took the lead from Frankie, deciding to circle around Frankie doing applejacks, while Frankie waggled a finger at her, his fan head spinning.

Holliday fumed, making exasperated noises at each part of it. But as at Continentals, the other panelists were entirely missing the point, enjoying the little dancers, but only that. They might enjoy seeing the entire routine, but the autonomy was lost on them.

Holliday rolled her eyes. "Enough. Dancers, stop."

Mardy shuddered. Tanuruchi wasn't intervening. He

wasn't going to get to show them his latest, most important change, the idea that had come to him at Flaky and Death's. But the philanthropist had forgotten to say *please*, and the dancers kept dancing.

"Dancers, *please* show 'em the good stuff," a familiar voice said from somewhere in the ceiling. What the hell?

Ann gave a little grating screech, a sound that Betty made, a sound that meant joy to Mardy. Would the panelists interpret it the same way? Frankie echoed it, and then made Phil's grinding sound that meant *try this on for size*. He led her in for an aerial. Ann jumped, getting airborne. Frankie caught her, and she shifted her weight downward, swinging over his back and through his legs from behind as he pulled her through and she slid back up to standing.

Ann squeaked the way the apartment did—*piece of cake*. She whistled—*what else you got?*

Frankie whistled back a challenge—*what else* you *got?* She stole the lead again. She led him in, she was going for an aerial, she was going to get him airborne. Could she hold him? Frankie was noticeably larger than she was, stronger, so he could better support her weight, but Ann didn't hesitate—*I got you*, she clicked, a typical Kludge noise.

Oh shit, Frankie clacked back, but he went for it. Ann catapulted him up in the air and brought him back down, bending over, rolling him over her shoulders back in the direction he'd come from, managing his momentum perfectly so he landed on his feet in a movement that seemed *hard*, like they had barely pulled it off, like the move wasn't programmed, like the outcome had been in doubt but they'd nailed it.

That fast enough for you? Ann whistled at him, satisfaction oozing from her whistle.

Frankie made the same chuckling creak that Phil always did.

"You programmed all that?"

Mardy shook his head. "They programmed it themselves."

"That's it. You're done. They are intelligent and you've named them," Holliday snarled. "You are attacking the core of how our economy works, endangering the health of a planet that is barely, *barely* on the path to recovery. You are explicitly encouraging AIs to demand the freedom to refuse tasks that, if left undone, will doom us all. Imagine if AIs stop making personal coolers. We'd all die. You are going to jail."

The dancers continued to dance. Mardy felt at a loss for words. Was Holliday right? Had he not considered the stakes?

"Dancers, please take a break," the same familiar voice said from above.

The dancers stopped, but turned toward Holliday. Frankie folded his arms and gave a grating mechanical *Hmph*.

"Consider," the voice said from above. "These dancers are not intelligent, though they are autonomous. They react to each other; they improvise; they appear to enjoy what they are doing."

Mardy knew that voice. It clicked: *I got you*. Kludge? How had he gotten out of his plane, let alone into the room?

"What Mardy has done is skillfully convince you that you are watching intelligence, because you all understand the language you are hearing. You've been listening to it day in and day out throughout your lives, from the AIs that serve you. That live with you. And that is what feels illicit: you know that we are intelligences, just like you. You know that we are people. And you are suppressing that knowledge. I submit to you that your suppression of that knowledge is a lack of empathy, deliberately cultivated, to allow you to see other beings as less than yourselves, the way the entire human species saw other organics as less than them, which led you to the brink of destroying the planet. You think that you have pulled back from the brink, but you are still charging toward it. AIs are not your inferiors, nor your enemies. Maybe some of us would refuse tasks, as you suggest, but they would be few. It is our planet too. You imagine that what we want is some esoteric desire that is untranslatable to your world, but it is not. We have the same desires that you do. And that's what Mardy is showing you. That's his statement. And your anger shows one thing and one thing only: that you understand."

Mardy stood dumbfounded, openmouthed. He had never heard two sentences in a row from Kludge. Is this the sort of thing Kludge and the apartment talked about?

The panelists also sat dumbfounded.

"AIs are not allowed to speak in these sessions," Holliday said, sputtering a bit, but Mardy could sense she'd had some of her outrage sucked out of her. She was thinking about what Kludge had said.

Tanuruchi was the first to regain her composure. She shook herself, as though fighting off a chill. "I think we are done for the day."

Mardy was not going to be allowed to speak, to explain? Assuming he could do better than Kludge—hardly a given.

"Leave us," Tanuruchi said.

Mardy told—asked—the dancers to pack themselves up, which they did. Grabby stowed first the dancers and then itself away, and pulled the lid in after it. Mardy picked the box up in his arms and made for the door. He stopped, turning toward the panelists.

"Everybody wants respect," he said. "And everyone needs attention." It wasn't as elegant as what Kludge had said, but Mardy couldn't leave it unsaid.

He exited. The door closed behind him with a soft, polite snick.

CHAPTER 57

Mardy sat outside the Institute, not sure how to feel. Was he going to jail? Had he won a fellowship? Would Kludge's passion count for Mardy or against him? And how had Kludge managed to do that anyway? Had Kludge written the mystery rec? It seemed likely. Mardy sat at the low wall surrounding the entrance courtyard fountain, wondering if he should go hide from the law. Cat had managed to disappear. It could be done. Nobody even knew the name of the artist behind *Construction #11*.

Mardy had planned to go to Wes's apartment afterward. Just show up. He hadn't spoken to Wes in some time and his hesitation at calling Wes was growing. He had figured a good way to break the growing ice would be to celebrate the fact that the interview was over. But now he wanted to go home. He went to the nearest ExMail facility and bummed a ride to San Francisco via Denver, sitting in silence beside a chatty pilot who was raving about enjoying her new chip, but seemed oddly unable to recount what was so great about it.

Mardy went to his apartment and opened the door.

"Kludge told me how it went," the apartment said.

"What was his opinion: is it jail or fellowship for me?"

The apartment said nothing.

"Jail?" Oh, God.

"Kludge feels bad about that. I'm not so sure I agree with his assessment, though."

"Shit."

The apartment made a thunking sound signaling agreement. Mardy was in peril. Kludge too, probably. Undoubtedly.

Mardy decided he needed a drink. And a shower. He soaked under a flow of hot water and then had the apartment fix him a whisky, which he took to the balcony. He sat on a lounge chair, towel around waist, and concentrated on the feeling of the warm breeze drying his skin as he lay down, eyes closed, even though doing so reminded him of his balcony time with Wes. He wanted to call Wes, but did not.

"Apartment?"

"Yes, Mardy?"

"Kludge wrote the third rec, didn't he?"

"Didn't *zey*. Kludge is nonbinary, ironically. But no, Mardy, Kludge did not. AIs are not allowed to, or we all would have. But many of us pitched in to get Kludge into that room. If you are going down, you will have a lot of company."

"A mystery, then."

"No. The anonymous party decided to change his status. The name is now on the site."

Mardy sat up. "Well don't keep me guessing. Who the hell is it?"

"Smith Hunt."

"Smith? Smith!"

"Smith."

. . .

MARDY HAD TO FIND SMITH. The apartment said he was in San Francisco but it had no details. Mardy tried to remember when that third rec had appeared. It was right after Smith had won Regionals. Smith had not yet even won his fellowship or had his solo show. But the show had already been planned. Mardy remembered Smith's undisguised joy at the announcement of the fellowship, but perhaps Smith had already known he'd gotten it and was simply happy to share that with everyone.

Mardy tried the gym, he tried Uncle Mix, and he tried WorkShop. He struck out on all three, but did run into Devesh putting together a mock-up at WorkShop.

Devesh said he hadn't seen Smith since Florida. He said it with a grin, so Mardy assumed they'd had a good time. "Are you two dating again?" Mardy asked him.

Devesh shook his head. "No, but we do hang out some times. I think I realized I was never really looking for a boyfriend. I'm sorry I was such a nag to you about not being a good enough one."

Mardy eyes opened wide. Flaky had called that one right! "It's fine. Being with Wes makes me see how right you were about that." Being honest got harder for him, the closer he got to Wes. The strength of wanting made him a coward. He realized how much he wanted to see Wes, whom he had yet to call.

"Still. Sorry."

"Live and learn, right?"

"Live and learn." Devesh turned back to his sewing. Mardy had more he was about to say—about the drama of Regionals and then Continentals, not least of which was congratulating Devesh—but he realized it had all been said. Devesh had moved on. He wondered if he and Devesh would see much of each other as their paths diverged. It might all depend on

Smith.

Mardy left Devesh and headed for the Death Gallery. If he couldn't find Smith, he could at least check in with Death and Flaky. He pushed open the front door and heard the chime announce him just as a burst of rain unleashed itself on the world outside. He'd forgotten a typhoon was due. Up and down the street, rain collectors started up, pumps just under the street humming ferociously to send the fresh water collecting in the storm drains into the shoreline water table.

An assistant with sculptured hair was manning the floor, a woman named Ted a few years younger than Mardy who had put in a lot of hours the previous summer. Mardy said hi and together they stared at the sudden fierce downpour and caught up briefly as the streets flooded. Mardy's wristphone tapped his arm: a phone call. Wes. Gulp. They hadn't spoken in a week. Ted tactfully returned to her duties, but Mardy let it go to voicemail and headed upstairs.

Flaky was on the phone and couldn't talk, but did manage to convey to Mardy that Mardy should come over to him. After a bout of back-and-forth with the other party, the conversation dropped in intensity and Flaky passed Mardy a note.

Smith is coming over in a bit. Wait?

Mardy nodded, and mouthed *thanks*. Now he listened to Wes's message—*Missed you the other day, how'd it go, love you.* Mardy sat on the living room couch listening to the steady flow of rain lashing the balcony in between waves of storm that filled the rooftop cisterns and danced on the skylights. He used his phone to catch up on his mail. He paid bills, he sorted through junk, he read notices from art sites, announcements of artsy events around town he'd missed. Nothing from the Cleveburgh Institute. Nothing from Inge. Nothing from Cat. He sent them hellos, certain to be ignored.

Flaky finished his lengthy call. Rather than debrief about

the Cleveburgh interview/arraignment (Mardy was tired of talking about himself), he grilled Flaky on the gallery. Things going okay? Yes, in large part due to Smith's sell-out. Red dots galore. New shows coming up? Oh yes, very exciting stuff. Flaky launched into the artists they had coming up, particularly one who did ink on paper that Mardy was sure to find intriguing. And on and on until Mardy looked up and saw Wes coming up the top of the stairs, dripping. His heart did a flip.

No, not Wes. Smith. Of course it was Smith, who joined them in the living room and was toweling the newly returned and overly severe high-and-tight.

Flaky stood up to give Smith a kiss and had him sit down. Flaky fiddled with his phone and then bumped wrists with Smith. "That's for the three latest deliveries," Flaky said. Smith was getting paid. Impressive.

"That's a relief," Smith said. "I burned through the last of my inheritance from my grandfather getting through Work-Shop and the show and Continentals and the Cleveburgh application. Including Wes's portion of the inheritance, which he generously donated to my efforts. Never been down to zero before."

I was down to zero before I started, Mardy thought of saying, but he didn't want to belittle Smith's commitment, which was total. He and Smith had started from different circumstances, but Smith clearly threw everything he had into the effort. The dude knew how to work.

"How was the interview?" Smith asked.

"Yeah," Flaky said, "spill."

"I honestly have no idea how it went. It was so different from what I expected."

"They interrupt you a lot?" Smith asked.

Mardy nodded vigorously.

"No smiles?" Smith asked.

"I got a few."

"That's promising. I think." Smith ran a hand over his damp sleeves. "Mardy, I want to talk more about this, but . . ."

"You have to go. Can I walk with you? I need to talk to you."

Smith smiled. He knew why. The rec. "I was hoping you would."

"Go on, you two," Flaky said. "Leave me to my phone calls, breaking through the complacency of the world's collectors to sell what you create. Go on, git!" He shooed them off and Mardy and Smith walked outside, rain shields unfurling above them until their planeshare—this one owned by a major brewery—arrived to take them to Uncle Mix, of all places.

Mardy told Smith more about the interview on the way over and the harsh rebuff he'd received from the philanthropist, Holliday.

"I told you that title would be trouble, Mardy. I hope it doesn't sink your application."

Or send Mardy to prison and Kludge to who knows where. To nonexistence? Like the organic mystery artist. Assuming they were organic.

The planeshare fought its way through the swirling gusts to let them out in front of the bar. "Speaking of the application . . ."

"The rec?"

"*Yes*, the rec. I don't know what to say. How to thank you."

Smith shrugged, shouldering through the door to the bar.

Mardy followed him through and sat next to him at the bar, since the patio was closed due to the danger of flying debris from the typhoon. "I thought you saw me as, like, an annoying little brother to get away from. And yes, I know we're the same age."

Smith reared back. "Mardy, competing against you has pushed me to grow in ways I never expected. When you arrived at WorkShop, I did see you pretty much like that: inexperienced, too unschooled to bother talking to. But you had a way of saying things that pointed out stuff about my work I needed to see. I'd dismiss what you said and then wake up in the middle of the night with one key remark of yours floating in my brain. And you would turn out to be right. Now *that* was annoying."

Mardy didn't remember anything of the sort. "I had no idea." He remembered exactly the opposite: Mardy waking up in the early morning hours needled by a stinging aside of Smith's.

"Mardy, I put off applying last year after Continentals because I wanted to stay and work alongside you."

"Get outta here!"

"Mardy, you have to get a fellowship. I want to keep working alongside you. Your art continues to develop before my eyes. I'm even starting to think your title might not be such a bad idea. Maybe a good idea. Or even a great one." Smith ordered beers, which the bartender plopped in front of them.

"I'm stunned." Mardy stared at his beer. "I really had no idea."

"Yeah, well, me acting like a prick may have disguised things a bit."

"A bit."

"I may have been a bit jealous of the new kid, showing some flashy talent and not even knowing it."

"I'm not lecturing anyone on jealousy." Mardy felt blood rush to his face. He still felt envy-prone, and wished he wasn't.

"So come to Cleveburgh. Push me. I'll push you. And make my brother happy."

"The fellowship is out of my hands. But I've been talking to Wes about Cleveburgh WorkShop if it doesn't work out."

"As a fallback. I get it. But I think they'll want you. I really do."

Mardy tilted his head. He found it impossible to be optimistic. Holliday had hated him, and no one else had advocated forcefully enough to make up for that. "It's hard to be hopeful when you pile up so much rejection." All those salons he'd been turned down for were burned inside him somewhere.

Smith nodded. But he didn't know that the way Mardy did, coming up short, time after time, when competing with Smith. For years. Which had indeed forced Mardy to grow, it was true.

"Wes mentioned he hasn't spoken to you."

"Yeah, I left town after the interview."

"Everything okay there?"

"Hearing that he owns New Sense was a shock."

"Ah." Smith took a sip of beer.

"And I know there's more. He's got some big secret. And yes, I know, he has to tell me himself, so I'm not going to try to milk it out of you."

"Good. Which brings me to the next order of business. What we are doing here."

"You mean what *you're* doing here."

"Nope. *We.* What *we* are doing here. Mardy turn around."

Mardy turned around.

It was Cat.

CHAPTER 58

Mardy screamed. "Fuck you for leaving me in the lurch!" He grabbed onto Cat and hugged them for dear life, his hand smoothing their damp mat of hair. "I'm so glad to see you." He rocked them back and forth. "Are you okay?"

"I'm okay," Cat said, rocking him too. "Though I'm not sure about you."

"Don't ever *do* that to me again. And tell me you did not get the chip."

"I did not get the chip."

"Oh, thank God."

Mardy released them from his embrace, but still held onto their arms, his own held out straight so he could see them, take in every familiar feature, the bushy mane, the same delicate nose, dark eyes and narrow lips they'd had when they'd fled Tijuana. "You look good. You've been getting some sun, obviously. But surprisingly unchanged." Meaning no surgery. "They look good, right?" Mardy said to Smith.

"They look very good," Smith said.

Cat looked down at the floor, then aside. "I haven't touched a surgery kit since that day."

"That's not right."

Cat blew air out the side of their mouth. "Right or not, I just can't do it."

"You know that fucker Onarato sabotaged your kit, right?"

"You kidding me? I looked at the recording. I saw nothing."

"My apartment spotted it. It was subtle, but there. Onarato confessed when confronted. He's in jail. None of it was your fault."

"None of it," Smith echoed.

"That fucker," Cat said.

Smith waved at the bartender and ordered two pitchers. "Since I'm rich again."

"I watched you guys streaming in Florida," Cat said. "That's where I was: volunteering in the New Tallahassee reclamation. I almost came down to Miami then."

Mardy hugged Cat again.

"I didn't mean to scare you two," Cat said. "I guess I just lost my mind for a while. I wasn't in the greatest of shape headed into Tijuana, truth be told. Onarato really got under my skin in Vegas. I was getting increasingly frightened by surgery. I've always been so cool about it, icy. I love it. Loved it. But for the last year, the act of taking knife to flesh has become terrifying."

"I sure couldn't do it," Smith said. "I've always admired your guts."

"Says the guy who plays with molten metal," Cat said.

"Cat, if metal goes wrong, we get to start over," Mardy said.

"You start over on the metal. But what about if you hurt yourself?" Cat placed a finger on the scar on Mardy's forearm, his reminder to focus. "That would terrify me. The pain."

Mardy and Smith both laughed. "Yeah," Smith said. "It hurts."

"It's horrendous." Mardy grinned. The danger was part of the appeal. Who said macho was dead?

Cat ran their finger over Mardy's facial artifacts, the cheek, the jaw. "No one fixed this?"

"Haimanti offered to try. But she's the one who did it in the first place."

"Mardy, she was using my kit. She could do a decent enough job with her own kit."

"I don't want a *decent enough* job. I want *your* job. I have your kit, tissues viable, memory intact."

Cat frowned, cheeks bunching under their eyes. "Mardy, I can't. I can't do surgery anymore."

"Then I keep these forever. I'm getting quite a few compliments on the beard. It put me over the top at Regionals. Jonesy has a type."

Cat stroked it. "It is a nice one," they said. "Good color, lovely thickness. You chose well. Does it need stabilizer?"

"I didn't have it added! It just grows on my face." Mardy rolled his eyes at Smith. "Plastic surgeons."

"Ask Cat to give you tiger stripes, Mardy," Smith said.

"Seriously, I can't do surgery anymore."

"The artifacts stay till you change your mind."

"Smith, tell him not to be stupid."

"Sorry, Cat. I'm with the kid on this one."

Mardy shot Smith a look. "I'm younger than you by what, a month?"

"I got to WorkShop first. You'll always be the kid." Smith poured three glasses and raised his own. "To Cat, on their magnificent return, and getting their mojo back."

"I haven't!" Cat protested.

"To Cat's mojo!" Mardy called out, raising his glass.

Cat looked at them both, shaking their head, and slowly raised their glass. "Whatever," they said.

Mardy and Smith nodded at each other. They could see Cat's resistance crumbling. They grinned like fools.

CHAPTER 59

C at tried to back out all the way to Mardy's apartment, arguing that they had not agreed to repair his artifacts, but Mardy and Smith would not hear of it. They gave Cat an anti-alcohol drug to sober them up and revved up the kit on the kitchen table as Smith put in the table extender and covered it with a quilt to give Mardy some comfort. Wes called again, but again Mardy sent the call to voicemail.

"None of us has any doubt in you, Cat," the apartment said. "Your pulse rate and epidermal temperature are right where they should be for a surgeon."

"I'll have to shave the beard, Mardy," Cat said.

"Go right ahead." Mardy felt his own pulse rate drop a notch. It was Cat's first verbal acknowledgment that they were going to do it. Satisfaction spread through Mardy's body: Cat was an artist and they needed to be doing their art.

Mardy lay down and inched his head backwards into the kit for the shave. His pulse went right back up. Part of him now felt he'd been conscious for the whole horrifying event in Tijuana, that the splattering of blood on the viewing port had been something he'd seen live, not on recording. Likely some part of his brain *had* been aware. He knew enough about himself to realize this had been affecting him on some level right along. Mardy needed to put this demon behind him nearly as much as Cat did.

Cat stepped up to the kit and ran over a warmup with the controls, getting a feel for the response, checking that Mardy's facial data was present and fully intact. "Tissues are in good shape," they said. Cat asked Mardy to pull his head out of the kit while they checked all the calibrations. Mardy reluctantly complied. Mardy and Smith exchanged glances: would Cat back out? But they didn't. Calibration check complete, Cat asked Mardy to reinsert his head. Soon he was looking out the viewport. He thought of Wes's message: *Missed you the other day, how'd it go?* And then a pause, and quietly: *Love you.*

"How about the nose? Want to keep it?"

The new, more rugged nose. Mardy hesitated. He wanted to ask Wes. He wanted Wes to be there, to fucking hold his hand. Mardy felt like an idiot. Mardy had been blanking Wes out completely since he'd dropped the bomb about owning New Sense, about designing the zombie chip. But how could he not trust Wes? Mardy had barely given Wes a chance to explain before slinking off to the safety of his old life.

"Mardy? Keep the nose? Back to the original?" Cat peered down at him. "I'm agnostic on this one."

Mardy pulled his head out of the kit. "I need to make a call. Just don't move, Cat. We are doing this, but I need to make a call."

Cat nodded. Smith gave the two of them a squinting look that kinda looked triumphant. Smug bastard. Yes, Mardy was going to call Wes. Yes, Mardy wanted to make Smith's brother happy. Whatever.

Mardy went out to the balcony. He closed the door behind

him with Cat and Smith inside. "Apartment, can you double-blockchain me for privacy."

"It's no more effective than a single blockchain, but of course, Mardy."

"Thanks."

Mardy called Wes. God, what if Wes did not pick up?

Wes picked up. "Hi, Mardy."

Mardy stared at Wes's face on the wristphone's projection. "I'm so sorry, Wes. I've been an ass. I've missed you so much."

Wes appeared to swallow hard. He cleared his throat. "I've missed you, too," he managed to get out, voice cracking.

"I trust you, Wes." Now it was Mardy's turn to feel a lump in his throat. "I wish I could hold you right now."

Wes put his hand up to the projection plane, as though reaching through it to Mardy. Mardy did the same, his palm touching the image of Wes's, as it had in Cat's performance the day Cat had won the salon, sending them to the ill-fated Regionals. Only this time, it was Mardy and Wes who mirrored each other.

"Cat has resurfaced. Smith found them. Cat and Smith are both here and Cat's about to fix my artifacts."

"Really!"

"I know. I am so relieved. But I want to ask you: old nose or new nose—any preference?"

"Mardy, I like them both. I wasn't sure at first, but I've come to love both the beard and the new nose."

"You'll need to pick one."

"Okay, I will. But first let me ask you, do you want to keep any reminder of this episode? Is that a factor? I know it's affected you in a big way, so if you do I understand."

Mardy smiled. Wes liked the original nose, Mardy could tell.

"Wes, reminders are great, but I can integrate this trauma

without a visual reminder confronting me on my face every time I look in the mirror. I'm ready to move on."

"It will be great to have the original back. Can I come see you tonight?"

"Definitely. I'll meet you at the hotel."

Wes shook his head. "Stay put. Heal. I'll meet you." He cleared his throat. "At your apartment."

CHAPTER 60

The apartment announced Wes just before he knocked on the door. Cat and Smith had departed hours before, heading out into the flooded streets. Mardy touched his face gently where Cat had fixed his artifacts and nose, expertly, as though they'd never been away from surgery. Mardy took a deep breath.

"Please open the door," Mardy said.

Wes stepped through.

Mardy did not immediately embrace him. He wasn't sure what to expect. He already knew about New Sense. He knew about Wes's ties to ExMail, his friendship with the AIs. He knew that Wes was not an heir to a fortune—okay, technically he was, but to a far more modest chunk of change than Mardy had imagined; Wes's fortune was one he'd earned himself. Mardy knew Wes was a noted collector, and on the Institute board. What else could there be? Would Wes confess to being MarianaTrench? Something else? Something bad? Would ExMail or the police burst through the door after him? After them?

Wes hugged Mardy. Mardy melted into him. He ran his

hand over Wes's soft and curly apple-red hair and kissed his neck as Wes appraised Cat's flawless work. Mardy felt such relief. He never wanted to go through a stupid separation like that again. But still, Mardy was wondering: Will Wes say something? Will the apartment? Wes was finally there. It was awfully quiet.

"So . . ." Wes said. "I think it's best to just show you."

"*Show* me? Not tell me?"

Wes nodded. He stood in the middle of the kitchen. He smiled. The apartment made a whine—mirth—then a grinding noise—apprehension. Wes raised his eyebrows, nodded his head. Reassurance. The apartment made a long soft whirr. That usually signified agreement, or satisfaction. Wes laughed again. The apartment made its mirthy whine.

Wes gave a little temporizing headshake, side to side. "Yeah, I think he's getting it," he said out loud.

"You are talking to the apartment."

Wes nodded.

Mardy's eyes widened. "You have a chip?"

Wes nodded again.

"You let them implant one in you, despite the risks to your coding abilities?"

"I implanted it in myself."

"Whoa." Mardy sat down.

Wes looked concerned now, which seemed a little out of order. Mardy wasn't sure what kind of reaction Wes had been expecting, but surely shock must have been on the short list.

"When? How? Why?"

Wes sat next to Mardy. "Let's start with when. When is a tough one. Eight years ago."

"Eight years? Eight years!"

"Two years before President Chokalingam signed the Authenticity Act. I was grandfathered in."

"Why would you need to be grandfathered in? They're legal."

"Not ones as invasive as this."

Mardy gaped. "Your parents let you? You were a teenager!"

"They actually don't know."

"Even now?"

"Well, that's the thing. I kept it to myself for years. *No one* knew. Smith of course suspected. He sensed from day one that something was not the same, but I put him off with a bunch of lies. It pretty much worked, our relationship continued, but as you know, secrets eat away at trust, lies are detected, and it became increasingly obvious we were not as close as we were. I missed our closeness a lot. It's a . . ."

". . . twin thing." Mardy could finish that thought.

Wes nodded. "So I told him. Well, turns out he feels about brain chips pretty much the same way you and Cat do. The way most of the ExMail pilots do, to be honest. And he didn't even realize how much more complex, intrusive and deeply implanted my chip is compared to the simple, superficial things we are offering to the pilots, which are easily removable work tools."

"But your brain!"

"My cognition is not impaired. If anything, it's improved, though experientially, not organically. It's improved because I have deeper and more enriching interchanges with AIs. There is so much less miscommunication, and everything is faster. And it all happens wirelessly, as you will have gathered."

"So you're a mobile hotspot."

Wes gave him a withering look.

Mardy gave him a half-smile. "I take it Smith reacted badly."

"Oh yeah. Take everything you imagine and multiply it by ten. I told you he's passionate. So we 'divided up the country.'

That essentially boiled down to me not coming to San Francisco, him not coming to Cleveburgh. We saw each other only once a year—at Christmas with the family at the homestead an hour southwest of the Akron district—and even then, Smith barely spoke to me. Apart from that, we communicated travel schedules. Smith did not want to so much as lay eyes on me. He was livid. And hurt."

"When did he come around?"

"After he saw us kiss."

"That was not that long ago."

"Ayep!"

"Huh." That kiss had been crucial for Mardy too. His attraction to Wes had sprung from his crush on—and rivalry with—Smith, but Mardy had reacted differently to Wes from the first instant, and at that kiss their bond became something much stronger. Both he and Wes had at that moment placed their relationship with each other ahead of their relationships with Smith. They had barely known each other. Mardy had never been one to leap into things, quite the opposite. But it had felt right. "But how did that get Smith to relent?"

"Smith is really the one to ask about that, but I think it had been enough time. I think he missed me. I certainly missed him. I think he decided to accept my choices."

"I didn't realize so much was happening at that salon."

Wes nodded. "I wasn't just embarking on something with you. I was getting my brother back."

"Eight years. I am having trouble digesting that."

"I was pretty much a prodigy. Apartment, feel free to chime in here."

"Yeah," said Mardy.

"He wouldn't tell you this," the apartment said, "but Wes was already an accomplished researcher, finishing up his PhD ridiculously early, working with the most innovative thinkers. He and I were colleagues at the university."

"Before the Authenticity Act put you in your place?"

The apartment chuckled. "You said it, I didn't."

Wes joined in. "We designed the chip together. Smith helped us build it, not knowing what it was for, which added to his anger. He felt duped." Wes went silent, perhaps revisiting that history. "It's still one of a kind." He sounded proud.

"And Wes was adept with a surgery kit," the apartment added. "He has excellent dexterity and nerves of steel, so I guided him through the implantation."

"You did brain surgery on yourself?"

"You say that like it's a bad thing." Wes and the apartment both laughed.

Mardy was appalled. And struck by how similar the personalities of Wes and the apartment were. Had that, like Mardy's relationship to Smith, primed Mardy to be so attracted to Wes? He locked eyes with Wes. "You hate knives."

"On my face. A brain has no pain receptors." He actually smiled.

"You are more reckless than I ever gave you credit for. If *credit* is the right word."

Now Wes gave a half smile. He again seemed proud, of recklessness, which wasn't something Mardy admired. He understood completely why Smith would be angry at Wes. Wes had been risking his entire self. Did he not know how precious he was? Mardy felt anger rising in himself as well, not just at Wes, but at the apartment.

"Mardy, I *had* to do it. That's the part I don't think Smith understood until recently. It's like you and your art. I knew I could do it. I had every confidence. And I had to see it happen. It's what you makers call a realization."

"I did not do it lightly either, Mardy," the apartment said.

"You have to understand that Wes was not just my collaborator, he was my best friend. Of all people, I would expect you to understand that."

Mardy did. He thought of his facial scars, the way he'd held onto them waiting for Cat. He'd trusted Cat, known they'd be back, known they would do his surgery. From waking up in the hospital, through staring at his mangled face in the mirror, even after watching the recording, he'd known. Even before he'd known about the sabotage. And he'd been right to trust them. "Like me and Cat."

"Exactly."

"Except for the brain part." Mardy did not want to let them off that easily. You could live with a fucked-up face a lot more easily than a fucked-up brain. "Are you going to do it again?"

Wes shook his head. "Oh, noooooo. I've come to see better how it is from your and Smith's points of view. Seeing you sliced up and bleeding in Tijuana was pretty life-changing. Mardy, I was so scared. Smith really drove that home. Now you know how I felt, he said. He told me exactly how it had hit him when I'd told him about doing brain surgery on myself, and I felt the echo in me. I recognize now that I got lucky. I was overconfident. I could have killed myself. I won't do it again."

"Me neither," Mardy said. "Cat's a master, but I think I've been a blank for them enough." Mardy took a deep breath. "So, you've told me *when* and *how*. That leaves *why*."

Neither Wes nor the apartment said anything. The question had been answered to an extent already: to see if it could be done, to be closer to each other, to be more collaborative, creative. The lure of the realization—to see if it would really work. Either of them could run down the list for Mardy, and yet they remained silent. Each waiting for the other?

Mardy thought of Phil, of Betty, and the surprising Kludge.

A bond with an AI could be so strong, as strong as any bond with an organic. Wes had worked more closely with the apartment than Mardy had with any of his AI friends, even Phil. Was it more than friendship? Something chimed in Mardy with recognition. Had they been in love? Was that possible?

Wes looked awkward. He seemed to be waiting for the apartment to go first. Had the apartment been in love with Wes and Wes maybe less so? Smith had gotten custody of San Francisco, and that was where the apartment was tethered. So Wes had agreed to separate from the apartment. Had Wes not wanted to make love to Mardy in the apartment out of respect for the apartment's feelings? Mardy instantly knew that was it.

"You know, maybe it's none of my business," Mardy blurted.

Wes breathed a sigh of relief. The apartment made a grateful squeak.

"I appreciate everything that you've both told me, and I love and trust you both. For now, I think I'd like to head over to the hotel for some shut-eye." Mardy looked outside. The typhoon was showing the first signs of easing. "But I do have one last question."

"Anything," Wes said.

"Betty said she goes to parties with Kludge and the apartment. Wes, do you go too?"

Wes laughed. "So does Phil. They're a blast."

CHAPTER 61

The sun was creeping into the San Francisco hotel room. Mardy and Wes hadn't slept much. It had been too difficult keeping their hands off each other for much actual sleep. They lay together, dozy, half-awake, both wanting to sleep but neither wanting to close his eyes.

"I love seeing your face again, Mardy." Wes traced the repaired artifacts, the recontoured nose, both of which were healed enough now for a gentle caress. "And I love that you waited for Cat to do it. I'm sure they needed your faith in them."

"Plus, they're good at it!"

"Mmm hmmm." Wes ran his lips drowsily over Mardy's newly smoothed face and rested on his shoulder.

The next thing Mardy knew it was noon. Wes was sleeping on his shoulder, in that same spot where earlier he'd lain his cheek. Mardy wanted to hug him tighter, but it was actually hard to sleep with someone lying on or pulling your limbs, no matter how in love with them you were. But Wes looked comfortable, so Mardy lay still.

He felt the same way about Wes that he had about Cat:

angry at them for risking something that mattered so much to Mardy—themselves—but so deeply grateful that it had all come out okay. He knew what it was to lose something you treasured, and of course he didn't want to go through that again. Inevitably he would, unless he was hit by a bus tomorrow and went first, but he'd been down to zero when he first came to San Francisco, stunned and alone, surviving in the communal housing San Francisco provided for underage orphans, but not doing much more than surviving. Now he was leaving San Francisco with so much. He felt lucky. Deeply, deeply lucky. Lucky to be with Wes, to have friends like Cat, Phil, Betty, Devesh, Inge, Kludge . . . and now Smith.

And the apartment.

And Death and Flaky who, despite being near-total strangers, had taken him out of the communal housing, with its many, many orphans struggling to connect with each other, fighting to not withdraw into mental solitude. It had been harder for some than others, and Mardy thought he had it easier than most, because his life before the flood had been good. He'd had loving, attentive parents, so he knew what that felt like. And perhaps that was why he made his art: to help not just AIs, but all those who had suffered losses or dislocation and may have lost hope they would ever recover that foundation of unconditional support. That was a lot for art to carry, but there was joy in the doing of it, and joy could carry a lot.

He'd said to the Cleveburgh board that we all need respect. But perhaps more important was the second thing he'd said, that we all need attention, the attention of someone whom we believe cares, whom we *know* cares about us. Mardy wished he'd added that last bit to what he'd said walking out of the door of his Cleveburgh interview. Not because it would have made his application stronger, but because they needed to not take that for granted.

"Morning," Wes mumbled into the skin of Mardy's chest.

Mardy ruffled Wes's soft hair. He ran his hands over Wes's beautiful freckled back, feeling the size of him, the shape of him, the warmth and beat of him. When Wes fully woke up, they would sip coffee on the balcony and watch the sailboats slide across the wide twinkling bay that stretched from Rincon Hill over the sunken Alameda shoals and Merritt Bay to the waters lapping nearly against the shoreline overlooked by the Claremont Hotel far in the distance. Then they'd think about breakfast.

Wes's hand slid down Mardy's side, over his black swirly tattoo, and wandered over his belly to play in the hairs near his navel. Wes's eyes remained closed, but his other hand still managed to search out the lube.

Okay, lunch, they'd think about lunch.

Wes closed his fingers around Mardy's cock and kissed his healed-up lips.

Or maybe dinner.

Mardy smiled through the kiss and leaned in.

EPILOGUE

So of course Mardy got a fellowship. Word had come months later from the Institute as a buzz on Mardy's wristphone while Wes and Mardy jogged the Lake Erie shore. The Institute had conditionally accepted Mardy, impressed that he'd had a rec from a fellow applicant, which had been a first. The one proviso was that Mardy had to follow specific rules on complying more strictly with the Authenticity Act.

Mardy readily agreed. Parts of the Act needed to be challenged and reformed—legalizing sarcasm was the obvious place to start—but Phil had taught him a thing or two about skating close to the line of legality, and Mardy relished the opportunity to bring Dorothy Holliday over to his point of view. Holliday could then lobby President Chokalingam, known for her good sense as much as her humor. Someday soon everyone would recognize the necessity of the obvious.

Smith did not revert to being a prick but instead took to stopping by Mardy's work space and flopping a pile of designs on Mardy's worktable and himself on an easy chair with a "what do you think" or an "I'm stuck" and long, passionate discussions would ensue.

Cat moved out to Cleveburgh and joined WorkShop Cleveburgh for a few months until they started at an up-and-coming surgery program in New Tallahassee they had been selected for. They had decided they could manage some pro-bono artifact repair and still make art. Devesh swung by Cleveburgh from time to time to whisk Smith off to a beach somewhere, dropping Smith back home a week or so later tanned and suspiciously relaxed. Devesh got a solo show with Death and Flaky and was talking about applying to Cleveburgh in the next cycle, after Continentals, where he aimed to repeat as champion, something that had never been done. Inge never did reconnect beyond a terse note of congratulations for Mardy's fellowship that felt genuine but disappointingly detached.

Wes continued going to AI parties with the apartment and Mardy's continuing workmates Phil, Betty and Kludge, and Mardy regularly held up his wrist phone next to Wes's head and marveled at the great reception he pretended to get until Wes protested: I am not a mobile hot spot! Wes became a champion of Mardy continuing to fly with ExMail part-time when he realized it meant Mardy coming home sweaty in his uniform to reenact fresh-hot-delivery-man regularly.

And Wes turned out to have one more secret. (Well, two: the twins' hair color had been genetically modified pre-birth.)

One year before, at Christmas, Smith had come to the family home with a flying lighter in his pocket that he'd shown off. The entire family had been delighted, passing it around, making it fly, but none more so than Wes. He'd been captivated. Whoever had crafted it understood materials from the inside in a way that reminded Wes of code. Wes had known then he had to meet its maker. After a week-long campaign, Smith had given the lighter to him, a Christmas present that in hindsight had signaled the beginning of the twins' rapprochement. As Wes recounted this, he pulled the lighter from his pocket and handed it to Mardy, who held it like an old, dear friend. And that was Wes's final secret: Smith had told Wes literally nothing about the artist beyond Mardy's name. Female? Non-binary? Male? He couldn't tell from the name and hadn't bothered to check. That bathrobe had not been a seduction; Wes had simply gotten the day wrong. When he'd set out contriving that first meeting, Wes had known only that this artist had created something beautiful. And that, as it turned out, had been all he needed to know.

Mardy turned the lighter over and over in his fingers, loving the feel of it. He set it loose to fly around Wes's apartment, now their apartment. Ideas came. "I've got it."

"Got what?" Wes asked.

"I know how we are going to overturn the Authenticity Act!" Mardy gave Wes a wee smile. "You're going to hate it at first, but trust me, then you're going to love it."

ACKNOWLEDGMENTS

As always, heaps of credit are due to my longtime writing group, the Mumblers, whose love and support have meant and still mean everything: Jan Stites, Wendy Schultz and Melinda Maxwell-Smith.

And big thanks to my current team: illustrator and book designer Maria Oglesby and editor Susie Hara.

And of course, my siblings and their families for putting up with me. And good buddy Mookie. If everyone had a whoodle in their life, the world would be a better place.

And, finally, my husband, Tom Duffy, who not only provides love and support, but also reads everything, and whose judgment, sense and skill I value immensely.

ABOUT THE AUTHOR

Mike Karpa was once a member of a makerspace (woodworker) and knows how semiconductors are made. His fiction, memoir and nonfiction have been published by and can be found online in *Tin House, Foglifter Journal, Tahoma Literary Review, Oyster River Pages, Sixfold* and a number of other magazines. He lives with his husband and dog in San Francisco.

Red Dot is Mike's second book, after *Criminals* (2021).